One Night at the Astoria

The Friends and Adventures of Rocky Star

Hayden Richards

ISBN: 9781723710865

Thank you

Chris, I cannot thank you enough, stay curious.

Jenny, without you it would just be a jumbled mess.

All my friends, there is a little bit of you in every bit of this.
I'm sure you will find it.

Enjoy x

1

James slipped his arm from under his chest where he had been lay on it for less than five seconds, at the same time he crossed his legs back into the place they had been only a few seconds before. He moved his head on the pillow, all of these movements had been done several times in the hour that he had been in bed. He could still hear noise in his ears and lay there hoping he didn't have tinnitus. The crisp, white sheets and heavy duvet were keeping him warm from the winter outside. The cold and rain that hit the huge, full length windows, kept the room cool as the heating system in the converted Victorian townhouse seemed to be none existent. The heavy cast radiators were not giving off any heat. His face was cold and he drew the duvet up to keep it warm. The man lay next to him.

He had passed out as soon his head hit the pillow and all of James' wriggling around hadn't managed to wake him. Normally this would be James' signal to leave and make his way across town to his place. He lived in North London were rent was much cheaper than this posh west end flat; his place was also even colder, as there was no heating what so ever. He did have a small fan heater that he was scared to use, due to most of his clothes being piled high in stacks everywhere. There was no room for furniture to house everything. He had imagined many times waking in the night to find the place in flames. There would be no way to escape, the window opening was tiny and the fire exit on the landing looked as if it had never been opened. In fact he wasn't even sure if there were steps on the other side for him to flee. He made a mental note to himself to check that when he got back.

The other people on the floor must be worried about it too. He shared a bathroom with three other rooms on his floor all of which were occupied by foreign couples, only one of the women spoke English. She was Russian and he had guessed her partner was too but had seen him shopping in the Polish shop down the road; he seemed to know all of the products and what he wanted to buy. He had heard them several times having sex through the paper thin walls of his bedsit. Taking stock of his current situation, a slightly warmer flat, en-suite bathroom, kitchen and living room was an improvement. It was Saturday morning, nowhere to go and he had a man next to him that he had decided early on in the evening that he really liked. He was staying put, even if he couldn't sleep and was lay in bed waiting for this guy to wake up. If only he could remember his name.

Last night he had spent several hours watching the man dance. For a short time he had been watching someone else dancing until he had realised it wasn't actually him. He had then set off from the dance floor leaving his friends behind to go and find him. It had taken him about 20 minutes until he spotted him at the bar. He walked past and smiled at him and then ordered a coke. His five foot nine frame leaning up to the bar, spiky blond hair, blue eyes and thin set face caught the eye of the man he had been following. James was an attractive twenty eight year old, sometimes a little camp when he was in the right company generally people could guess he was gay upon first meeting him. In fact most of the people that he worked with had made an assumption based on his friendship with Mark, his closest friend and work colleague. Mark happened to be very open about his sexuality at work. James came from quite a conservative family so when he flew the nest and moved to London he embraced the gay scene but was the type of person to discuss it incessantly. Since moving to London four years ago he had wanted to find a boyfriend and settle down. In the last year alone, he had fallen in love three times and had his heart broken each time within weeks. Right now, his head was in a haze as he groped in his pocket for some money. The ecstasy tablet he had taken earlier was being to wear off but he still felt the lovely fuzzy feeling it had given him. The woman behind the bar had a thick wedge of spiky hair at the front of her head and the rest was shaved, James had spent a little too long staring at her and felt uncomfortable when she smiled to reveal a mouth full of gold teeth. As he had leaned over to hand her the change, having not heard how much she had asked for, the guy, who was now lying next to him had reached over and paid, taking James' hand and pulling it close to his face.

'Who you smiling at?' he said in a thick London accent. He looked just like Daniel Craig.

James was thinking how much he had fancied him in Layer Cake. In fact he fancied him a lot in James Bond too but much more in Layer Cake.

Maybe that's why he fancied this bloke? He had a look of a gangster about him. He was about 5'10', slightly taller than Daniel but that didn't bother James. Blond short cropped hair, shaved, but looked like it had started to grow back, square jaw and big, big muscly arms. James was blissfully taking in the sight of the man as he felt his pull. He liked the Diesel t shirt he was wearing. Diesel was a trendy brand and a bit out of his price range.

'Oi, I'm talking to you' He said looking directly in James' eyes, only a few centimetres away from his face.

'Erm' he stuttered, 'it's you' as he realised he sounded like Jason Statham. James was feeling more confident than usual due to the drugs he had taken; he was normally quite shy when it came to speaking to men, especially older, sexier men. He was thinking to himself what it would be like to show him off to his friends as his boyfriend. He wanted to take the guy back to the dance floor and show off.

'You what?' He said to James, screwing his nose slightly as if in mock disgusted. 'You, erm..... asked who I was smiling at?' James replied back the man, aware that his north east accent jarred. James had moved to London from Newcastle, he had a thick Geordie accent. He looked cute and sounded cheeky, a style that had served him well over the few years he had been out on the scene in London. Using his boyish charms was a sure fire way to pull, and it was going to work for him now.

'Oh right, you can talk then?' the man said with a slight scowl. 'So, why you smilin' at me?' He moved in closer. James attempted a reply but his voice was stopped by the man pressing his lips hard onto his mouth and then followed by pushing his tongue deep inside his mouth.

O... M... G... James spelt to himself as he thought about the kiss; this was the single horniest kiss he had ever had. He wished his friends could have seen the man he was with at the bar. He had even bought him a drink which was a novelty nowadays. He liked the fact that the man had forced himself upon him. It was new to him. Normally, he would take hours talking to people and flirting, but this man knew exactly what he wanted and James was very happy to let him have it.

James felt like he had been kissing the guy for hours and his chin had begun to itch from the man's stubble, he found himself thinking again of his friends he had left behind on the dance floor. He hadn't even seen them to say goodbye or show off his new friend, but right now, he did not want an audience. He was back at the swanky west end apartment before he knew it; it was 5am in the morning.

No sooner had he entered the apartment doors, the man had begun to take his clothes off, kissing him hard in each place that clothes had been removed. Very quickly they had found themselves naked in the shower exploring every inch of each other. After a long, hot shower they had moved naked but for towels back to the lounge, where the man had lifted James in the air and allowed him to wrap his legs around his waist. He then slowly, without breaking eye contact, lowered him down onto his lap and entered him. Face to face, they kissed as the man slowly lifted James up and down as they found the intensity of their pleasure heighten. The sex had lasted for hours. It was a record for James and by far the most pleasurable. They hadn't used protection and James had been very aware that for some reason he had trusted this man and that it would be okay. It was at this point, right there knowing he trusted the man that he realised he was in love with him.

O... M...G... he spelled out to himself as he made a final thrust. He pulled James up higher than before, withdrawing quickly from deep inside him and ejaculated over his arse and balls, just the feeling of cum all over him made James reach orgasm. His cum shot satisfyingly, over the man's chest. Moments later, the guy stood up, pushing James to stand with him and walked through the duplex apartment.

'Time to sleep, are you staying?' He said as he disappeared into the kitchen and down the set of stairs towards the bedroom and the bathroom where James had already been.

James, knowing when he was onto a good thing sprang across the room and followed the man down. He walked into the bedroom to find he had already gotten into bed and was almost asleep. James crept in beside him and had been there for almost an hour tossing and turning wondering if he would ever fall asleep, wondering how this man had managed to fall asleep so fast. He had never been able to sleep after a night out dancing. He had only taken two pills before he had met the guy and still he couldn't sleep.

'Stop fucking wriggling about!' the man said from under the mass of pillows and duvet. James had a rush of adrenalin as the excitement of knowing he was awake ran through him.

'Why? What you gonna do about it?' he said, as he looked over the bed to him.

'Send you home......... or' the man said as he raised himself with his right arm to make space under him, his left arm moved across James and his hand cupped around his waist pulling him into the space under him. The man was once again hard, as James drew his legs around his waist. He either didn't hear, or he just chose to ignore the sound of James' whisper of 'I love you' through the duvet cover.

2

Ben lay in bed, waking up slowly. The light of the room began to creep into his consciousness and his body began to wake as he moved. He rolled from his back onto his front and pulled the pillow over his head in an attempt to fall back to sleep for a while longer. It didn't work. The more comfortable he tried to make himself the more alert to his surroundings he became. He heard the dull beat of life outside his bedroom on the street below. A car horn sounded bringing him even closer to starting his day, as the distinctive sound of a bus pulling away from the stop that stood right outside entrance to his flat. More sounds began to fill his morning, people walking by and talking about their lives on the street below. He heard a baby crying and then he could hear word perfect what the mother had to say to the angry child. He realised he was now wide awake and there to be no more sleep for him. This was the difficulty of having such a great location for a flat. He lived on Upper Street in a trendy, converted warehouse loft apartment, just a minute's walk away from Angel tube station. It was a very up and coming suburb of Islington, North London. He had paid a fortune for the privilege of being able to live alone and be so accessible for everything.

It meant he had to watch every penny he spent, but it was worth it to have such a great pad. A great shag pad as he told anyone who had ever visited. The majority of the apartment had been stripped back to bare brick and had a modern industrial feel to the way it had been renovated. The only rooms that had plaster on the walls were the bedroom and bathroom, which were mostly tiled. It was small but had just enough room for a walk in shower that would fit two people, three at a push; it had been tried at one point. An undersized sink and a toilet that you could just about sit on with your knees centimetres away from the opposite wall and a window that you had to stand on the tips of your toes to see out of. All tiled in slate with shiny chrome fittings with white porcelain giving it the expensive look it deserved.

The whole flat looked expensive and it was this expensive taste that was fast becoming Ben's main stress. He had never suffered much with worrying before. Money, work and sex had all come quite easy to him. He didn't have a high powered job and didn't want one, middle management suited him well. Working at the bank was easy and he didn't have to think too much about what he did. He got paid what he needed and he had plenty of sex. Or so he thought. Lately it was becoming apparent that he no longer earned enough to keep up the lavish lifestyle that he had. Last night was the first time he could remember coming home alone from a club. What was going on? For as long as he could remember he had always got shag on a night out clubbing. It didn't even matter how much he had to drink or any substances he consumed, he always went home with someone. He loved sex. He also loved sex with himself. From being around the age of 11, when he had first got an erection. Having found out what it was actually for, there was no stopping him.

Several times a day he would wank and this went on for years. Until one day, he got caught by one of his school 'friends' who then forced him into wanking him off instead. This he found was even better than playing with his own. Playing with someone else's was great. In no time at all he was, on a regular occasion, wanking off 3 of the older lads that attended his boarding school. By the time it was graduation, he had realised not only was he gay but he really couldn't get enough sex to keep him satisfied and so this continued into his late teens. When all the lads around him had started to slow down, he continued his regular masturbation with unrelenting vigour. It was just before his graduation that the rumour had gone round that Ben Smith-Monroe would wank and suck you off anytime and anywhere. This tantalising information soon fell on the ears of his Geography professor who then called him to his office. It was during this meeting that whole new world of sex had opened up to Ben. It was the best two hours he'd had in a long time.

Buggering the teacher in his mid-50's with salt and pepper hair, a very hard chest and a very, very big dick had sent him straight to his desktop computer and for the first time he googled gay sex. The rest, he likes to tell his friends and anyone who will listen, is history. Recently, by his own standards, his sex life was extinct, or maybe he was just being dramatic, he had left his friends in the club last night as he wasn't enjoying the music. From the messages he was getting, he realised they'd had a great time and he had gone to bed. He rolled over trying to block out the noise of the baby crying in the street, reached down the side onto the floor and pulled up his shiny MacBook. He revered the apple name and his new toy in the same way that devoutly religious people saw God. The shiny casing and the technology it used, the iPhone which was also languishing on the bedside table, were the perfect accessories for his lifestyle. Opening up the laptop it pinged into action within seconds and the website opened up in a new safari window. Gaydar! This was the place where he spent hours and hours talking to and connecting with people. Well maybe not quite connecting, but finding a shag at least.

3

'Cock!'

'No he isn't' he said with a giggle.

'Listen to me,' Mark said as he looked down at Tom who lay across the bench with his head on Mark's legs.

'Yes he is' he continued to say with a huge grin on his face taking a cigarette from the packet with his mouth and continued to talk with it between his lips.

'He is, because no gay man in their right mind would go out dancing for the night wearing skinny black jeans and black shoes that look like the Child Snatcher from Chitty Chitty Bang Bang.' Tom laughed hard enough to make him need to sit up.

'And?' he said

'White socks! The cock is wearing white socks' Mark was trying to light his cigarette now his arm had become free from Tom moving. They both looked over at the man they had been talking about and observing for the past few minutes. He was stood leaning against an outdoor heater on the other side of the yard they had entered about 10 minutes before. Mark wanted a cigarette, and in his words, 'assess their progress.'

It was around 5am on Sunday morning, they had been out since 8pm on the Saturday night, where they had had a usual night out with the group of friends that were fast becoming a usual crowd. They had gone on to Fire in Vauxhall to go dancing. Mark and Tom had been friends for about seven or eight years. They had instantly hit it off one night when Mark's then boyfriend had introduced them. Paul, the boyfriend, now ex, were still good friends and had met Tom on a skiing holiday with hundreds of other gay men.

When Tom had moved to London he had gotten in touch with Paul and been introduced to Mark. Paul became an ex very soon after, but Tom had very much stayed a friend to Mark. Mark saw Tom as his best friend. They had exactly the same taste in almost everything and had the same sense of humour. If you were stood in the yard now, watching the two of them as they laughed and joked, you would think they were a couple and had been together for years. In fact, never once had it crossed either of their minds that they may want to be together like that. Tom, still laughing at Mark's outburst and staring at the guy in the white socks turned to his friend.

'Make him take them off.'

He hadn't realised he was pointing his finger at the guy with the white socks while he said it. Mark suddenly sat on his hands like a naughty school boy and looked at Tom as if he had done something wrong and was about to get found out. Tom slightly puzzled, trying to work out what had happened jumped when the man in the white socks said from behind him.

'Can I 'elp you bois?' This said, in a thick French accent. Tom turned and as quick as he was, didn't demonstrate one bit of the shocked state he was in.

'No thank you kindly! On your way love, oh and by the way....... wear dark socks in future.'

The man not quite knowing what was said or if the joke was about him, looked quizzically at the boys on the bench.

'Au Revoir' he said and walked on. Mark held his hand up to his mouth in a camp shock pose.

'It'll get the better of your sharp tongue one day love' he said rolling his eyes. At which point a tall woman with a short bob of bouncy brown hair glided into the middle of them and sat down.

'Now then Pip' Mark said to her. 'What do you have to report?' Pip looked both of them up and down and took out her purse from the hip pocket of her figure hugging jeans. 'I bet Pip would never wear white socks with black shoes.'

'Oh sweetie, who on earth would do that?' Pip said in her west London posh accent.

'Some French geezer' Tom said to Pip as she nuzzled in between the two of them.

'Who would like one of these, it's all the rage on a Saturday morning don't you know.' Pip produced 3 ecstasy tablets from the purse and offered them up to the boys. A huge grin came over Mark's face. 'Young Tom' Pip continued. 'Kindly tell me what is on the front as I'm afraid I seem to be unable to see that close up.' It took Tom a minute to get his eyes to focus.

'It looks like a wizard's hat..... I think. It's pink anyway.'

'Yummy' Pip said 'I've been looking for these babies,' before even finishing her sentence she had pushed one into each of the boy's mouths and was pouring water into Tom's mouth to wash it down.

'I guess we won't be stopping anytime soon then?' Tom said to his companions.

'Bloody grannies secret purse will be the death of me' Mark replied.

'Stopping!' Pip said in a high pitched shrill, 'Stopping! Who said anything about stopping young Tom? The night is still young..... Well, the day is still young and we have dancing to be done.' With this, she jumped from her seat and disappeared back through the door from which she had appeared. As the door swung open, the thud of the bass line from the club banged out to the crowd smoking in the yard. A tall man with his top off wearing jeans that hung off his hips, perfectly, walked through the door. He had olive skin and looked like he worked out. Tom was admiring him, looking at the tattoo on his arm and the muscle that it covered. He noticed that the man's skin looked soft and the part of his chest that was visible had just a few hairs.

'Bet he wouldn't wear white socks.' Mark said noticing that Tom had been watching the guy.

'Bet he has a huge cock too.' Tom said as he slid back onto the bench to be on the same level as Mark. During this time, the man with the tattoo noticed the two of them talking and looking at him. He walked over and sat down beside Mark.

'Can I help you boys?' he said. Re-occurring question Tom thought to himself, knowing that the guy had chosen to sit next to Mark because he fancied him. And who could blame him though? Mark looked after himself and was damn attractive, shame really, he found this guy horny.

'We are doing grand love, how about you?' Mark said to the man with the tattoo.

'Having a brilliant time, the tunes are bangin', the man with the tattoo said in an Irish accent that made Tom fancy him even more.

'What's with your mate?' The man with the tattoo said to Mark. Tom realised he was just sat there staring. Had that pill started to kick in already? Or was he just still wasted from the last one a few hours ago.

'He's got special needs' Mark said as he pushed both his hands between his legs and pulled a sad face at Tom.

'Oh yeah, and what are they?' said the tattooed man

'Mostly Irish men with tattoo's and no tops on' Mark said.

Tom suddenly realising what Mark was saying and still unable to speak, blushed.

'Oh yeah? I think I could help him out with those needs.' The man with the tattoo said.

'Right then!' Mark jumped up from his seat making room for the Irish man. 'Move over, there's work to be done, see you boys on the dance floor shortly' and with that he walked through the door where Pip had disappeared minutes earlier. The pair sat on the bench together. Without a word the Irish man leaned into Tom, he made himself comfortable, and put his lips on his. His tongue slipped into his mouth and they began to explore each other. Tom thought to himself that this was a far better way to spend time than dancing. He soon forgot all about his friends. For some reason he couldn't stop singing the tunes to Les Miserables in his head. Still kissing the Irish man with the tattoo and excellent tongue, he had a conversation with himself in his head about why he was singing show tunes whilst kissing this man. The conversation in his head finished swiftly when the Irish man with the tattoo pushed his hand down Tom's trousers. Tom wasn't surprised that he had an erection.

4

Ben surfed through several pages of the 'Who's Online' section and started to pop messages out to guys he hadn't seen online before. There were always loads on a weekend. Lots of men came into London on a Friday night to go clubbing and hung around for the weekend. Luckily for him it seemed most of them hadn't pulled last night either. A few messages were replied to and some started a conversation. He got a message from the guy he had spent Thursday night with, suggesting that he came over again. He was going to keep that at the back of his mind, going back was better than not getting shagged at all. He checked his phone for any messages and as he sat back a message came through. It was a response to his standard 'Hi, how are you? New in town?' that he always sent to new potential prey.

Received:

Hey! Thanks for the message. Are you just visiting here too? I am pretty central?

Ben quickly checked the messengers profile out. He seemed like a guy who looked after himself, probably went to the gym a lot and it said on his profile he was a runner. Looking at the pictures of him with his top off, he was beginning to feel hornier. The guy was about 5'8' with a shaved head, about a number 2. It said on his profile he was a German American. Wow! What a mix. Wondering what his accent would be like as he checked out his square face and distinctive brown eyes. He messaged him back.

Sent:

No, not visiting. I live near Angel tube station. You know it? Are you visiting? Where from? You look well horny!

Seconds later another message came back. Ben knew this meant he was interested and began to ignore the other messages coming through for a minute to see if the guy was up for it.

Received:

Ok cool. Thanks Mr.

Glad you like my pictures, I've been working here for a couple of years, and I know Angel. I'm near Farringdon on the same tube line.

Sent:

Cool, so you know your way to Angel then? What you looking for on here?

Received:

Well, I was chatting and seeing what's happening. If anything else was offered then I would look into it. I'm not looking for anything in particular. Just cool dudes to hang out with, either for a beer, or a naked beer!

Sent:

Where do you get naked beer?

Received:

Well at home, I guess

Sent:

Hang on a minute, at 10 in the morning?

Received:

Yeah! Main thing is not in public...it annoys the locals :)

Sent:

I think you would probably need to show me so I can understand it better. My place?

Received:

Haha! Well, I am not so shy about that. Lived in Germany too long ;)

Sent:

Wanna come over? I can text you the address?

Received:

Naked beer? Yeah, why not! Just so you know though, I have a girlfriend and don't really go far with guys. The most I've done is have beers, hang out, watch some porn maybe, hang out... naked. That sort of thing. Wanking. That kind of thing, not very exciting for most gay guys, I know.

Ben sat up in bed and read the message again. This guy was a bit different. He remembered the countless number of straight guys he had had sex with in the past and those school chums that had been so happy to have his mouth give them a work out. This guy would be no different. Happy to say he was straight and has a girlfriend, but also plasters himself across Gaydar and pretty soon him.

Sent :

Here is my number, come on over. Text me and I will text you the address

Ben jumped out of the bed and strolled naked across the flat. He passed the window and into the shower room. All the way his erection stood proud from his body. As he climbed into the shower he heard the distinctive buzz of his iPhone as he received another message. As the hot water sprang into action and washed down on to his skin, he wondered to himself what the guy was called.

5

Sam Rockwell loved his name. Well he liked being called Sam, he had never cared much for Samuel, it reminded him too much of a previous life. A life, on reflection, which was much stranger than the one he had now. London was a great place to live, the city had a great vibe to it and providing you stuck to the places you knew and the crowds you love then you would be safe. There were always some idiots out there looking for a fight or an argument because you might be slightly different to them.

He could handle them. He could handle anything after the strangeness of his childhood. Growing up in a small fishing village near Plymouth, it may have been near Plymouth, but the mind set and culture of the people in that town was on another planet. His earliest memory of being a child was around the age of five and being taken to church. He knew he had been plenty of times before but this was the sole memory of going at such an early age. He was dressed in his Sunday best, despite it being Tuesday and he was walked to church by his parents, Patricia Rockwell, then a secretary at the local infant school and Mr Rockwell, his father.

Sam was to always refer to his father, Mr Rockwell, as Sir, never dad, daddy or father. He knew his name was David. It was printed above the door of the Undertakers three doors away from their family home. His father was a formidable character and for most of his childhood Samuel had been scared of him.

They lived in a small terraced house with two small bedrooms upstairs, one for him and one for his parents. Downstairs was a lounge room that was dressed as formal as if the Queen were about to visit unannounced at any time. Next to and divided by a set of stairs, was a larger kitchen with a huge pine table at the heart of it. Sadly, Sam thought that there was no heart in this kitchen. There was a poster the size of five year old Samuel on the wall depicting Jesus with the burning Heart. His parents belonged to a devout religious sect, a branch of the Catholic religion that many people in town were all part of. On this crisp Tuesday morning, Sam recalled, he had been dressed in his finest and marched over to the Church up the road. The sea wind was strong and salty and Samuel, holding his mother's hand asked where they were going. The crack of his father's voice whipped Samuel knowing that he should not be asking questions and he kept quiet the rest of the way.

Arriving in church he was taken to the alter and the Priest, a fat old man that sometimes talked to Samuel with a detachment, as if he was another person was stood quietly. On this occasion, he knew exactly who Samuel was. Samuel had always thought him strange and several years after that, he had realised that the man was losing his mind and had no clue about the things he did or had done. The Priest spoke with his parents and they all kept turning and looking at him. Samuel was made to stay in the old wooden pews, waiting to see what was going to happen.

The day before, although Sam couldn't quite remember the exact details, Sam had been caught out of the house without permission playing near the beach. He had found what he believed to be a Sony Discman with a CD in. The recording artist was called Madonna, an artist he now sees as being the one greatest to have ever lived. He had never heard music that was not sung in the cold church on the hill. He was found stood on the beach wearing only his underwear and having listened to the songs over and over, was singing at the top of his voice for the whole village to hear. The song was called Holiday. He was beginning to realise that he was about to be punished.

The punishment hadn't lasted long. He was plunged into a pool of cold water while the priest tried to cast out any demons that had tried to seduce the young boy. The Discman which had probably been left on the beach by one of the walkers that often took their lunch to the beach, was taken into the vaults of the church and he assumed was burnt. The burning he assumed would never let the demon into the village again.

Five year old Samuel spent several years after this event wondering why Madonna would be a demon when she had such an amazing voice and had the same name as Our Lady herself. He was taught about that at school. He never asked for fear of going back into the plunge of cold water. Samuel was a fast learner, he knew from a very young age that his parents where not the finished article, so to speak. He realised that they were slightly different to the rest of the people in the village, and all the others were all a load of nutters.

At the age of 15 he was sneaking out of the house when his parents were asleep in bed and going on the late bus to the nearest town to begin his education into the real world. He had seen most of the recent films at the cinema and spent time walking through the streets and looking into shop windows, seeing all kinds of new and fantastic things. He loved to look through the window of the woman's clothing stores and see the statues of women dressed in bright clothes with shiny shoes. Clothes he had never seen in his home or his village for that matter.

It was around this time that he had realised his parents had totally lost all grips on reality, when one night at tea, his mother, who was finding it hard to control her excitement waiting for Mr Rockwell to come home from his day at work told him their strange news.

'You are the second coming.' She said in a haze of excitement.

'I'm what?' Samuel looked back at his mother fearing the worst, knowing what was coming.

'We have spoken with Father Rowlands. Your father, Mr Rockwell has been discussing this for years and now it is time for you to know.

'You're Jesus' His mother looked at him intensely. She wasn't joking, why would she? She didn't even know what a joke was.

'Jesus!' He said it in shock and blasphemy, not in answer to her.

'Yes, my son, the son of God. You will be so wonderful.' There was a glaze over her eyes as if she was drunk on the knowledge.

'Jesus' she said as she looked at him.

Samuel had been distracted, wondering what madness had got into them. He was so shocked that he answered to the name.

'What?' It was a curt reply with no pleasantness at all. It was the harsh crack of his father's voice in the doorway.

'The son reborn of God does not speak to his mother in that manner.' Mr Rockwell said. He walked into the kitchen smelling of embalming fluid from the funeral home.

'Jesus.' Samuel said again,

'My son' there was strange warmth in his father's words that he had never heard before. 'I know I have done my best to be a good father to you, your real father however, The Lord our God, will have plans for you.

'You are the saviour!'

Samuel, in a slight daydream due to the distinct amount of shock was unfathomably wondering what Tom Cruise would do in a situation like this? He had seen him in a film just days before where he had made cocktails on a sunny island holiday. That's what he would do and that's what Samuel needed to do right now. It didn't matter what Tom Cruise would do, it mattered what he was going to do.

For now he decided to go with it. He had been planning his escape from them for a while and this sealed his fate. He could use this to get the few things he needed in order to make a run for it. He couldn't be the re-born son of God, unless he was in the habit of wearing pink frilly knickers with a soft lace trim under his school uniform. He doubted that very much.

6

'You know what he said to me? Hahaha, you won't believe what he said to me.' Fred said to Tom and Mark as they walked arm in arm down the street behind Pip. Frederica, Fred to her friends, was the same age as the boys with shoulder length brown hair and amazing green eyes. She was attractive and men often chased her. She wasn't interested being happily married, but did enjoy being chased a little. Pip was on a mission to find a fast food place she had been told did amazing food.

'He leaned over and whispered in my ear.' Mark was already laughing. He had heard the story about an hour earlier when Fred had dragged him to the toilet. 'I'm gonna take you home and do some serious damage to you, and you're gonna love it.' Tom stopped in the street breaking free of Fred's arm and held himself up on the wall and began to laugh loud enough for passers' by to look at the group of friends.

'What a twat!' He said as he began crying with laughter, Mark was already laughing and the three of them fell into each other. Pip turned to see them all laughing uncontrollably but didn't get the joke. She often didn't get the joke between these three. Not many people did. She had always loved that they had such a close friendship, that they got each other so well. Deciding not to bother to find out, she turned and saw the fast food shop.

'Here it is' she declared to the comedy trio. They all looked up, calming the laughing down to see the dirtiest most grubby fast food place they had ever seen. The look on their faces said it all. None of them had even wanted food and the trip from the club in Vauxhall to London Bridge had been all Pip's idea. Fred had wanted to carry on dancing somewhere else, Tom wanted to go and wake up Ben who had left the club very early on, so that they could all pile into the hot tub in his apartment building. Mark was still pretty high from the mixture of drugs that had been consumed and was happy to do what he was told. Right now Mark could feel the laughter he was trying to hold back, once again surging up inside him.

'You want me to eat from there?' Fred questioned. She was more surprised that Pip found it acceptable to eat there. Pip and Fred had been friends for many years. They had lived together at Manchester University when Pip was studying Business and Fred was studying Fashion Design. During their years together, she could honestly say she had never seen Pip eat fast food. In fact the food bill for their normal meals with Pip could have bought everyone in the queue in this shop their meal. Pip had made a lot of money in the various business ventures she was part of, a few years ago she had lost everything and then built it all back up again. The two of them had hit it off straight away. When Fred had moved after graduation to Milan after receiving an amazing job, Pip had been the first person to go visit.

She had stayed with her in Milan for 8 weeks during which time; she had moved Fred from a hovel of an apartment, into a fresh one bedroom flat. She had realised then, that Pip was one of life's heroes.

Pip never quite made it to where she planned to be, yet she was always were she needed to be. She had given up on the Business degree but still hung around the university and started her own coaching business. Now, ten years later after several rises and falls, she ran a highly successful life coaching and professional development consultancy. As well as several other businesses. Pip always seemed to have the next big idea and worked hard to be successful.

Fred's one bedroom apartment long been forgotten and during the past ten years she had become a highly regarded Fashion designer and now lived in Paris with her French lawyer husband and children, Jerome and Etienne. The two of them ran a business together using both of their talents. A few years previously, Pip had come to Fred to discuss an idea she had for a business venture. Now almost 3 years had passed and Dressed for Dinner was a runaway success story for both of them. Their client list was long and loyal as they were to them. They catered for a small, but growing community of high flying successful men, who liked to dress as women. From the studios in central London the gentlemen would come for the day, have a whole make over from an exclusive team of experts and then an evening of dinner and entertainment was provided in a safe, luxury environment. The business had grown over the years and now offered accommodation in a boutique hotel and once a year a celebrity chef came to cook the dinner. The pair loved to be ladies that lunch together, often making trips to amazing restaurants in Paris, London and all over. Which is why, having flown in from Paris almost twenty four hours ago to have a longer weekend with her friends, she was shocked that Pip wanted to eat fast food from a dirty chicken restaurant down a back alley in London Bridge.

Fred had grown up with Tom in Leeds; they had both left at the same time. They both went to University in Manchester. After University Tom had moved to London, where he met Mark fast becoming best friends just as Fred and Pip were in Paris. They had spent many years stomping about dance floors together, now they got the opportunity to venture out as a foursome only once or twice a year. Pip and the boys were out every few weeks.

The boys were in as much shock as Fred right now, the thought of solid food right now was repulsive.

'It's got a great following, fast food is the new Michelin star don't you know?' Pip said as she walked through the door and pushed through to the front of the queue. Three lads in the queue asked what she thought she was doing and she turned and fluttered her eyes at them.

Still stood outside Tom was wondering what was happening and Mark was still laughing.

'The dirty cow, how can she even eat?' Fred said walking into the shop. She was greeted by the sight of Pip being pushed to one side by three lads that looked like they would kill for the food on the floor. Pip, brushing herself down, mumbled the word brutes to them as they placed their order. It was soon Pip's turn to order.

'Chicken and Chips please waiter.' The man looked at her as if she had just parked her spaceship outside.

'Ain't no waiter here.' He said with a Greek London accent. Pip just smiled back and turned to Fred.

'Anything for the lady?' she asked as Fred was joined in the shop by Tom and Mark. Both still amused by their earlier fit of laughter.

'Are you really gonna eat summit from ere?' Mark said looking at Pip. The Greek stepped back and looked at all four of them. He placed a pizza box on the counter and the three young men ripped the box open taking a slice each, one of them grabbed the box and they all walked out in unison, almost getting stuck in the doorway.

'Salt and vinegar, chicken and chips?' The man said to Pip, Fred was stood next to the counter now and turned on her heels.

'No thanks sausage and pie.' Mark erupted in laughter hearing Fred's reply. He fell back to the wall and slid down. Tom fell forwards into Fred who had also erupted into laughter, slipped on a patch of grease and was holding herself up on the counter. As Tom hit her they hung together on the side of the counter. Pip was also laughing hard, her laugh was high pitched. She had been called a Hyena in the past, the sound of it, made the other three laugh even more. Tom dropped to the floor first, which made Mark point and laugh even more, tears were rolling down his face. Fred lifted herself back to the counter now the weight of Tom was gone to find herself face to face with the Greek.

'Ain't no sausage, ain' no pie, juz chicken and chips' Pip threw a five pound note over the counter.

'Sorry, I'm so sorry' and ran out of the shop followed by Fred and Tom, all three looked round to find Mark crawling out of the shop door covered in dirt and grease with tears rolling down his face and a box in his hand that looked like it may contain Chicken and Chips.

'What the bloody hell did I miss?' said the sexy Irish guy with the tattoo 'I only went for a piss.' He walked up to Tom and planted a kiss on his lips. Tom was still laughing and looking at Mark, who was trying to get off the floor. The sexy Irish guy with the tattoo grabbed his arm and lifted him, taking the parcel from his hands.

'Ahhh, food! Excellent!' All four of the friends looked at him disgusted.

'What was I thinking?' Pip said as she walked into the road and started to flag a taxi.

'Yuk! How can you eat that?' Fred said walking to the Hackney Carriage that had pulled over. 'Come on boys, no time to be stood about in the street.'

As they walked towards the taxi another one pulled in front of it and a head popped out the window and shouted over to the group.

'Morning all' It was a friend of the group, Paul. As he spoke another head popped out the window next to his, it was Pauls best friend and housemate Chris.

'What are you all up to?' Chris asked giving a funny look to the sexy Irish guy with the tattoo eating a pizza. 'we're on our way back to Munty Towers. We lost you in the club. Are you coming back?" He asked. Paul Langston and Chris Ancell had been friends for many years and shared a house in North West London. They threw the most amazing parties, bringing all their friends together for many different occasions. They also had great after parties which is where Tom, Mark, Pip and Fred often ended up after a night out with them.

'We are on our way over to Sam's' Tom had walked closer to speak to Chris and Paul.

'Ok" Paul replied 'Well maybe come over once you've found him' Chris sat back in to the taxi and Paul blew a kiss to everyone and they drove away.

Tom walked back to the taxi they had waiting and the group took their seats in the taxi and drove off across London Bridge. As they turned the corner they drove past a queue with about 20 people in it at a very lush looking food outlet called Mess Hall.

'OOhhhh' said Pip as they drove passed, realisation setting in 'I think that's the place!'

7

At the exact same moment that the group of friends drove from London Bridge across town to Maida Vale, Ben was about to open the door to this morning's visitor. He had received a message whilst in the shower. The guy seemed pretty confident for a straight 'I don't do anything with men' lad and Ben figured that this conquest would be an easy one. He strode up to the door as the buzzer sounded, having already let him in downstairs. He stood in the doorway in shorts and t shirt, hair still damp from the shower.

'Hey man, find it ok?' he said to the guy as he walked to the door. Ben leaned forward as he came in, his usual greeting to a visitor would be to kiss them on entering, he was met with a firm hand that he shook and the guy walked past.

'Yeah, it's pretty easy,' he replied 'your directions were spot on.' He spoke with a slight American accent. He looked like his pictures, dirty blonde hair a bit longer than the pictures and a rugged face. He had hairy arms and Ben was thinking that the rest of him must be much the same.

His profile had said he was an outdoors person, into climbing, walking etc. He fit the bill, his brown Merrill walking trainers looked worn in and his combat style shorts looked the part for starting a walk up Snowdon or going off camping for the weekend. Ben had never been interested in the outdoors spending most of his earlier years in a boarding school where country walks were forced upon pupils daily. Any holiday he could get now, involved a beach and a hotel with a high star rating.

Shall I sit over here?' the visitor said, the accent was obvious now. He walked to and stood thoughtfully next to the brown leather sofa.

'I thought you said you were German?' Ben asked as he moved closer to the sofa 'You can sit were you like.' He finished with a sly wink at the man.

'Oh man, no, not at all.' The man said with a laugh. 'I lived in Germany for a few years, no man, I'm American. Lived in Europe for over 10 years now, so I guess I class myself as just European really.'

The American was now sitting in the middle of the two seater sofa. Ben was eyeing up if he could squeeze in on either side, deciding he couldn't, he opted for the chair to the side of him.

'And the man becomes more interesting.' Not really knowing what else to say, and also not really caring as he was trying to get himself at an angle to get a good look of the man and imagining what lay beneath his clothes.

'Shall I crack open a beer?' The American said as he reached down and pulled out two one litre bottles of German beer. It took Ben a minute to compute what was happening, the guy had actually brought beer, what was going on? Did he really come over just to hang out? What was he going to do now? This had really thrown him. By this time he was normally in the bedroom or halfway there. He would certainly be naked. Naked! That was it.

'I thought we were supposed to be naked for the beer?' Ben said, thinking he was getting things back on track.

'Well, yeah, we did say naked beer didn't we?' The American said. 'So, your name's Ben, right?'

'Yeah I'm Ben, do you often go round to guys' houses you just met on Gaydar and have a naked beer?' Ben was intrigued to know what was happening and what this guy enjoyed. He knew he could take the fruits of this conversation into his bedroom.

The American laughed. 'Well not too often, have a mate I watch porn with sometimes' Ben noticed that he didn't make eye contact as he replied, he watched the news that was on T.V on mute 'I'm not gay, never had sex with a man just enjoy a naked beer and beating off to some good porn.'

'So you like to watch men wank?' Ben said wondering if this guy was for real. Had he really never had sex with a man?

'Erm, well I guess so yeah. Kinda horny watching porn with another guy and beating off.'

'Gay Porn?' Ben asked.

'Any kind of porn really, gay porn is good, you can see all kinds on the internet now' the American said, he looked over at Ben and smiled. It was just a smile, Ben wondered if it was a cheeky smile and whether maybe the guy was just teasing him, sadly however, it wasn't and Ben was beginning to realise that this guy was for real and did in fact just want to come over and hang out with a naked gay guy and watch gay porn. This realisation gave Ben an instant erection and the thought of getting this guy naked and then sucking on his cock was the biggest turn ever.

'So, you' Ben thought for a second 'have never had sex with a guy, what about wank a guy off?' he asked.

'Never done it' the American answered.

'Had a guy wank you off?' Ben delved deeper 'Had a blow job?'

'None of the above Officer' the American made a salute signal to the side of this head with his right hand.

'I've never been interested. I just like to hang out naked, have a beer and watch porn.' The American took a long gulp of the beer he now had opened. He put it down on the floor, took the other beer, opened it and passed it to an ever increasingly horny Ben. 'What about you Ben? You gay, straight or Bi?'

'Gay as they come me.' Ben focussed on the conversation again rather than his hard on that he had surreptitiously been playing with in his shorts pocket. 'I have never even been near a woman, what about you? Bi, I take it?'

'No man, as I said, I just like to hang out, don't like to do stuff. I got a girlfriend' the American was beginning to confuse Ben now. Normally, he would not have been confused however the increasing damp patch of pre cum around his cock was too distracting for him.

'Right, does she know you hang out with guys naked?' Ben asked

'No, not at all, this is just a thing I do every now and then' The American was a very confident guy. He knew exactly what he wanted and what he enjoyed and was by no means in the closet. He wasn't even gay. Ben on the other hand was now very much like a horny teenager, who had just worked out what his cock was for. There was no reason or understanding any more just his rock hard cock and this guy.

'I feel like I'm breaking the rules drinking the beer with my clothes on.' Ben said, hoping this would begin to seduce the straight American.

'Let's take them off then Ben.' The Straight American stood up and took off his shirt. It revealed a toned chest covered in the same dirty blonde hair as his head. Ben Jumped from the seat as the straight American folded his t shirt and put it on the chair. Within about two seconds Ben was stood naked in front of him with his dick out in front, dripping. The Straight American was unlacing his trainers and putting them to one side. Ben still stood in front of him.

Then he stood up and removed his shorts, revealing that his legs were also as hairy as his arms and he wore loose fitting boxers. Ben still stood in front of him with his dick out in front. Finally he took off his boxers and folded them next to the rest of his clothes. His hairy pubes held a large ballbag and his dick was disappointingly flaccid and not at all as excited as Ben's was.

'You're not hard.' Ben said

'You are I see, that's a decent sized cock you have there Mr.' The Straight American said.

'Go ahead, touch it if you want' Ben looked directly at him.

'I think you might blow your load too soon if I did Ben.'

The Straight American sat down again and took another large gulp of the beer, his bottle was now almost empty and he reached down and grabbed another from his bag.

'How are you doing with your beer?' FUCK, Ben thought to himself, what the hell was going on? This guy is actually for real and all he wants to do is drink beer whilst naked. Ben thought fast. PORN!

'Shall I put some porn on? I've got some vintage stuff.'

'Yeah that sounds great! I like the vintage stuff..... More of a storyline' The American pushed himself back into the sofa and stroked his cock that was beginning to become more solid.

After putting the DVD in, Ben sat on the arm of the sofa that the straight American was on. His dick was still hard, as he looked at the guy who was watching the TV. The porn was going through some opening credits. It was a 1970's film Ben had picked up as he fancied the older guy on the cover. It looked like his old geography teacher at school, someone Ben had wanked over many, many times. The guy in the film was a traveling sales man who wasn't doing very well with his sales. His narrating voice over was explaining that his wife and him just didn't understand each other anymore. The straight American watched the TV, Ben watched the straight American. The guy in the porn got picked up by a younger guy and they went back to his place and within minutes they were sucking each other off. The straight American was fully hard now and wanking his dick with one hand whilst drinking his beer with the other. Ben was wanking himself and was almost ready to cum but wanted so much just to suck this guy off.

'Wanna let me do that?' Ben asked as his slid in next to the straight American.

'No way man, I'm cool on my own' he said as he moved over to give Ben enough room and so that they weren't touching. They continued to watch the porn both enjoying playing with their own dicks, the guy on the screen was being fucked now and Ben loved this scene but was distracted by the guy next to him wanking. All he wanted to do was touch him, grab hold of his dick and wank him off.

'Let me give you a blow job, you'll really like it' Ben said

'Nah man, I'm pretty close anyway' the straight American said. Ben thought to himself that he was too was pretty close and had been for ages.

'Go on please, just let me finish you.....' Ben couldn't finish the sentence for as he spoke, the guy roared back on the sofa, arched his back and pushed his cock forwards. He grunted and roared again and his cum ejaculated from him and across onto the floor in front of him.

He moaned several more times and then sat back into the sofa. At this sight Ben wanked himself hard and did much the same. Still in shock from what was happening he didn't enjoy the orgasm like he would normally would, and came down his own leg. He sat there staring at the guy for a minute longer and was only broken from the shock by him getting up and beginning to get dressed.

'Oh right, so like, that's it?' Ben said as the two men on the screen reached their climax.

'Man, that was great, we should do this again sometime' the straight American said. He had put his clothes on faster than he had taken them off. Ben stood up and walked with him to the door.

Still slightly shocked and not realising he hadn't dressed or cleaned himself up. The straight American opened the door. 'You should really clean up Ben and put some clothes on, we have finished the beer now' he winked.

'Right......well...... Fuck man I SHAVED MY BALLS FOR THIS!' Ben shouted.

'Take care!' With that, he was gone.

'What the bloody hell was all that about?' Ben said out loud as he walked back to the sofa and removed the two empty bottles of beer and then looked over to his bottle which had not been touched.

8

James still hadn't managed to fall asleep, after the man from last night had pushed him out from under him. He had kissed him hard on the mouth and let James know that he was satisfied, turned over and fallen asleep. James too had then drifted off himself, wrapped in the warm fuzzy glow of just having had sex with a man. He was now officially totally in love with him and the drugs had begun to disappear from his system and were not keeping him awake. He woke just a few hours later to find that the man was still fast asleep, snoring loudly and would be for a while. He reached down to his phone and was disappointed to find that none of his friends had messaged or called him to find out about the new man. He had sent them all a message earlier on to tell them he was with him and not one of them had acknowledged it. Deciding it wasn't fair that now he had found the man of his dreams, none of them were interested.

He got out of the bed and looked for his clothes. Instead, he found the shorts the man had been wearing at the club the night before and his boxer shorts, he put them on. The man wouldn't mind, why would he? They could share everything now. He walked out of the bedroom and crossed the large living area and into the open plan kitchen passing all his own clothes as he went.

Downing a huge glass of water he began to look around the apartment. Exposed brick walls, a huge leather corner sofa in the middle of the room, a massive knee high glass table in front of it and the biggest television James had ever seen. There were several DVD's on the floor and some Xbox games but he couldn't see a DVD player or an Xbox. With his phone in his hand, he typed out a text message and continued to look around the apartment, occasionally looking down to see if he had spelt something correctly.

Guess you're not bothered if I'm alive or dead then?

He sent the message to Dean. Partly because he knew he would get a response. Dean was a text addict; phone constantly in hand, texting everyone every minute of the day. Partly because he knew Dean would be following his cousin around as he generally does and would be relaying messages to them wherever they were. It didn't take long for a new message to come back. James had taken a seat on the sofa and was looking at the DVD's which were mostly European porn, and by the looks of it, quite rough looking skinhead porn.

'What happened man?'

'What do you know?'

'U still wit bloke from last nite?'

It took James a minute to read the text; Dean had a way of adding several words together, thinking it made him cool. In fact it probably did make him look cool with the rest of the people he went to college with who were all 18 years old and spoke like this to each other constantly. But for James, who had realised on his 30th birthday that he was no longer classed as a 'youth', automatically obtained a lack of understanding of what a 'youth' was talking about.

'You ok? We is juz 'avin a drink int' crown' Dean had messaged again.

'Yeah, I'm really good. A..MAZE..IN night with this bloke. Think it could be something' James replied.

'Way cool man! You gonna come 4 drink?' Dean's reply was almost instant.

'Who's there?' James asked.

'Just few of us man, Mark, Tom, Pip, Fred, Sam (as a man) an sum bloke with tats. plz come I think Mark is with tat bloke :-('

Dean had had a crush on his cousin's best friend since the day they had met when Dean was just 13. James was well aware of this and teased Dean about it all the time. Everyone else was aware of it too but didn't play up to it as much as James did.

'You come here if you want. My fella is asleep. We can leave here together then. It's not far.'

James had decided Dean would tell everyone where he was going and thus spark up enough interest for him to then make his way over there and tell everyone all about his new relationship. The conversation ended with James giving him directions and a quick look out of the door to make sure he had remembered correctly where they were. 28 minutes later Dean walked up the stairs inside the impressive and expensive block of flats and knocked on the door of 1A.

On his 13th birthday Dean had been at a football match with his Dad and arrived home to find his Auntie Linda had arrived with presents. With her were all of her family, including her son Tom. Dean had always got on with Tom. He had looked after him many times whilst growing up. They were good friends. With him, was his friend Mark as they were later being dropped at the train station for a night out. It was at this very moment that Dean had realised that his crush on the PE teacher was nothing compared to meeting Mark. From that day on, he had spent more and more time with Tom, in the hope that he would then get to see Mark more and more. A few years after, when he had been told that the two of them were gay, he had blurted out that he was too. No one had took him seriously, apart from Mark who had sat down and discussed it with him and told him to think about it more before he told too many people. Mark was amazing. In Dean's eyes he could do no wrong. Dean had seen Mark with plenty of guys over the years and more so in the last six months since he had moved to Tom's flat in London while he continued his dance scholarship. He was dedicated to the life and the prospect of being a professional dancer. Hours and hours of dance training every day, a strict diet and absolutely no drinks or drugs. He didn't understand one bit why any of Tom's friends would want to take drugs. Maybe he would ask Mark about it one day.

'What are you day dreaming about, Tom and his tattooed lover?' James said stood at the open door.

'Don't be a dick, and he is with Mark anyway' Dean said sounding upset.

'No he isn't, he is with your Tom, I saw them together last night...shhhh.' James cut in 'He is still asleep I don't want to wake him, you know what he'll be like.'

'I've never met him' Dean said with a puzzled look on his face.

'WOW! Nice pad man' they had now walked into the main part of the apartment. Dean always the hyperactive one, was now running round pretending he was a plane.

'Bloody huge, you could fly round this room.'

'Sssshhhh, I told you to keep it down.' James closed the bedroom door as Dean began to open cupboards in the kitchen and explore the contents. 'Stop it Dean, they aren't yours.'

'Look at this man, he has got all kinds of cool food' Dean was now stood looking at the rows of neatly stacked food cartons and tins.

'Come out of the kitchen' James walked towards him and began to get carried away with himself 'OMG it's all from Harrods and M&S. Well you know us Dean; we like to eat good food.'

'I thought this was the first time you had been here?' Dean said and jumped passed James. He began to open doors to cupboards and other smaller rooms off the main room. There was a dining room behind the kitchen and a laundry room next to that. He jumped over the sofa and opened the bedroom door where the man from last night was sleeping.

'Close the door, he is asleep in there.' James ran at Dean regretting the idea of inviting him over but liking the fact that Dean had now seen his new man.

'Soz man, what's in 'ere?' Dean walked to the next door along the wall from the bedroom.

'I don't know, stop now. We will have to go in a minute' James had found his underwear, swopped them over and found his jeans on the floor. He stepped over and picked them up and realised that Dean had gone quiet. Turning to look he saw Dean's back outlined in the doorway. Standing still and staring into the room. James stepped closer.

'What shut you u.....' he didn't finish his sentence. He looked into the room in as much amazement as Dean.

9

The room was very brightly lit, yet the windows weren't transparent. They had an opaque film over it, so that you could not see in or out. The walls were white, the dark oak wooden floor the only hint of colour in the room. A rectangular, glossy black table about 6ft long and 3ft wide sat in the middle of the room, with four identical glossy black chairs around it. On the table was what had stopped Dean and now James in their tracks. Sat piled up high in the middle of the table was the largest pile of pills either of them had ever seen!

On one corner of the table there was a box full of small plastic bags about one inch square in size and on the other side of the table was a sealed heavy duty plastic bag containing at least double the amount of pills on the table. James grabbed the door handle and closed it. James and Dean stood in front of the closed door in disbelief. Neither of them said a word. As if he somehow needed confirmation of what they had just seen, James opened the door and once again shut it slowly when the sight of the pills confirmed no mirage.

'What the fuck is that all about?' Dean was the first to speak 'I mean I don't think they are for a bad head!'

'Definitely not for his head' James said in a distant sounding voice. He knew exactly what the pills were. The man last night had been generously giving James Ecstasy pills, to the point that some of them James had not taken and they were in his pocket right now. He slipped his hand into his jeans and pulled out one of the two in there. Dean saw this and his mood began to change.

'Are you a drug dealer?' Dean said as he stepped back from James. The horror was evident on his face.

'No, don't be stupid, it's the first time I've ever been here' James looked at Dean, trying to work out in his own head what was going on. Last night's love of his life was clearly the dealer. He needed to get Dean out of the flat now.

'So then your boyfriend is a drug dealer?' the question was rhetorical.

'James, your boyfriend is a drug dealer and you have loads of drugs on you, Are you addicted to drugs?' Dean was beginning to sound panicky. Drama was Dean's default function. He was going on and on saying the same thing and James knew he had to get him out of the flat now.

'Oh my God James, I'm really scared for you, I have seen this on the telly and everything and you will...'

'Stop it' James said firmly.

'This isn't the time or the place to have this conversation. You need to leave. You go back to the pub and I will meet you there'

'NO!' Dean shouted. He grabbed the handle of the door and flew into the room. His diva rage flared as he stomped across the room banging into the table and sending the pile of pills flying everywhere. He grabbed the big bag of pills and shot past James who was grovelling on his knees, trying to catch the pills that were bouncing everywhere.

James jumped up and raced after Dean.

'What the fuck are you doing? What are you doing with them?' He shouted at Dean who had disappeared into the laundry room.

10

Sam slipped out of his bed and chuckled to himself as he remembered the thoughts he'd had the first day his parents had started calling him Jesus. He had loved them for all their faults and knew that they just lacked intelligence and will power to make their own decisions. The devoutly religious group, or cult as it had since become known, prayed on the weak minded to bring them round to their way of thinking. That's what Sam thought anyway. As fate transpired, Father Rowland's had been found out years later, apparently sharing some of the same dress sense as Sam but also it appeared that he had never actually been ordained into the Catholic church. Frilly knicker wearing or not, 'Father' Rowland has made up his own religion. As he got older, Parkinson's had set in and one day, confused and thinking the man he was talking to was his long lost son and not a reporter for the Sun Newspaper told him everything he had ever done in the village.

When Sam had read the report in the Sunday newspaper he had felt for his mother and father so much that he wanted to return to them and make sure they were ok. He decided not to though on the account that their son who was reborn of God, the child they had brought up till the tender age of sixteen was actually not the new Messiah but a massive raving tranny. His mother would have a heart attack.

Sadly it was only one year after the expose in the sun that Mr and Mrs Rockwell were taking a Sunday drive to their new church in the next village when, ironically, they had a head on collision with a Hells Angel group on a motorbikes and thus were destined to be with the God they had talked about for so long. Sam wasn't sad about their deaths; he knew that being with their God was the best place for them. He now had fond memories of his parents. As he rolled across the bed and began to think about attempting to get out of it, he pulled from his left eye lid an oversized eye lash extension with a pink diamante on the end and thought back to the day he had left home.

They had returned from church on the Sunday morning and everyone in the congregation as always had been calling him Jesus and touching him hoping that somehow some of his mystical powers might rub off on them. Samuel knew this was the day. Everything had been packed during the night and concealed in the garden.

Given that he was fast becoming quite a dramatic character, he knew he wanted to go out with a bang. Being dramatic he laughed to himself in bed, everyone thought I was bloody Jesus, how much more drama do you want? And so, on the return from church he went to his room to pray as did his parents in the lounge room downstairs. Whilst they were sat praying Samuel crept down the stairs and from outside the old wooden door said to his parents.

'I have learnt a new word' his mother was the first to look towards the door as Mr Rockwell stood up and straightened out his suit jacket.

'Jesus, do come in and tell us of your new word' his mother said expecting this to be one of many future lessons that Jesus would give. She had been waiting for this day for so long and the excitement, like the first day they had told Jesus who he was, began to rise within her and she could barely contain herself. His father, feeling a sense of pride that he too thought the preaching was beginning stepped closer to the door wanting to hear as much as possible.

'Fabulous!' said the voice from behind the door.

'Fabulous?' both parents said this at the same time and then Mr Rockwell added 'Jesus, what does this mean, Fabulous?'

Sam stepped from behind the wooden door to reveal he was dressed head to toe in a red, sparkling evening gown, a blonde wig that was curled and waved to that of a 1950's lounge singer, the look Sam had been going for. His size 8 feet almost crippled and rammed into a pair of fiery red 7 inch stiletto heels and the best make up with glossy red lips he could apply. His mother stood first the look of shock on her face.

'Jesus, you're......' her words trailed off and it was Mr Rockwell's face that said it all. He was fast turning as red as the dress his son was wearing.

'But, you're.......... Jesus.'

'I know, but I'm also fabulous darling' Sam said to the two of them.

His mother clutched her chest and fell to the floor. Mr Rockwell had no reaction to his wife passing out he stood looking at the doorway, where Jesus in the red dress was stood.

Sam rushed passed Mr Rockwell and was picking his mother up from the floor.

'Mother, are you ok? I think you've had a funny turn' Sam said as she opened her eyes.

She took one look at the beautifully groomed face and the big red lips and passed out again.

'I think she'll need the smelling salts Mr Rockwell' Sam said as he stood defiantly in front of his father.

'But you're Jesus' was all his father could say.

Sam touched his father's arm allowing him a close up of his immaculately manicured hand and the gloss on his finger nails coordinating well with his lipstick and dress.

'You were supposed to be praying' His father finally said.

'Well, Mr Rockwell, I think we both know that the reborn son of God isn't going to get many people following him in a red frock and 6 inch stilettos' Sam said holding his father's arm.

'What's a Stiletto?' Shock had kicked in with his father now.

'It's a heel darling, I think I'd better be making tracks. I don't want to miss my train' Sam said as he picked up the hand bag he had dropped when attending to his mother who was now pulling herself up to the arm chair.

'But where are you going Jesus?' She asked

'He isn't Jesus, he is the devil' Mr Rockwell said with venom in his voice.

'I love you mother, Mr Rockwell I'm quite fond of you too, but it is high time we stopped thinking I'm the saviour of mankind and realise how fabulous I look in my new dress. Please do look after yourselves.'

Sam opened the front door and walked out into the windy sea air. That was the last he had seen of either of his parents. He lay in bed wondering if that had been the right thing to do. Knowing the shock they would have been in the heartache it must have caused them. He also knew that just leaving in the night would have been worse. At least this way they knew who he was and why he had gone. This way they knew that Jesus wasn't coming to that small village stuck in the early part of the last century.

11

The laundry room that Dean had walked into was just as stylish as the rest of the apartment. It looked like a complete fitted kitchen with white glossy doors and a huge Belfast sink. Behind the doors were many appliances and in the middle of the room was a clothes horse with some clothing drying on it. Dean skidded into the clothes horse and it dropped to the ground along with its contents. James arrived at the door to find Dean stood over the Belfast sink trying to rip the bag open. He darted straight to him and tried to snatch the bag back.

'No.....I......Won't....' Dean was struggling with James to keep hold of the bag. 'Let..... You.'

'Give it back to me Dean, give it back and we can leave.'

James continued to struggle with the bag but he stopped suddenly and stood back, making Dean Stop and wonder why he wasn't fighting anymore.

'If gorgeous guy woke up and finds this he will probably kill both of us.'

'I can't let you be a drug addict James' Dean said, there were now tears rolling down his face.

'I'm not a drug addict Dean, you know that. If we put the bag back we can both leave.'

James was trying to reason with Dean, all the time he was looking over his shoulder hoping that the door to the bedroom stayed shut.

'All those drugs' Dean was still trying to open the bag. James now realised that it was quite a thick plastic and he wouldn't be able to open it without a knife. Knowing this meant he had more of a chance of getting it back to the other room without the man ever finding out.

'Look, I didn't know he was a dealer. If we put it back now we can leave and he will never even know you have been here.' James was trying his best; he was still in shock at Dean's reaction to the drugs. James was beginning to panic now too. He had never seen Dean like this and was unsure of what to do. The man he was in love with was a drug dealer and he had been taking his drugs all night. What did it make him? Could he be arrested for this? What if the police were watching the house, what if they were watching them now? He closed the laundry room door behind him and looked at Dean. 'You have to give me the bag so I can put it back. We are going to be in all kinds of trouble if you don't.'

'Ok' Dean said, as he pulled the bag up out of the sink the edge caught on the edge of something sharp on the granite worktop and ripped a hole in the side. As he saw what he had done, Dean's eyes widened in shock. The bag then freed itself from the snag and jolted forward sending half the contents flying through the air in the direction of James. Hundreds of little tiny pills were flying through the air. It was like everything went into slow motion.

'Noooooo' James dived across and grabbed what was left of the bag, wrestling it from Dean's hands to find that the majority of what was left was now slipping down the wide open plughole of the Belfast sink. He tried to grab as much as he could but they disappeared faster than he could grab.

Dean and James sat on the floor of the laundry room. Dean shyly with his head down and James looking around with the same look of shock on his face as he had when Dean had first opened the door to the room where the drugs had been kept. Hundreds of tiny little pills were scattered across the floor and over the granite worktop. Thoughts were racing through James's mind. What do we do now? It's not my problem, Dean can sort it? Dean can't sort it, it's my problem. What are we going to do now? Shall we just run? Tidy them up and put them back, he won't notice a few missing, who are you kidding he is a drug dealer, and then he saw it.

The end of something, it was showing only slightly, under a pair of Calvin Klein pants. The red banner of the underwear draped over the black barrel of a gun. He pushed the pants away with his foot to see that it was held in the leather holder. How had he not seen it before, it must have been hung on the clothes horse. Dean had now seen it too and looked up at James, he was beginning to shake. Shock was setting in at what he had done.

'Sorry' he whispered.

'Sorry isn't going to get us out of here!' Hundreds of thoughts were flying through James' mind; he had to think more clearly. His shoes were near the entrance, his jacket on the sofa and his phone on the table.

'Do you have everything you brought with you on you?' he asked Dean. Dean put his hand in his pocket and checked he had his phone and then nodded at James.

'Right then.' He had a plan. 'We are going to get up and walk out of here' he said calmly.

'My coat is on the sofa and my phone is on the table. I will get them; you head straight to the door. My shoes are next to it. Pick them up and walk out. I will follow you.'

'But what about your boyfriend?' Dean said with tears running down his face.

'Stop crying, you did this, stop fucking crying. Doesn't look like he is going to want me to move in when my so called friends do this.' Dean began to sob.

'Right come on!' The two of them stood up, more tiny pills falling off them onto the floor as they did.

'Shouldn't we try to clean them up?' Dean looked down to the floor.

'There must be about 2000 of them!'

'How many do you think were in there to start with?' James asked.

'More than double this!' Dean was now looking down the sink.

'Then out of respect, we need to clean them up and put them back where we found them.'

James' mind was racing again. Oh, Fuck, Oh Fuck, Oh Fuck. He had never known any drug dealers before. In fact, whenever he had taken drugs they had been bought by other friends. He wouldn't even know how to find a drug dealer, and now he had spent the night with one, fallen in love, to find that not only was he a drug dealer but he was a drug dealer with a gun.

'Respect?' Why should we respect him?' Dean stopped James's train of thought.

'I hear you, but it might be the only thing that doesn't get us killed.'

'What do you mean killed? This ain't some East End Guy Ritchie film you know. This kind of stuff just doesn't happen.' Dean tried to make James understand by holding his arm.

'Oh my God Dean, you're more naive than I am. Of course it fucking happens, why do you think he has a gun? Why do you think he has thousands of pills in his flat?' James shrugged Dean off.

'Well he is pretty careless if he is going to bring some boy back with him and then let him invite his friends round' James almost dived on Dean when he heard him speak.

'Well, I thought I was in love, he probably did too and now you've fucked it.'

'Sorry!!' Dean's whiney voice set James teeth on edge.

'We gotta get out, oh God' James began to worry. They both knelt down and began to put pills back into the bag.

'How many have we got?'

'About two hundred and fifty maybe eighty' Dean was holding the bag up in the air.

'So what, you reckon the bag normally has about five hundred in it?' James asked.

'I guess so if they come in five hundreds, do they?' Dean quizzed James.

'You fucking numpty' James said to Dean 'Get up, were going?'

The two of them headed to the door that led out into the main apartment. They were about to step through into the kitchen but were greeted by the bar chest of a not so impressed looking drug dealer.

'Who the fuck are you?' the thick deep cockney accent filled the laundry room.

'And what the fuck is going on?' He was staring directly at James. He turned and looked at Dean who was now shaking with fear. The man made a move to step closer so he could look. This small movement was enough for Dean to vomit with fear at the man's feet. The sick splashed across the floor and onto the bottom of his jeans. 'FUCK!' he shouted stepping back. As he did, he grabbed hold of Dean by the neck and dragged him into the kitchen.

'Who the fuck are you?'

'De...' Dean tried to talk but a mouth full of sick and the hand pulling tight on this throat stopped him. The drug dealer looked back James. He looked angry, no actually he looked demented like he was about to rip out Deans throat and then start on James. James, was still confused, he couldn't quite work out what had just happened. Thirty minutes ago he was as happy as he could ever be and now he was watching his friend about to be killed by the man that had made him the happiest he could be. How was he going to get out of this? He was always pretty good at flirting with blokes and being able to chat up an older guy but this was extremely different, but worth a go.

'Hey babe...' James attempts at flirting were halted by a fist flying out from the man's free right hand and meeting with his face, sending him crashing back into the laundry room. The half full and broken bag of pills landed on top of him and once again scattered across the floor. Blood began to trickle from his nose and the pain slowly moved across his face like frost biting into him, pretty soon the frost was burning hot and the pain shot through his head. He could hear somewhere someone cry out in pain and realised it was coming from him. Still dazed from the punch, he pulled himself up and started to scrape together the scattered pills again. It was just an instinctive reaction to get them back into the bag. He hadn't yet turned to see what was happening to Dean. He was too scared to know. Slowly he looked up to see the drug dealer looking down menacingly at him. He was still holding Dean who was now frozen to the spot, by his throat and unable to move. He looked back and continued picking single pills up and adding them to the bag. As he did so, he noticed the black cold barrel of the gun sticking out from under the red banner of the Calvin Klein's on the floor. Thoughts began to race through his mind about killing the drug dealer stone dead. He could free Dean and make a run for it. Did he know what to do with a gun? Yes! Of course. He decided he wasn't going to shoot it, he'd use it to scare, just enough that the drug dealer would let Dean go so they could get out.

12

'Haha, that's hilarious....did she get caught?' Sam laughed as he sat back on the sofa; Fred curled up next to him.

'Did who get caught?' Fred asked 'I wasn't listening.'

'This woman who works with Ben' Sam said to Fred pulling her closer into his arms

Ben, Sam and Fred were sat in the lounge of Sam's apartment where they had been since crashing through Sam's doors about 3 hours ago. Ben had arrived soon after.

'No, she didn't work with me, no one knows who she was' Ben explained.

'So some woman walked into your office, went round with a card getting everyone to sign it and putting money in an envelope and then left?' Sam asked in mock shock.

'Yeah' Ben lay back on the couch laughing.

'Whose birthday was it?' Fred asked.

'What?' Ben sat up and reached for the drink on the table, almost knocking it over.

'The birthday card, whose birthday was it?' Fred was now sat up looking over at Ben, who clearly needed sleep as he was looking jaded from the night out.

'It said Karen on the card but there wasn't anyone called Karen with a birthday. She had made it up; she just come into the office and did it.'

'You want to complain about that, can HR not do anything about it?' Fred was beginning to come round more 'In fact, that's rubbish go and find her and ask for your money back.'

'No one knows who she was' Ben replied. 'That's my point.'

'What the fuck! You let some bird you don't know fill out a card for Karen who you don't know and then go and get her present?' Fred quizzed Ben 'What was the present?'

'There wasn't one, SHE ROBBED THE MONEY!' Ben slowed his words down hoping that Fred would get what he was saying.

'Well she sounds just charming' Fred got up and walked to the kitchen, Ben shot a look at Sam, both were laughing, 'Poor Karen, bless... she doesn't deserve that.'

'Who the fuck's Karen?' Ben shouted through to Fred.

'Oh god, the poor girl just had her card and present stolen at work and now you can't be bothered to remember who she is' Fred walked back and slammed a glass of water in Ben's hand. 'Here you go!'

'What's that for?' Ben looked puzzled. Fred looked at him, took the water back and gave it to Sam.

'Thanks sweetheart, but I didn't ask for it either' Sam was laughing.

'Oh bugger, it must be for Pip' Fred took the drink and put it on the table. 'Pip love' she reached over and tapped Pip's toe. Pip was fast asleep on the sofa on the other side of the coffee table. A duvet had been wrapped around her earlier as she had dropped off to sleep. 'Pip love, I got your water.'

'I don't think she's awake' Sam pulled Fred over to the sofa and back into his cuddle.

'Tell Karen happy birthday from me on Monday, we can take her for lunch or something.'

Fred said as she sat back and closed her eyes, sleep was creeping up on her.

'Yeah alright love, I'll do that' Ben and Sam laughed. Suddenly Pip jumped up from the sofa, looked at the two of them as if she had no clue who they were and where she was and then walked to the bathroom.

'The car is double parked you better move it' She shouted as she disappeared into the bathroom. Sam was the first to burst into laughter and then Ben. Mark and Tom came back to the seated area accompanied by the sexy Irish guy with the tattoos who they had now found out was called Gavin.

'Whose car is double parked love?' Mark said as she passed him. He turned to the rest of the group.

'We are gonna make a move and head back home, Fred.' He waited for her attention.

'Are you and Pip stopping here or do you want to share a taxi?' It took Fred a while to work out what she had just been asked.

'I think the fact that it took me a minute to work out what you were saying and that Pip thinks she is double parked when she ain't driven a car in about ten years means we should stay put.' She snuggled up to Sam. 'Is that okay? What time will Dave be home? Will he be bothered?'

'That's fine love; I'm just chilling out here today so you two can get in bed. Dave is away'. Dave was now Sam's ex-boyfriend, Fred was aware they had split but obviously forgetting this in her drugged up state.

'Aww he is dead lovely you're Dave, how long have you two been together?' Fred asked.

'Eight years.' Sam said quietly, sad to think about the end of the relationship.

'WOW!' Fred almost shouted 'that has flown by. I remember when you first met him. I hadn't known you too long' Fred sat up to continue the conversation.

'Where's our Dean gone?' Tom asked Sam, changing the conversation seeing that Sam was getting upset.

'He left about an hour ago to go meet James, said he would bring him back here' Sam looked round at Tom. 'I could do without them two hanging about all day.'

'Right, I will give him a ring when I get in the taxi and tell him we have left' Tom said pulling his phone out.

'Can't see him wanting to come back if Mark has already left' Sam winked at Mark.

'Right then' He said laughing 'We are off, give us a tinkle later on and we can meet up for some scran.'

'I think Pip may have gone for a little sleep' Gavin said 'she just passed out on ya bed Sam.'

'Oh thank the Lord' Sam said raising his hands 'We won't have to talk her into it now.'

13

Mark walked out of Sam's apartment block with Tom and the sexy Irish guy Gavin, they stepped into the windy street and Tom walked forward to grab a taxi. Mark was looking down the road at a face he recognised. The man strode towards him wearing a fitted grey Armani suit that hung well across his broad shoulders. It made his white fronted hair with darker grey sides stand out. Mark noticed how the shirt under the suit was fitted perfectly to the man's chest and pulled just enough over his hard chest to make Mark think of what lay beneath.

He recognised him as the man he had met at a night club about two weeks ago. He had spent the majority of the night talking to him and being totally turned on by him. He'd then lost him in the crowd at closing time before he could exchange numbers. Now he was thinking about what indeed lay beneath that shirt and how great it would be to slowly take that suit of him. The man was now a few paces closer to Mark and stopped in a shop window to take a look at something. His tanned skin, made his whole appearance look even more distinguished.

'In the taxi' Tom had grabbed Mark's arm and had been saying something he hadn't heard.

'Earth to Mark, come in Mark your transportation is waiting' Mark looked into Tom's eyes slightly confused.

'What?' he said, then looked down and saw the sexy Irish guy with tattoos and big arms looking up at him from a taxi.

'Oh right yeah, erm' looking back at the suited man he made a decision 'I'll take the next one' he said to Tom.

'What the?' It was now Tom's turn to look confused.

'We live in the same building.' He then noticed which direction Mark was looking in.

'Oh right I get it, I'm pretty sure that on the day businessmen stop working on a Saturday I will get your attention.'

'What you on about?' Mark looked at Tom with a big smile on his face.

'You and your bloody suit fetish.' Tom said as he stepped into the taxi. 'Be good little man.'

He turned to his Irish partner in the taxi. 'Now then, tell me what your name is again?' and with that the door was closed and the sexy Irish man with the tattoos and big arms forced his face onto Tom's, his tongue travelled into his mouth and the taxi began to drive away leaving Mark stood on the street wondering what he was going to do next.

It didn't take long. The suited man started to walk towards Mark with a cheeky grin on his face. Mark began to admire his face, his chiselled jaw line with a slightly pointed nose. The white hair at the front of his spiky fringe framed his face perfectly. His smile was great but his intense stare right into Mark eyes all the time he was walking towards him made Mark melt even more. The fact that he was wearing a sexy tailored suit made him start to go hard.

'Good morning Mark, I didn't expect to see you again after we last met.'

'Hey, how are you?' In the state that Mark was in it was hard for him to remember his own name never mind the suited man's but he was thinking back to the night they met, Steve, Simon.....Stuart!! 'It's Stuart isn't it?'

'I'm impressed. I didn't think I had made that much of an impression on you the other night but you've remembered my name.' Mark moved slightly closer having been pushed in the back by a woman trying to negotiate the high street with several children, one of whom was in a buggy. They stood close together now looking into each other's eyes, smiling. There was a few seconds, of lovely comfortable silence.

'Where are you off to in such a good looking suit?' Mark asked, still very turned on by Stuart and the suit.

'Oh, this?' He ran his finger and thumb down the lapel of the suit and across his chest. 'Like the suit do you Mark?' Stuart said, the smile on his face turning to a grin.

'I most certainly bloody well do, you look well horny in that Mr' Mark ran his fingers down the same lapel that Stuart had just been touching.

'Mark...' Stuart's voice had changed, still interested and still intense but a little further away.

Mark noticed he had moved slightly further from him and thought he had then misread the signals and this wasn't the chat up he had wanted.

'Maybe this isn't the place for us to be........ so flirty?' Stuart said. Mark relieved, that flirty was what he wanted said 'Shall we grab a drink?' Stuart turned to look at the pub a few doors down.

'Great Idea' Mark wanted to get to know this guy a lot better, but not here. Knowing that a group of his friends were upstairs and highly likely to be in the pub later he decided they had better go elsewhere.

'Really not a great place though. We won't be able to get to know each other half as much as we would like in there,' quickly thinking whether to invite the guy back to his place.

'I have an idea Mark' Stuart said to him. Mark liked the way he used his name, quite direct, almost like giving a command. 'Erm....' Stuart was hesitant. 'I know a gentleman's club not far from here; in fact I was on my way there when I saw you. We could get to know each other as much as we so desire there. I'm not sure if that would be your thing....'

'You mean like a sauna?' Mark said understanding what Stuart had in mind.

'Well, you know the type of place Mark but this is far from a sauna. It is a Gentlemen's Club, so no steam rooms and hot tubs. I guess some of the same things go on there. What do you think?' Stuart said back to the cheeky smile, his hand now on Mark's shoulder once again being quite masterful.

'I guess I could give it go.' Mark now extremely interested in the idea of what this place might be.

14

The walk only took them 10 minutes, during which time Mark had told Stuart that he had been out all night with friends and could really do with freshening up before he entered the club. Stuart had explained the setup of the club and also that there would be a place for him to take a shower and he would also be able to borrow some suitable clothing for the occasion.

Mark spent the rest of the walk wondering what the occasion was. As they arrived, Mark saw a door set back from the street. It was the kind of door that you never usually noticed. The door was set back in an alcove with black and white tiles on the floor and the rendered walls were an exact matching colour to the grey door that looked solid and old. There was no identification on the building apart from a small golden plaque next to the door with a logo carved into it.

'Institute of Gentlemen' Stuart said to Mark noticing he was paying attention to what was written. Stuart took a key card from his wallet and waved it passed the handle of the door and they both heard the familiar sound of a lock mechanism opening. They entered into a dramatic marble mosaic inner hall that extended for about 50 feet to a large masculine looking reception desk.

They walked towards the desk where a man of about 50 years stood from his seat dressed in formal wear and definitely looked every bit the butler of the building. Mark was taking in his surroundings while Stuart spoke to the butler. A magnificent staircase that Mark had not noticed on entering was above him. It angled away from the main entrance door and led round the wall wrapping the whole of the room and reaching a balcony landing high above.

'Do you have any identification with you Mark?' Stuart was now stood intensely close to Mark once again. 'They need to make a record of you joining me today'. Without saying a word Mark took out his wallet and handed over his driving license to the gentleman behind the desk. After a few more minutes the card was handed back.

'I have booked you into room 214, the items you have requested will be waiting for you and today's event will be taking place in the large library room, is there anything else I can get for you sir?' The gentleman behind the desk said to Stuart, never once speaking to Mark.

'Thank you that will be all I need.' Stuart turned and walked towards the stairs, looking back at Mark. 'Come this way.' The cheeky grin was back and he was speaking to Mark with an authority that he was beginning to get very turned on by again. As he walked up the stairs to the balcony he noticed the paintings on the walls. When he had first looked he had not looked close enough just noticing paintings that you would expect in such a historic looking building. On closer inspection however, he noted that the paintings must be modern but with a feel and style of history. Not knowing much about paintings he didn't try to guess the age they were, instead he noticed that the people in the paintings were all men, all in suits and all depicting some form of sexual act.

They walked along a corridor off the balcony, there were doors lining the long passageway all deep set into the walls with deep modern frames holding the large oak doors in place. They stopped at a door with no marking on. None of the doors had markings but Stuart seemed to know where he was. Once again he took out his key pass and opened the door, entering a room just as impressive as the rest of the building. Deep pile red carpets, a huge window with a view across the Thames and the top of St Paul's Cathedral and a huge four poster bed in the middle of the room. The bed looked like an antique and had expensive looking bedding.

'So' Mark said as he walked across to a wardrobe to look in. 'Is this a hotel then?'

'No' Stuart said assertively.

'Oh, right. It looks like a hotel. We checked in like a hotel..... and there's a bed' Mark said looking into the wardrobe to see a black suit hanging inside joined by a crisp white shirt. There was a shelf with socks and a Calvin Klein box of underwear and a few other items.

'They are for you; I believe I have got your size correct?' Stuart said.

'It's not a hotel Mark. As I said it is a Gentleman's club.'

'There's a pair of Calvin's in here, what kinda of club supplies underwear?' Mark had them in his hand looking at Stuart. Very excited about this new place he was discovering.

'Guess you want me to wear all this then do you?'

'It's the kind of place I pay handsomely to be a member of and by doing so they supply whatever I wish.' There was an emphasis on whatever and Mark wondered what else the man on reception would be able to arrange. Still feeling slightly out of it from a night out partying, but he was still very much in control of enjoying this new experience.

'You can take a shower in here' Stuart opened the door to the bathroom and walked in. When Mark joined him he was checking himself in the mirror. 'I think I'll do.'

'You most certainly will, so have a shower' Mark began to remove his clothes and drop them on the floor.

'And then put that suit on. What you going to do then Mr.... erm? I don't know your surname.'

'You don't need to know it, you can call me Sir' and with this Stuart grasped Mark's shoulder, turned his naked body round into a standing spoon position and sunk his tongue deep into Mark's ear. At the same time he reached over and turned on the shower and slowly eased Mark towards it. 'There is a little event we can attend down the hall before we come back here and I will show you what happens when you call me Sir.'

Mark was becoming increasing more curious of what was about to happen. Knowing that this wasn't going to be dinner and drinks with work colleagues, he showered fast, Stuart stepped out of the bathroom.

15

Dean shot past James, both running as fast as they can, James pulling on clothes as they were going. They ran along the busy high street unaware of the people around them. Just seconds before they exited the flat of the drug dealer having almost been killed inside. Both of them began to gather speed. Every noise they heard, they thought was the drug dealer following them. Keeping pace with each other they turned the corner into an alleyway and Dean disappeared. James holding himself up against the wall was looking for Dean and all of a sudden his hand came out, pulling him back behind a set of bins. They huddled together for a few moments both of them desperately out of breath, their hearts pounding up into their throats, soaking wet with sweat. Desperately trying to catch his breath James was trying to say something to Dean.

'What the...... What...... What... Did... You... Do that for, you fucking idiot?'

Dean just sat there holding onto the side of the bin and James's arm desperately trying to gather his breath, not saying a word. He was shaking, maybe from the shock or maybe from the fact that his body was beginning to shut down after having run so far at such a speed. James began to gather his breath now his heart stop pounding so much.

'As if things weren't bad enough, what was that about?' James whispered over to Dean.

'I just erm......... Panicked' Dean replied back shaking even more.

'Fucking panicked? Panicked is getting up and running out of there. Panicked, is not stupidly opening a bag of drugs and scattering them across a floor. Panicked! Dean! Is most certainly not taking a gun and firing it at a drug dealer!' James said staring at Dean who had now begun to cry.

They could hear footsteps in the alleyway and wondered if the drug dealer had now found them. James looked down the alleyway and realised that there was a couple sorting through some shopping bags.

'We're gonna have to make a run for it!' James said.

'No! No! He's out there he's gonna get us' Dean sobbed.

'No he isn't he's gone the other way, we've gotta make a run for it' James stood up pulling Dean with him 'We can go to the pub and find the others.'

'This is all your fault, James. What you doing with a drug dealer? Why is your boyfriend a drug dealer?' he cried.

'My fault? How can you say this is my fault? This is your fault, if you'd just let things alone, everything would be fine. I can't believe I'm stuck in this mess after just meeting the man of my dreams and now find out that he wants us dead.' James pushed Dean up against the wall.

'Don't you dare blame this on me, if you hadn't been there none of this would have happened' Dean tried to argue his way out but it wasn't working. James got more and more angry, at which point he grabbed hold of Dean's jacket wrenching him away from the wall and threw him across the alleyway. Hitting the wall on the other side, Dean bounced back on top of James and punched him in the face in exactly the same spot where he had been previously hit. The pain rushed to his face and down across his body once again and James began to feel lightheaded.

16

Mark finished drying himself having spent a little longer in the shower than he had first planned. As soon as the hot water hit his skin he began to relax and enjoy the heat. He stepped into the bedroom to find that Stuart had left. The suit was lying on the bed, the underwear had been removed from the packaging and it had been joined by socks, and two small boxes. One box contained a pair of cuff links and the other a pair of sock suspenders. Mark laughed as he took them out thinking he had found someone who took suit sex much more seriously than he did.

He sat on the bed and pulled on the underwear, as he did so he saw a glass of champagne sat on the dresser with a note under the glass. The note told Mark that once he was dressed then he should join him in large Library room. There were directions, not just how to get to the room but also how to wear the suit and the important sock suspenders. Laughing to himself and feeling that rush of excitement again he drank the champagne down in one and dressed for Stuart. Once dressed he realised his footwear was not going to do, he had a pair of trainers with him that he had been wearing for the last 16 hours. Sat on the bed wondering what to do, the wave of tiredness came over him.

'What the hell are you doing?' Mark said out loud to himself and lay back on the bed. He closed his eyes and began to feel sleep creeping in; maybe the long hot shower wasn't the best idea. Not quite sure how long he had dozed for he was startled by a knock at the door. It must be Stuart coming to look for him he thought as he jumped up and opened the heavy door.

'Sir?' Mark was shocked to find the man from the reception stood in the doorway.

'I was asked to check if everything was ok Sir?'

'Erm' still a little puzzled Mark replied 'Yes, all if fine I'm just about to go to erm....'

'The Library room Sir?' The man said.

'Sir, I took the liberty of preparing these for you. It looked like they may have been required?' The man handed over a pair of black polished shoes.

Expensive black polished shoes.

'Thank you, that is exactly what is needed' Mark was beginning to feel excited again.

'As I expected Sir' the man replied.

'If you would like to put them on Sir, Then I can show you to the event' Mark leaned against the wall and slipped the shoes on tying them whilst holding his feet in the air. He didn't realise the butlers distaste at this slack way of putting the shoes on.

'Right then' Mark thought to himself about posh hotels and tipping 'I'm afraid I don't have any change for a tip' Mark said.

'That won't be necessary young man. This way please.' The butler continued down the corridor where Stuart and Mark had stopped to enter the room earlier. After following the man round a few corners Mark began to realise that they may in fact be the only people in the building, as he had not seen another person the whole time he was there. His feeling of unease soon passed when he rounded another corner to see the large open doors of the Library in front of him and could hear the volume of many conversations taking place.

'Erm, excuse me' Mark asked the butler 'What type of event is it I'm attending?'

'You will see soon enough young man, I'm sure it will be to your taste.'

The butler turned to Mark at this point and brushed the shoulders of the suit and buttoned the front together. 'A great fit I think. Have a good day young man' and with this the butler disappeared along the corridor where they had come from.

17

The sound of the intercom was high pitched and hurt Sam's ears every time he heard it. It was worse right now as some idiot at the entrance was holding their finger on it so that it buzzed continuously.

'You better have a good reason for...' Sam began to speak.

'Open the fucking door Sam' A loud shout came through the intercom, Sam thought he recognised who it was but wasn't sure.

'It's Dean, fucking open it!'

'You're too late love, the boys have gone, and watch your language when you....' Cut off again, Dean shouted back.

'Please, open it now!' Sam pressed the button, wary that his neighbours would now be listening in. The lady in the flat below was older than the building itself, frail in body, strong in mind and her hearing seemed to get better every day. Unless she had the flat bugged which he doubted, she seemed to know pretty much word for word every conversation that had ever been had in the building. Sam could now hear footsteps on the stairwell, two sets. Bloody James was with him. Whatever they had done this time he certainly wasn't getting involved. The pair needed to stop getting into trouble. Sam was pulling his phone out of his jeans pocket getting ready to call Tom to let him know Dean was here when they burst into the room. Dean red faced looking like he was about to be sick and James a footstep behind him pushing the door closed and running the window that over looked the entrance and looking down pushing Sam out of the way as he did so.

'What the hell is going on here?' Sam said in a tone that showed he was more than upset.

'It doesn't look like we were followed, I can't see anyone' James was looking out the window talking to no one in particular.

'Followed?' Sam dragged James's shoulder and flipped him round 'Followed to my house?'

'Who is following you? Have you been hit?' James stood red faced catching his breath and shocked. He didn't know what to say. Sam looked over to Dean who was leaning against the wall. The redness of his face was going and a new colour was appearing, a green and white face. Just as Sam realised what was happening it was too late. Dean was sick from his standing position, hitting his feet, it splashed up against the wall and over the door to the bedroom he was stood in front of.

'Get in the bathroom' Sam shouted at Dean, James tried to walk over to him, but Sam caught his jumper and dragged him back.

'Not so quick, what's going on? What's wrong with him and where have you been all morning?'

'I met this bloke. I stayed over at his place and I think love him. No, I know I love him and he loves me. It was so special. We like, totally trusted each other. We didn't even need to use a condom and then we went to sleep, well he did, I couldn't as I was wired.'

Sam listened to James talking faster than he did when he was on drugs and began to get confused with the story.

'And then Dean came over to meet him and there were drugs everywhere, I mean like everywhere, thousands of them and then Dean went crazy and then the bloke came out and the gun was shot and then we just ran and this was the first place, well we just thought everyone would be here.'

James stopped speaking and held his hand over his mouth. Sam stood in shock looking at him.

'You shot a drug dealer?' Fred was stood in the now open doorway of the bedroom looking down at the sick in front of her.

'James, tell me you didn't shoot a drug dealer and run away?'

'I don't think he was a drug dealer, he is really nice and I really....' James began to cry.

'I'm not quite sure what to say' Sam looked over at Fred, his eyes bulging asking her what they should do.

'You better call Mark and tell him to come get Dean James...' Fred shouted harder.

'JAMES' he looked at her wiping his eyes. 'James, what state was the bloke in when you left and where did this happen?'

'He was really, really pissed off' James was nodding his head.

'Yes I should imagine he was, two teenage queens had just shot him and.... exactly what had you done to his drugs?'

'They are here!' Dean walked into the room holding the plastic bag containing about half the pills from earlier. Both Sam and Fred jumped away.

'No! No! No! No! 'Sam was pointing at the bag and looking at James.'

'You didn't steal the drugs?.... You stole the fucking drugs and shot the man and then came here?'

'We didn't shoot him, Dean shot at him.' Everyone now looked at Dean 'He missed!'

18

Mark entered the room and instantly noticed the amount of sexy suited men that were stood around, drinking various drinks. Whiskey over ice, glasses of Champagne and several with long drinks too. He scanned the room looking for Stuart, but found himself checking out all of the men. He didn't recognise a single person. He looked around seeing men in groups talking. Some were couples talking as close and intimately as he had been with Stuart earlier. Each and every person was looking extremely good in their suits. They were openly admiring each other. As he was looking one particular guy up and down, thinking to himself that his suit fetish had moved on from just watching suit porn at home. This was in fact some kind of grown up suit party. He had been to night clubs before where everyone wore suits and generally end up shagging each other but this was totally different.

The air was still as sexually charged, but it was calm and very, very horny. He continued into the room and was offered several drinks from a waiter he had not previously noticed. Taking a glass of champagne and thanking the waiter he walked further into the room and noticed there was a huge leather chesterfield couch in the middle, with no one sitting on it. Everyone was around the edge of the room with most people on the other side of the couch. He stood next to the back of the couch with it behind him and continued to check everyone out. He had seen Stuart sat on a tall stool leaning on a tall table; he was almost stood up perching on the edge of the seat. He had seen Mark walk in and the attraction he already felt for him grew stronger. He watched the other men in the room taking notice of him in the black Armani suit sipping the champagne. He watched Mark checking out the sexy crowd of businessmen here for the event. Mark looked directly at Stuart and they both caught each other's eye. Staying in their positions they looked intensely at each other, Stuart smiling and admiring Mark. He was very pleased that he had seen Mark on the high street earlier. Attending these occasions alone wasn't his preference. He had done it before and met other men here that did the same and enjoyed it very much, but he got very turned on by bringing someone to an event. He looked at Mark and Mark looked back at him. He went to take a step in Stuart's direction but was cut off by an older gentleman, probably in his late sixties but still trim and looking good in his suit.

'Now then.' He said in an eccentric calm voice. 'We haven't seen you here before have we Johnson?' He referred to the man stood next to him. Johnson was considerably younger than himself, younger than Mark's thirty one years anyway, he was probably in his mid-twenties.

'No Sir, we haven't.' he said to the man then directed his comments to Mark.

'No, I've never seen you here before.'

'I'm pretty new' Mark said looking over the man's shoulder at Stuart who sat patiently watching the interaction.

'Then I simply must show you around, you can stay with me sweetie.' The man then noticed the glint in Mark's eye and the fact that he was paying more attention to the man behind him.

'I see you may have already have found your date.' The man turned and looked at Stuart too who nodded in acknowledgement at the man.

'And what good taste you have. Stuart certainly is a fine specimen. Now you go over and say hi from me sweetie' and with this he gently pushed Mark's back as his hand slid down and patted his bum, he turned and ordered Johnson to follow him. Mark walked slowly to Stuart who stood, took his arms and planted his lips directly on his.

They kissed deeply and passionately for about 5 minutes. Stuart turned his mouth away from Mark's and kissed his neck as he had done so earlier, turning Mark round back into the standing spoon position and perching himself on the stool, holding on to Mark.

'I think you're really going to enjoy this' He whispered into Mark's ear.

'What exactly is this?' Mark asked as he watched a young man walk over with a pile of papers and sit on the couch.

'You'll see' Stuart said.

Mark realised that Stuart was now reaching round to put his hand down into his trouser pocket. Thinking that it might not be the best place to do this, in a bar full of horny men, he soon realised just how passionate everyone else was being with each other. There were a few men doing similar to him and Mark.

19

On Sunday afternoon at precisely three thirty-two, the door of the second floor flat at 32b Clearwell Drive, Maida Vale, swung open crashing into the wall next to it knocking the potted plant over that also held numerous umbrellas, sending its contents across the laminate hallway floor. Sat around the kitchen table in the room just to the left were Sam, Dean, James, Pip and a half full bag of around two thousand ecstasy pills.

All of them jumped, Dean screamed and each looked to the door, scared to find out what had just entered the flat. It had been a long day for everyone and now some new terror was about to explode into their lives, adding to the fear that had developed since this afternoon's events.

Earlier this afternoon, Sam had tried to eject Dean and James from the flat once he had found out that James had spent the night with the drug dealer and then Dean had stolen the drugs and shot at him. During the argument, Fred had stepped out of the bedroom leaving Pip asleep to see what was going on. Her head had now cleared from the partying the night before and she was ready for a shower. Standing next to James she stretched, put her arm around him and asked;

'What's all this about then?'

'It's a long story.'

'Maybe I don't want to know.' She looked at the pair and then looked back at James.

'Why they talking about shooting drug dealers, what on earth has he done now?'

'Oh shit Fred, Oh shit, it is all fucked up' James began to cry and threw himself into Fred's arms. Fred held him and listened. She listened to Dean explain exactly what had happened. He was pointing at James a lot and she could see that Sam was getting more and angry with him. Every few minutes Sam was typing something into his phone whilst screaming at Dean and then putting the phone to his ear. She guessed he was trying to call Tom. Deciding that something needed to be done to calm to situation down she stepped towards Sam.

'Sam love, come over here with me' she attempted to lead him to the kitchen.

'No I bleedin' won't, I want him and them OUT of here NOW!' Fred saw the bag on the table containing a hundreds of little pills. It wasn't taking much to confuse her at this point and Sam shouting wasn't making it any easier.

'Can someone explain what's going on?'

'I'll tell you what the fuck is going on shall I?' Sam screamed lurching forward onto his other foot to scare Dean, who jumped back over to James. 'I'll tell you what these two pairs of fuckwits have done. They managed to sleep with a drug dealer who just so happens to be a ruthless psycho who shoots people for fun! They however, SHOT at him and stole his drugs' Sam was beginning to calm down 'Did I leave anything out?'

'It was James that slept with him' Dean said. Sam Jumped forward to be pulled back by Fred.

'That's not helping Dean!'

Fred and Sam stood looking at the drugs on the table and then looking back at each other. 'Right Sam, get yourself a drink.' She turned to look at the other two.

'Tell me exactly what happened.'

When Sam returned he had calmed down, James had stopped crying and both he and Dean were sat on the sofa with Fred stood in front of them.

'So you just ran, and you know you only shot the gun at him and didn't actually hit him?' The pair nodded.

'Right then.' she looked at Sam. 'And you know who it is they are talking about?'

'Yes, he has a bit of a name for himself. A drug pusher, he has loads of kids working for him. Bit of a psycho, shoots first and asks questions later.

'But he was really nice, I really like him' James said looking rejected.

'That's very nice dear, but you were in love last week and the week before. If you really want this bloke then don't bring him round here' Sam sat in front of the bag of drugs.

'James, tell me honestly now. Is there any chance he might have followed you, or anyone might have followed you here?'

'I don't think so.'

'Oh fuck, we are fucked if he did. Would he know where you live, know who you are?'

James sat looking at Dean and then at Fred as if they would have the answer.

'No' He started to cry again 'I don't think he would even remember my name' James let out a huge breath at exactly the same time that someone knocked on the door to the flat.

Fred's eyes shot to Sam who stood up and looked her directly in the eye too. Both of them looked at each other, knowing what the other was thinking. James and Dean sat on the sofa scared.

'I'll go' Fred said. She began to walk towards the hall way.

'Don't be stupid' Sam walked past her.

'It's my flat' he said, hoping it was nothing to worry about. He looked through the spy hole on the door and saw the top of a very tight, grey perm. He let out a huge sigh of relief.

'No worries, it's just Mrs Potts from downstairs' He unlocked the door, took the chain off and opened the door.

'Hello, Dear!' Mrs Potts said through the door as she heard the lock being taken off.

'There is a lovely young man here looking for you, I thought I would bring him up' Sam pulled the door towards him to be greeted by a man in a beige suit with grey hair. He thought to himself that he had a look of Daniel Craig. Panic shot through his whole body when he realised exactly who it was.

'Now then Rockers, you look a little underdressed' He said to Sam as Mrs Potts retreated down the stairs. Once Mrs Potts was safely ensconced back in her own flat, the man lurched forward pushing the door with force enough to make Sam stumble.

Pip sat behind the bedroom door listening to what was happening in the lounge area. Fred had pushed her back into the room and told her to stay there when she had tried to come out forty five minutes earlier after hearing someone knock at the door. A lot had been said. Sam and Fred seemed to be doing most of the talking and she thought that Dean and James were there too.

There was another male voice that was doing a lot of the talking too, mainly to Sam and Fred. She couldn't place it yet but she had heard the voice somewhere before. Something had happened and he wanted money from 'these two', she assumed that meant Dean and James. The male voice had now moved closer to the bedroom and she heard him clearly now.

'You have until this time next week to get my fifty grand or I'll 'av both of these two little shits!' pointing to Dean and James.

Pip still couldn't place the voice but knew she had spoken to him before.

'Right Rockers, you know the score. You get this sorted or I'm coming for you!'

There was a loud bang as Pip heard the door to the flat slam back into its hole. Having sat next to the door for the last 45 minutes listening, she had figured this was the best place for her. The other man didn't know she was there and nothing had happened for her to have to save anyone from anything. She stood up and stepped out of the room making everyone jump as they saw someone her appear.

'What's happening?' She said in shock. The four faces looked back at her, all in shock, mouths open and no one quite sure of what had actually happened. Fred explained what had happened to Pip.

'So, I came out to find them arguing and that bag of drugs on the table' she pointed across to the table they were now sat at.

'And then he arrived and started on James, so we had to stop him!'

'Oh my God!' Sam said.

'I can't believe this is happening.' He held his head in his hands. Pip looked at all of them in shock and Fred rubbed Sam's back. He looked up.

'I'm pretty sure he would have killed you right here James. I think you have a lot to thank Fred for' everyone looked at Fred.

'You're a fucking dynamo you are, I can't believe you talked him down... what did you say... say it again' Pip and Sam looked at Fred.

'I just made him see reason. He wouldn't get his drugs or money back if James was dead.'

'So now you're in debt to the tune of 50K to a drug dealer?' Pip looked at James and Dean sat at the end of the table.

'What are you going to do?'

'I'm calling Tom. There is no way I am making my way home on my own' Dean said to the others.

Sam rolled his eyes and stood up to go to the kitchen. He held on to the counter, worried, and scared about the fact that he was now part of this. Wondering just how a great night out had turned into this chaos. Dean walked in behind him and Sam could hear him dialling Tom.

'Tom? Tom, it's me Dean, oh my fuck Tom everything is really shit. James shot a drug dealer and stole all his drugs and now we are....' pause 'why are you whispering Tom? I said James had this thing with a guy who turned out to be a drug dealer and I didn't like it and then all the drugs got spilled out and we had to do a runner.' He paused again, tears now welling up in Dean's eyes. 'You have to come and help' Dean sobbed. 'Ok, ok, will you come and get me, I don't want to come home on my own … he is here too.' Dean turned from the corner of the room and walked towards Sam. 'He wants to speak to you.' Sam took the phone and pushed Dean back to the dining room table where everyone else was sat.

'Hello dearest, everything has gone to shit and these silly little boys of yours have got themselves into a whole heap of trouble…. Ok, see you soon'. Sam took his seat back at the top of the table. Pip, Sam and Fred looked at Dean and James sat at the end of the table. This is where they had been sat for the last hour just staring at each other in silence, unaware that something in the hall way was about to come crashing through the door.

20

Sam was the first to do something. He jumped out of his seat. Everyone else yelped. The loud crash behind the closed hall way door was frightening.

'I'm forty four fucking years old, why the fuck, am I scared of this shit?'

He walked passed everyone sat around the table and looked towards the door.

'Come on then!' he shouted to the door.

As he approached it the door burst open, once again shocking him and making him jump back towards the group. As he did so he looked up to see a figure stood in the doorway holding on to a large suitcase that seemed to be bursting its contents out from its sides.

'You won't believe the chuffin' day I've had!'

Caroline was Sam's flatmate. At six feet she was taller than most of the other girls, she carried a bit of weight too and no one seemed to mess with her. Her thick north Manchester accent also held off anyone who may have wanted to try. All of which were exactly the opposite of what she was actually like, each and every person that got to know her realised she was the nicest person you could ever get to know. She would go out of her way to ensure everyone was happy and often got taken advantage of. Her ditzy nature often got the better of her, but more often got the better of everyone else as she also knew how to use it to her advantage, when she put her mind to it. The last 24 hours had been an example of when she didn't put her mind to it.

In the mid-eighties Caroline had married the love of her life and having finished her nursing degree, moved to London as part of his medical degree. She packed up and moved with him without a second thought. What she hadn't realised at the time is that she wasn't the only nurse that had had the intimate pleasure of Dr Borring's company. She later found out soon after the move that he was referred to as Dr 'Boring' once most had had that pleasure. They tried for several years to build a life together, most of which was because she ignored the fact that he slept with most of the nurses she knew. After a few years she fell pregnant and she had twins. Life changed and they grew further apart. On their 10th anniversary, she came home to find Dr Boring in bed with two nurses and decided she had had enough.

By 1996, she was a single mother bringing up twins in a house she couldn't afford with an absent ex-husband who had quite quickly moved into the house of one of the nurses whom she had found in bed with him on that fateful day. Caroline never took it to heart and moved forward with her life. However, it was this life changing event that had born the realisation that Dr Boring was in fact dull in bed and that she had never realised it. Caroline's second life changing event came in 1997, when after a drunken night out with work colleagues. She ended up in bed with the same nurse as Dr Boring. To the nurse, she was a twenty four year old sexy blonde who was just trying something out when drunk, to Caroline, it was like the calling. She finally understood why people actually enjoyed having sex and also totally understood why Dr Boring liked to have sex with so many women. It was during her exploration of being a lesbian that Caroline met Sam and they became best friends.

They had suffered hard times and been there for each other each step of the way and enjoyed many happy times together. Everyone often joked about them really being married and both realised that they would grow old together. When the twins had decided to move out and go traveling, Caroline had sold the family home to help support their dreams and moved in with Sam in his flat in Maida Vale. The twins had settled in Melbourne, Australia and found themselves wonderful Aussie girls.

'Oh my God Caroline, you scared the bleedin' life out of me' Sam said supporting himself on Freds chair clutching a hand to his chest.

'What the bloomin' heck? What's wrong with you lot? You won't believe what kind of a day I've had, it's been bloody ridiculous. Sorry I wasn't back in time for last night I have been stuck with security at Adelaide Airport. Rox, are you alright? You look like you're having a funny turn.' Caroline aimed her question at Sam but didn't wait for an answer. She took a seat on the sofa, turned to them and began to tell everyone about her journey. 'So this cheap ticket I got, to go see the boys in Oz, aww it was dead nice seeing them and their girlfriends are both dead nice too, I well miss them. Sam sat back in his chair, the group all gobsmacked at the addition to the room. Caroline continued talking without even noticing them.

'So I had to fly through loads of different airports because it was cheap, it was like a bus or something with loads of stops. So, when I got to Adelaide and I didn't know this right. When I got there I had to change from domestic to international right. So I get off the plane with all my stuff and off I trot. Only I don't know where I'm going and the domestic airport isn't really all that big. So I followed this little woman who was doing the same as me. I knew because I had spoken to her on the plane right, so off we go. And this guy tells us that international is just through these doors. We head through and realise that we are in a staff bit so just nip out through the exit and into the international bit of the airport. Well, that's where it all went wrong' Caroline looked at everyone a little puzzled but carried on anyway.

'So this big security guy come running over and rugby tackles us both to the ground and starts to arrest us.' She looked back at everyone to get a reaction. None.

'Right' beginning to wonder what is wrong with them. 'So we get hauled over to the security rooms and they strip search me.' Still no reaction.

'Are you listening to me? Strip searched' realising there was no reaction.

'What is up with you lot, have you had a really big night out and now feel rough? I am gutted I never got the night out. What's happening?'

'It's a long story, you better sit down again.' Sam got up and walked to the sofa with Caroline.

21

Detective Inspector Jack Daniels sat at his desk and read the birthday card from his ex-wife and three daughters. There was a black and white picture on the front of an old woman holding a tray and a joke underneath that made reference to her bra not being able to hold her breasts. Jack did not get the joke and wondered if it was his ex-wife's way of somehow insulting him. There was a picture of his three daughters inside the card, he reached over the desk and took the frame that held the picture sent to him last year by his daughters and replaced the picture with the new one. He carefully added the old picture to the album kept in his desk drawer. The next card he opened was from Detective Sergeant Alan Jones, his direct report. The card was of a picture of the famous Bourbon, Jack Daniels and made reference to the similarity in his name and the name of the drink. Once again Jack was not amused by the joke and realised that at age fifty three the joke had been around for too long and looked like it would never leave him. He had been in the police force for 34 years. He had passed the minimum age for retirement, a time at which most of his counterparts took their large pay, federation pension and enjoyed their retirement playing golf and moving to warmer countries. Jack however, had no intention of leaving the police force that he loved so much. He knew he was a good inspector; he knew the law in minute detail and was happy to teach younger officers the right and the wrong of police work. Sadly, he had little or no self-awareness and didn't realise that most of the new recruits were part of a new police force that had somehow passed Jack by. He reached for the machine vended cup of coffee he had bought before entering his office and took a sip. The bitter, burnt taste barely noticeable over the searing heat as it burnt his lip. He wiped coffee from his pencil thin moustache and swore under his breath at the burning feeling.

He didn't often work over a weekend these days. He didn't much like dealing with the drunks and druggies that come through the police station on a weekend but as he taught the younger officers, policing is a twenty four seven occupation. Crime doesn't take a break and nor should he. Which is why, when it was not his responsibility to do so, he had decided he was in charge of the report that had just come in. He had answered the phone to a young lady in the communication suit he knew to be new to the role as he had taken time to introduce himself on a recent visit. Natasha had taken a 999 call from a young man walking along the canal at Little Venice, who had come across what they believed to be a dead body. Natasha explained that most officers had been called out to an RTA and she could not get hold of the duty Senior

Inspector Daniels explained that it would be fine and he began to read the update on his screen having been given the crime reference number. Within minutes he had discarded the coffee and cards and called his sergeant into the office to get ready to leave. Five minutes later they were in his Ford Mondeo driving towards the scene of the crime. Jack had already decided this was a murder case and he was going to be the one to find the killer. Unaware that the dutiful Natasha, as Jack would say 'part of the New Policing', had continued her search for the SIO, finding her and relating the report. At the same time as Jack was driving across London to attend the scene, so were an entourage of police officers ready to attend the suspected crime scene. The SIO, Detective Chief Superintendent Kirsty Brown, was minutes in front of the Ford Mondeo and prepared for his arrival.

22

Mark looked around the room seeing that everyone was in the same mood he was. He was rock hard and Stuart had hold of his erection inside the suit trouser pocket. Every now and then he nibbled on Mark's ear or said something to him that made him feel even hornier. He watched the man on the sofa, not quite able to work out what was happening. He was sat down now going through the papers. Mark was thinking how odd this was, in the middle of the room where all these blokes were obviously here to get off with each other; this guy was doing some work. Another guy approached him. Mark was about to point out what was going on, but he sat next to him and began to talk about the paperwork. Mark twisted to look at Stuart who turned him back to look at what was happening on the sofa. The man who had joined the other guy on the sofa was now looking stressed with the results of what was contained in the paperwork. Mark could just about hear what was being said; he thought he heard the guy telling the younger paperwork guy that it just wasn't good enough and something about a big meeting the next day. Mark was intrigued to see what was happening but also wondering why they were having a business meeting here. His brain wasn't work at top speed at the moment having now been awake for about 36 hours and having spent about 12 of those off his face dancing. At any other point in time the penny would have dropped much sooner.

It didn't take much longer for him to realise what this was about. He heard the younger guy say to the boss type figure sat next to him. 'But Sir; is there nothing I can do to show you how much I appreciate the opportunity?' The boss sat back into the sofa and stroked his now bulging crotch, his cock was obviously hard underneath and he said something to the younger guy that Mark didn't hear but it didn't matter. He watched as the younger guy slipped onto the floor and unzipped the boss man's trouser taking out his hard cock and tentatively taking it into his mouth, all the time keeping eye contact with the boss man. Mark's own cock was as hard as it had ever been. Stuart had hold of it, stroking it, not teasing it, just holding it through his trousers. Bloody hell, Mark was talking to himself in his own head. I'm at a bloody suit orgy. He began to feel slightly uncomfortable wondering what was to be expected of him. Stuart could have told him what was going on, he had just kept on calling it an event but Mark was in no state to go to an orgy nor did he want to really.

He wasn't a prude at all but he had only just met this guy and wanted him all to himself. He looked back at the sofa and the two guys were taking their clothes off, the younger guy was bending over while the boss inspected his bum with his thumb. He looked on to see that lots of the other people in the room were enjoying the show. Other guys where now beginning to touch and feel each other, hands down pants, like Stuart was with him and others kissing each other.

'Don't worry. It's just the guys doing the show who will have sex in here.' Stuart whispered into Mark's ear as if he had known what was going through Mark's head. On hearing this, he saw what was happening in the room differently. The men around the room were all in couples, enjoying each other. Some were in threesomes. There were a few guys on their own who were now cruising other lone guys. Stuart grabbed Mark's chin with his free hand, twisted his head to his and kissed him, pushing his tongue deep into his mouth. After the kiss had finished, that, seemed to last forever, Mark turned to see that the guys on the couch were now totally naked apart from their socks and sock suspenders. The younger guy was now preparing to fuck the boss. Mark was now totally turned on and could feel Stuart squeezing his own cock ever so slightly. It was a good job too as if he was to do anything else he would cum straight away.

This was like watching live porn from the Men at Play website. Who were these two guys that were so happy to be watched having sex in this room? Stuart's hands moved from in Mark's pocket and he was turned round to face him. Mark noticed the bulge in Stuart's trousers now, it looked huge which excited Mark even more. He needed to calm down, he was getting really hot now and wanted to rip Stuart's suit off him then and there.

'Come with me.' Stuart said as he stood up and led Mark back to the entrance of the room. Mark noticed that other people were beginning to leave the room too. He passed the camp guy he had spoken with earlier who was kissing a younger guy with Johnson knelt between the two rubbing his face in their crotches. Stuart and Mark walked back along the corridor and after several stops, Stuart pinned Mark to the wall and kissed him all over his face they made it back to the room. His head was spinning. The after effects of partying all weekend and then the drinks he had been knocking back during the live show were now taking hold of his senses. The alcove doors felt huge as did Stuart's hands on him. The door hadn't even closed when Stuart pushed Mark onto the bed and kissed every inch of his body through the suit. His hands slipped around Mark's waist slowly turning him over, Mark's back pressed into Stuart's chest and his warm lips touched the back of his neck. His large hands came round to explore the outline of his chest as he pushed his hands behind himself to explore Stuart too. They turned to face each other, their lips meeting as they looked into each other's eyes, Stuarts tongue pushed deep into Mark's mouth. His slight stubble feeling good as it brushed over his chin. It took them an hour to slowly remove each other's clothes. Stuart was clearly enjoying taking the expensive suit off Mark, just as much as he had enjoyed seeing him in it. They were naked in each other's arms on the bed pushing their bodies together. Stuarts toned body pressing against Mark's. His tanned olive skin pulled soft across hard muscles with just a few grey hairs on his almost bald chest. They kissed passionately for long periods, moving up and down each other's bodies, exploring every inch.

23

Detective Chief Superintendent Kirsty Brown stepped forward and directly into the path of the silver Ford Mondeo driven by Inspector Jack Daniels who slammed his foot onto the brakes pushing Sargent Alan Jones forward stopping himself with his hands on the dashboard.

'You stupid fucking woman' Daniels shouted out, quickly releasing his seat belt and jumping out of the car 'Do you know who I...' His words trailed off when he realised who it was.

'Oh! Hello Ma'am. How are you?'

'I'm very well, thank you Daniels, can I ask what you are doing at my crime scene?'

'Well, Ma'am.... earlier today I took a call from dispatch who reported a body found here in the canal.' Kirsty Brown cut him short.

'Yes, yes, Daniels. I know exactly what you did. But can you tell me why someone from community policing in Central London is now here in Maida Vale looking into a reported dead body?' Her words cut deep into Daniels. Being part of the community policing team was to him not policing at all. In fact the reason why he came after this call out was, as he saw it, his right to do some real policing. He knew he could do it better than some woman who had risen through the ranks too quickly, probably sleeping their way to the top or probably even a lesbian.

'Well... Ma'am,' It pained him to be polite knowing she was his superior.

'No, Daniels I didn't think you could.' Kirsty stepped forward, came close enough for Jack to smell her perfume and that she had recently had a cup of coffee, look him directly in the eye and spoke with a cool calm voice. 'Listen Daniels, you are one of the most odious, self-satisfied, misogynistic men I have ever met! Your kind of policing is not welcome in my kind of police force. If you want in on this investigation then you toe the line, fall in rank and do what the bloody hell you're told. Do you hear?'

'Ma'am.'

'Now you have a bloody good Sergeant sat in that car that could go far and I intend to do my upmost to support his career. Tell me Daniels, do you want the same support?'

'Yes Ma'am.' Jack was beginning to feel uncomfortable, he had never liked that this woman had gone so far in the force, and now this jumped up over promoted bitch was trying to tell him how to be a police officer. Using fancy words that he didn't understand and he suspected she didn't either.

'Well then.' Detective Chief Superintendent Kirsty Brown's demeanour changed almost instantly. 'I think we are going to start to get along Daniels. Now if you two boys want to be part of this investigation then that is great, as it is a big one.' She looked over to the car.

'Come on Jones, out you get, there is work to be done.' She began to walk away from the car and towards the group of police officers and detectives stood further along the path and close to the reported dead body.

Jack stood in the same spot thinking this is why women shouldn't be on the force. Just like his ex-wife, this one runs hot and cold, one minute all nasty and demanding the next all sweetness and wants to be your friend. He watched her walk away shouting out orders to the group, pointing to areas asking it to be cordoned off. He thought to himself for a moment, she is probably like that because she fancied him.

'What was that about?' Allan Jones was next to him on path.

'Bloody women... if she wanted me on the case all she had to do was ask. She didn't have to come down all heavy like she did.' Jack turned to Allan. 'Make your mind up woman, that's what I say.' Allan watched Jack walk towards the group and then turn back to him. 'We are on the case though Jones, we are on the case.'

'Daniels!' Kirsty Shouted over 'There is a witness, young gent by the name of Ben, do you think you can handle a statement?'

'Yes Ma'am.' The two of them walked in the direction of a small gathering of people being held off by two police officers. Jack walked directly to one of them and ask where the witness was. There was a member of the crowd stepping forward, a woman with bright pink hair.

'Is it The Pusher?' She shouted at the police officers 'has the pusher stuck again' She was referring to a urban myth that there was a serial killer working the canals around London pushing their victims in and holding them under.

'There is no evidence to show that there I any such thing as The Pusher' Said Jack to the woman 'It's a myth' He was right, there was no evidence to show that The Pusher was a real thing. There had been several bodies pulled from the canals around London, all of which had been accounted for as accidental deaths or suicide. There had also been one alive but partially drowned man pulled from the canal claiming to be the survivor of The Pusher. Later it was proved that he was drunk and had fallen in and a shopping trolley had gone in with him. However much the myth was out there all police officers gave the same information to the public. It is a myth. It didn't stop the talking about across the police stations of London, stories were told on a regular basis about The Pusher. Non of them true, most police officers believed it to be the myth that it was, some didn't and took it very seriously.

24

The sexy Irish guy with the tattoos stood under the shower, the water almost hot enough to burn, washing away the night before and enjoying the memory of Tom. They had returned to Tom's flat in Oval after leaving Sam's place in Maida Vale earlier that day. The sun had long gone and the dark night had brought with it a chill in the air that was sending out masses of steam from each open window. They had returned and sat down in the kitchen to make food, neither of them really feeling up to eating.

'Interesting group of friends you have there.' He said to Tom who was stood looking into the fridge aimlessly, unable to make a decision as to what to get out.

'You've seen them at their best too.' The sexy Irish guy observed Tom looking into the fridge.

'Do you fancy just getting some shut eye before we eat? You've been staring into that fridge and not produced anything for a while now.'

'That sounds like a better plan' he closed the fridge and looked at him.

'This way!' He walked out of the kitchen and into the bedroom opposite.

'I don't think I'm up to it.'

'Don't worry, me neither' the sexy Irish guy with the tattoos stopped Tom with his comment, acknowledging that he was in the same mood as him. 'For now that is.'

They stripped off their clothes climbed into bed, had a little kiss and both fell fast asleep.

As the hot water washed over him he smiled at how comfortable it had been to go to sleep. This really amazing guy, he was excited about getting to know him more. It had been comfortable to be naked with him with no agenda of sex, just the need for sleep and to be with each other. He had been woken when Tom had jumped out of bed to answer the landline phone that had been ringing on and off for a while. Overhearing the conversation he sat up in bed.

'Dean, what the fuck are you on about?' Tom whispered.

'James did what?'

'Where are they now?'

'You stupid twat.. Why is that my…..stop crying… ok, I will come over and get you. Where is James? Put Sam on the phone…. right, ok. I'm coming over, tell me about it then.' Tom hung up the phone and walked back into the bedroom.

'Trouble?' The sexy Irish guy with tattoos asked.

'It seems that way.' Tom started to pull his clothes out and look around for his mobile phone.

'Anything I can do?'

'Oh, right... erm... not really.' He found his phone and began to dial Mark's number. He looked back at the sexy Irish guy with tattoos sat on the bed. Noticing his muscles and knowing that this meeting had been perfect and was now being spoilt.

'My idiot cousin has got himself into a bit of bother and I have to go get him and bring him home.'

'Taken too many of the wee dancing pills?' he quizzed.

'If that was it, life would be good. He doesn't take anything but it does seem to be related to those little dancing pills' Tom sat down next to him.

'Do you need a shower or anything? I might be a while getting him and coming back'

'My cue to leave then?'

'No, no... Shit.' he kissed him 'I don't want you to leave, not sure what is happening yet. Can you stay? Do you have to be anywhere?'

'Na worry, I can hang out here and wait if you are ok with that, got nowhere to be until work tomorrow.'

'That's cool. Mark lives opposite he should be home, his answer phone is on at the moment... oh, hang on.' Tom heard Mark's voice ask to leave a message.

'Hi mate, call me back.'

God knows what's happened but Dean and James have got everyone into some trouble' He hung up the phone and looked back.

'So, he lives over the road, there is food in the kitchen and hot water in the shower. Knock yourself out' and with that he jumped up, pulled on his jeans and disappeared out the door. Less than a minute later he was back, came over to the bed, kissed the sexy Irish guy with the tattoo's and gave him a business card.

'It's got my number on it.' Tom said as he stood and walked towards the door to leave again.

'Ok there Thomas, IT Director.' Tom looked back and gave him a big grin, then was gone.

As Tom walked out of Warwick Avenue tube station at almost 6.30pm he felt the cold air hit him. He had left home wearing only a t shirt and thin jacket. The last few weeks had been warm for December, and he hadn't thought he needed much more. It seemed now the weather had changed and winter was kicking in. Tom loved summer in London, everywhere seemed so much better, endless possibilities and more options to go and see new things. That said; his favourite time of the year for the city had to be winter, the snow and Christmas. London became almost magical at Christmas. He walked on towards Clearwell Drive with a smile on his face and enjoying the evening air. It was almost dark when he made it to 32b, Sam's place. He tapped in the code for the door, a number he has used so many times he would never forget it. As he walked through the door to the downstairs flat, he heard a familiar voice.

'Tom, my dear. My dear, dear Tom. Said the elderly voice. You simply don't know how hard it is for a lady like me to be all alone.' This said with the drama of the stage career she had once had, and as if she had been mid conversation with Tom already. He thought to himself that she must have been waiting for him, by how quickly she had got to the door.

'Hi Mrs Pott's, how are you today? Have you enjoyed your weekend?'

'There is little for me to enjoy my dear. Just the small things like your visits.'

'I'm afraid I'm not here for you today Mrs Potts. I'm collecting my cousin.'

'Oh' she said we some distain in her voice 'The protégé, the up and coming star, the one we all need to look out for. Tell me Tom, has he won any awards? Did he star with Laurence Olivier onstage and screen?'

'No Mrs Pott's, no he hasn't, how could anyone but you have achieved such great things?'

'Oh Tom, it is lovely to know you are still a fan. Especially with it being my 90th birthday this coming Thursday and me having no family of my own to celebrate with.' Tom stopped trying to get past Mrs Pott's who had been blocking his way, realising that a 90th birthday was pretty significant.

'Mrs Pott's, your 90th is this Thursday? I would have never guessed you were that age.'

'Flattery Tom, flattery will get you everywhere!' She had a mischievous look in her eye and brushed her hands down passed her breasts and across her waistline.

'Well, I must make sure I swing by and say hello on your special day.'

'Tom, you must come by, I'm throwing a party, bring all of your friends. You gays do make such good company for a famous actress like me.' Tom decided not to tackle her on her reference to his group of friends this time, she was old school and it sometimes riled him.

'Ok, maybe a few of us can pop over?'

'No, Tom! All of you must come. Tell each of them that they simply must help me celebrate.'

I will do a finger buffet for 6pm, be sure to be here!' With this she turned back to her flat and closed the door. Tom listened as she retreated behind the closed door, singing Tuppence a Bag from Mary Poppins. Smiling, at how demanding his friend's neighbour had been and also a bit sad that all she had left now was the company of him and his friends. He walked up the stairs and pushed on the door to Sam's flat. The door did not move. He knocked on the door thinking it was strange. Normally the door to Sam's flat was always unlocked. He heard movement behind the door, the bolt unlocked and he was greeted by Sam's face.

'I think we have to go to Mrs Pott's birthday party on Thursday night.' Tom said with a smile.

'What, whose birthday? What the hell are you talking about?' Sam looked at Tom and was scared. Tom began to realise that the situation he was about to experience was far worse than he had first thought. He stepped inside the flat as Sam looked down the hallway behind him checking if anyone else was about. He closed the door and secured the bolt again.

25

'I'm guessing you must be Dean?' The sexy Irish guy with tattoo's said from behind the kitchen bench as Dean walked in to the open plan kitchen living room of Tom's flat. He had been there on his own for the last few hours and was wearing Tom's dressing gown. Having had a great shower, he didn't want to put his dirty clothes from the club back on. He had watched a bit of telly and then got hungry so started to look for food in the fridge, at the same time he had sent Tom a text message to see what was happening and had a plan to have food ready when they got back. Dean had walked through the door just as he was straining some pasta and adding in the meatball sauce he had made from the limited ingredients from the fridge.

'Oh my God! Who are you?' Dean trembled next to the door frozen to the spot.

'Hey, hey, it's ok young man. I'm....' The sexy Irish bloke was shocked to see Dean's reaction to him and was then cut off by Tom following Dean in to the room.

'He is with me, I told you he was here on the way back.' Tom walked in taking his coat off. Dean stayed next to the door.

'Wow, you cooked. I'm starving, what's for dinner?'

'It's more like supper, where did the time go, its gone 9 hasn't it?' The sexy Irish guy with the tattoo's looked over to Dean. 'Are you hungry fella? There is plenty for you all' Dean continued to watch from the corner of the room.

'Where did this come from, did you go out and buy stuff?' Tom asked

'It is amazing what you can do with the contents of someone else's fridge and freezer and a whole heap of time' He replied.

'Yeah, sorry about that, it took a while to get to the bottom of what had been happening and then get this one sorted enough to come back.' Tom looked over at Dean and rolled his eyes.

'Doesn't sound like a simple tale.'

'It's not a tale; it's fucking scary as fuck and....' Dean burst in to tears 'fuck... fuck...' he sobbed. 'Where's Mark? Does Mark know what is happening?'

'I've still not heard from him' Tom took out his phone whilst grabbing a bowl of the steaming hot food.

'Shall we eat on the sofa?'

'Sounds good to me.'

Tom and the sexy Irish guy with the tattoos sat on the sofa, all the time watching Dean and his actions. Dean collected his bowl of food and threw himself at an armchair in the corner.

'I shouldn't even be eating carbs this late. What's your name anyway?' he directed both comments at the Sexy Irish guy with the tattoos.

'Gavin. And I'm pretty sure you can have carbs this once,' he replied in his soft calming Irish accent.

'Thanks for dinner Gavin.' Dean began to melt in the warmth of Gavin's Irish glow. Tom sat back looking at Gavin and realising that up until then, he had not got his name. Gavin then looked at Tom and they both smiled at each other in realisation.

'So who is going to tell me the story of what you boys have been up to while I've been here cooking for ya's?'

'It's a bit of a long one.' Tom said looking over at Dean, who once again started to well up.

'Maybe a long story, I can tell you later?' Gavin smiled at Tom and tucked in to his food.

26

'Bit worried about you mate. Dean is ok now. Got him to go to bed. Can you call me? Doesn't matter what time. Just call.'

Tom hung up the call and dropped his phone on to the bedside table.

'Strange for Mark to be AWOL for so long, I'm a bit worried about him.'

'He seemed pretty happy with that chap; he dashed off with when we left him.' Gavin said dropping the dressing gown and climbing in to bed.

'Has your heating gone off its cold?'

'Erm, not sure, probably.' Tom Said

'Maybe you should come and warm me up then.' Gavin smiled at Tom.

'Oh right, I see what you did there' Tom was stood at the end of the bed wearing the towel he had tied around his waist having just had a shower. 'I'm sure Mark will be ok, I'm just concerned after the events of this evening.'

'Are you going to tell me what's happening then?' Gavin asked. Tom sat on the side of the bed and lay back on to Gavin's legs.

'Where do I start? I walked into Sam's apartment to be greeted with the carnage that was Dean. He was in a worse state than when you saw him here.'

'Did he go to bed?'

'Yeah, had a shower and got in bed.'

'He lives with you? How are you related?'

'Yeah, has lived here for just over a year, he is studying at Barbican. Cousin. My Mum's sister's... son. We are a pretty close family so it worked well that he came here when he moved down. He is pretty much a little brother.'

'I get the close family thing' Tom looked at Gavin 'I'm Irish. I have cousins coming out of my ears. I don't think I am even related to some.'

'Great, sounds busy' they smiled at each other again.

'Wait a sec, he is studying at Barbican?'

'Yeah, he is a dancer.'

'Oh right, pretty stereotypical, gay dancer,' Gavin said. Tom chuckled at the comment.

'I'm not even sure he is gay to tell you the truth. Never been kissed and kinda 'came out.'

No one in our family is bothered. He spent a lot of time following Mark around when he was growing up and just decided he was gay.'

'Interesting. I didn't get a gay vibe from him when we were talking.'

'Yeah, there is definitely an all about me vibe. You should see him when he talks to Sam's neighbour. Fabulous lady lives downstairs, she used to be a bit of a big deal in Hollywood. You would think they we leading ladies fighting for the limelight.' Tom laughed 'it's great.'

'I need to meet her.'

'She is great. So, we are in Sam's flat and everyone is a bit shook up. Sam goes on to tell me about this drug dealer coming round and threatening to kill everyone unless they cough up 50k by the following week.' Tom explained to Gavin and he sat up in bed.'

'What?' he demanded. His demeanour changed.

'I'm not sure. I shouldn't be telling you this. The guy I just met and really like and now going to scare him off by telling him some scary drug lord story.'

'You just elevated him from drug dealer to drug lord in about two seconds. I'm not going to be scared off by some story of a drug dealer; however I would be a bit concerned for ya.'

'Aww thanks.'

'You're welcome, so the drug dealer?'

'Yeah, Dean and James seem to have gotten themselves in a bit of bother with a drug dealer. James met him in the club last night. We all saw them together, he was pretty fit and off they went. James is pretty good at falling in love really fast.'

'Not sure who James is?'

'Oh right, he is a friend of the group. He works at Mark's place. He's a similar age to Dean, so they get on pretty well.'

'Ok, carry on.'

'Do you need to make notes?'

'Not sure yet.'

'So the girls are still there. Sam and Dean and Sam's flatmate is now back who you didn't meet. James has spent the night with a bloke who just happens to be a drug dealer. This morning he was showing off to Dean about this guy he is now in love with and wants to introduce him to everyone. He got Dean to come over to this guy's place. Dean arrives and whilst the guy is sleeping the two of them happened to find a bag full of those little dancing pills.' Tom looks at Gavin giving him a knowing look having used his name for ecstasy.

'Oh dear,' Gavin put his head in his hand pre-empting what is about to come.

'They didn't steal them did they?'

'Steal them? No, no, no. What they did is far more fucked up than that. If they had stolen them I might have actually had some weird respect for them. No, what they did was fuck everything up. Dean, who is pretty much against drugs, decided James needed to be saved from this guy who was going to somehow make him take them all and he decided to flush them.' Tom sat up and looked at Gavin who had now pulled himself up on to his knees.

'He didn't?'

'He tried.'

'What the actual fuck was he thinking?'

'That I am not clear on, but in part, saving James from being a cheap white ho. His words.'

'Oh right, so the pills got flushed?'

'In part, James and Dean had a bit of a struggle and the bag slipped, the pills went everywhere and some got flushed. The dealer then found them on the floor, pills everywhere and he was obviously not to happy.'

'I'll bet. How many pills are we talking about?'

'He wants 50k to replace the lot.'

'Shit man, that's a lot of pills to be spilled, and what about the ones that weren't flushed?'

'That's not the best bit.'

'There is a best bit?'

'They got as many as they could back in to the bag, I'm not sure of all the details but the not very happy dealer whom James was allegedly in love with, now has a gun and has scared the shit out of both of them. They grabbed the bag and made a run for it' Tom paused to think.

'The gun has been fired but I'm not sure by whom.'

'The drug dealer will have fired that at them, wouldn't you say?'

'I would imagine. These two do a runner across London and head straight for Sam's place.'

'Why Sam? What has he got to do with it?'

'At that point nothing and now Sam is full on storming because they went there. The dealer turned up at Sam's place.'

'Oh shit' Gavin gave slightly uncomfortable laugh thinking about it.

'What the fuck were they thinking?'

'They weren't.' The two men sat back on the headboard looking at each other.

'So, he turned up and threatens everyone, the girls, Sam, his housemate and the boys stating they have a week to get 50k sorted or they will all be shot... and then he left.'

'Do you believe it?'

'I saw the half empty bag of pills.'

'Oh shit man they still have the bag of pills!'

'Yep, on the table at Sam's, I got the impression Sam was about to force each and every one down the boy's throats.'

'Jesus, what're you going to do? Sounds like serious shit.'

'It is and I'm not sure. For now I intend to sleep on it and work it out in the morning.'

'Good idea, now come over here and let me help you out' Gavin pulled Tom close to him, holding his back tight against his chest, with his warm breath across his neck, the two of them fell fast asleep together.

27

Mark awoke alone in bed in the bright room. Even though the curtains were closed the sunlight filled the room through the gap and he wondered what time it was. He leaned over to get a drink from the bottle of water standing on the bed side table as his mouth was extremely dry. He pulled himself up in bed and looked around the room. The suit he had been wearing was hung over a suit stand in the corner of the room and there was what looked to be a note in the lapel pocket. He jumped out of bed and took the note from the suit.

Mark,

I had to leave. I hope you got a good sleep you deserved it after that performance. Your clothes are being cleaned and will be ready for you when you leave. Keep the suit, it looked so good on you, it would be a shame for anyone else to wear it. You can wear it for me next time we meet. If you want breakfast before you leave dial 1 on the phone.

Speak soon

Stuart

He read the note again. This really had been a different encounter, they were now cleaning his clothes and he had just acquired a really expensive suit. He climbed out of the bed went into the bathroom and took a long hot shower. He thought more about Stuart's note and the performance he had mentioned. Mark had been very surprised to find that Stuart was a bottom and had wanted Mark to fuck him in pretty much every position imaginable. What did the note mean about breakfast? Maybe Stuart had thought he would stay the night. He walked back into the bedroom dressed in the suit, collected the rest of his things and made his way back to the reception where he found the same man waiting.

'Hello young man, and how are you doing?' He said as Mark arrived at the desk.

'Very well indeed' Mark said with a knowing look on his face 'I really wasn't expecting any of that.'

'Not for me to comment young man' He said back 'I have your things in a package for you, will you be changing or leaving as you are?'

'I erm..... I think I will leave as I am.' Mark was still a little shocked that he got to keep the suit.

'Is everything in order with the suit young man, we can have it altered if needed?' Mark thought that this was getting stranger and stranger. A club for gentlemen that had live sex shows and expensive suits to hand out to the chance encounter of one of its members.

'How would I become a member of the club?' He asked.

'I believe you would be best placed speaking to your friend about that young man, the members of this club are particular about who joins and operate a voting system to gain membership. Members like their privacy you see.'

'Yes I'm sure they do, well I have had a great time. I hope to see you again.'

Mark took the brown paper package from the desk and walked towards the door wondering at which point someone was going to stop him and give him the bill for the suit. 'I don't suppose you have the time please? The battery on my phone has died.'

'Of course, it is seven o'clock.' The man on reception said.

'Seven! Wow it has been a long day' Mark replied.

'Seven in the morning young man.'

'Ok' Mark replied in shock, how could he have slept the whole night. No wonder Stuart had offered breakfast as part of his stay. He now began to think about what he was supposed to be doing today and where he would find his friends at seven on a Sunday morning. All of them in bed he would suspect.

'No doubt our paths will cross again young man' the butler was now at the door showing Mark out onto the busy high street as the light almost blinded him.

28

Mark stepped forward from the building still smiling at the excellent night he had had. He looked down at the suit he was wearing, almost a perfect fit. He felt great and had the whole of Sunday to relax and be ready for work tomorrow. He turned left into a line of people busily rushing forward. Mark then began to feel confused, why was it so busy at 7am on a Sunday morning. He thought more about the night he had spent at the I.o.G and with Stuart, it had certainly been horny.

By the time he had gotten in there it must have been way into the afternoon and the by the time he had seen the sex show early evening. Realisation began to creep in, it was Monday morning. It was Monday morning.

'Fffuuucckkkkk' Mark shouted without even realising. He turned back to the door of the Institute of Gentlemen and grabbed the handle. It was locked. The door wouldn't move. Mark began to search all around the door for a bell or intercom. There was nothing other than a small, black discreet key card tag on the wall, to the right of the door. A voice came from nowhere.

'Is there something else sir?' The man from the reception desk spoke over an intercom.

Mark searched to find where the voice was coming from but found nothing.

'It's Monday Morning, its 7am' Mark said in a panic 'I have work!'

'Yes Sir' the man said back. 'That would be the case' all Mark heard after this was an ever so slight hiss as if whatever the man on reception had been speaking into had been disconnected.

He stood back from the door and began to think what to do. He needed to get home, get ready for work and then get to work. He was now running, pulling out his mobile phone, no battery power.

'Fuck' he shouted again. Where was he? Mark stopped and looked around, panic setting in. 'Oh crap I have to be at work sometime in the next hour. He began to walk fast along the high street and then stopped and looked at himself in the window, he admired the suit he was wearing and instantly the panic began to go and calm set in. He did like the suit and thought he wore it exceptionally well. He stood there looking at himself and thought of the working day ahead. He was no longer bothered. He was well rested and now realised that he could go straight to work and have a stress free day. Even if he was carrying the weekends clothes in a brown paper bag, he realised he was even closer to work than he thought so he could take his time. Still looking at his reflection in the window, it looked like his head was jumping about. He blinked his eyes and realised it was a shop owner waving his hands and trying to move him on from the other side of the window. He waved at the woman on the other side, wished her a good day and turned back in the direction he had just run in a panic and headed off to work.

29

'Good morning everybody! Thank you for making it in this early on a Monday morning.' Detective Chief Superintendent Kirsty Brown grabbed a strong cup of coffee from the vending machine and looked at her watch. 7.28am. Having been called in on her weekend off to quite a bad road traffic accident and then on to a suspected homicide on the patch, she had spent the day chasing around the city, following leads and speaking with police officers who had attended the scene and taken witness statements. Then she had grabbed about four hours of broken sleep on the sofa in her office before hitting the gym and running for 30 minutes. She found it was a good break in thought pattern for her to focus on running and often came up with her best ideas. Today she was at a loss. Showered and new suit she was now in the major incident room and looking at her team of detectives. She was starting with a small team. A body found in the canal at Little Venice in Maida Vale looked very much like a hate crime was going to be a quick case. She had worked enough of cases like this to know. She was still feeling tense, crimes like this made her tense. There was no reason for it apart from one person's hatred of another person's lifestyle. She was going to catch who did this fast and make sure an example was set while doing it. She looked around the room at the nine people gathered for the briefing,

Detective Inspector Andy Grey was sat at the head of the board room table. He would be the lead on this enquiry and quite soon she would be handing everything over to him. A proud man was Grey. He was a stable officer who had worked his way up and made a name for himself in doing so. He was known as 'Pitbull' for his ability to act like a dog with a bone on a case. He never let anything lie until a case was solved.

Next to him was Shirley Keith an executive PA, here to ensure all administrative duties were taken care of. In her 60's, she looked great for her age but was focused on retiring to spend more time with her young grandchildren. She was currently showing pictures of them to the two ladies sat next to her. Sandi Singh and Jenna Alexandrov were the Police Officers, who were on duty at the time of the report and first on the scene. Young and athletic, they were used to walking the beat and not used to being sat in briefings first thing on a Monday morning. Next along was Inspector Joanne Rhymes, their boss. An attractive yet boyish looking forty something woman with short black hair cut into a spike, she now owned the crime scene and had a team of other police officers managing the scene and taking statements from anyone around the canal side area this morning that may have been around over the weekend. Then there were two detective Sargent's, John Barrack and Shilpa Manov. Kirsty gazed at them for a long while, the jewel in the crown of her. They worked so closely together and got results by doing so, an excellent pair to work alongside each other and also as a team. She looked at them both with fondness. John was a rugby player and his nose and ears told the story of many Sunday morning games, in his late 30's and Shilpa a similar age carrying a little extra weight but carrying it well. Kirsty wondered if these two excellent members of her team had ever been as close as they could have been. John was about to get married and his soon to be wife was expecting their first child. Kirsty dismissed the thought of them ever having been together as she realised she knew very little about Shilpa's personal life. And then her eyes fell upon the person she wanted so much not to see every day of her life. Detective Inspector Jack Daniels sat staring at her. How someone with so little common sense and narrow minded view of the world had risen to the rank of Detective Inspector was beyond her. She was saddled with him because no other place would have him and getting rid of someone like that was a human resource nightmare. Plus cases like this needed man power and he came with an extra pair of legs. Next to him was Sergeant Alan Jones, she knew little about the young sergeants personal life, she had heard great things about him as an officer and from what she had seen over the weekend, she wanted to know more. Anyone who can work alongside Daniels, in her eyes, was a saint. He had moved into the force about a year ago from Sussex his strong Irish accent gave away where he had grown up, yet his name suggested Welsh. She made a mental note to get to know him better. He could end up being a valuable member of the team. She overheard Daniels refer to the deceased as a 'fag', her blood began to boil and she slammed the case note file in her hands down on the table.

Everyone turned to look at her and she shot a glance at Daniels. The look told her enough that he knew he was in the wrong, slightly bowing his head in shame.

'I know it's early and I am also aware that some of you' she looked at the two police officers 'are due to finish shifts after an exceptionally long weekend.'

'So, early indications are pointing that this is a hate crime, I would like to say that it is a hate crime gone a bit too far. Julia at the Coroner's Office hasn't completed the autopsy yet but says there was a fight, there are defence injuries, a clean cut right to left opening up the victims neck that could be from a knife. Hell of a way to go.'

'Left handed perp' Alan Jones commented, everyone in the room looked at Alan and took in his information.

'Yes' Kirsty Said thinking it over 'Yes, you're right, a right to left cut would indicate a left handed attacker. Narrows the search down a little'. The door to the major incident room burst open and an older gentleman walked in, looking tired due to being ready to finish shift. Everyone looked at him. Tim Brown looked at the lady stood at the front of the bank of desks and realised that Detective Chief Inspector Kirsty Brown, his daughter, didn't look too happy to see him.

'Sorry to barge in, sorry I should have knocked' He looked directly at her 'Kir...' almost saying her name he corrected himself 'Ma'am, I thought you would want this information urgently. I have just taken a call from a resident of Notting Hill who wanted to report hearing a gunshot in the building next door to her on Sunday morning.

'Sunday morning, why wait until now to report it?' Kirsty said

'It is an anonymous report ma'am; the lady didn't want to leave details. When I tell you where the gun shot came from you'll see why.'

'I'm hoping this is the reason why I am going to want this information urgently, or I might start to get upset about you coming in here.' The rest of the team sat back and watched the interaction. All of them knowing it was the boss' father, most of them respecting the level of professionalism kept between the two. Jack Daniels on the other hand was disgusted at the way she spoke to her father, in his eyes a total lack of respect for him.

'Sure is' Tim continued 'the gunshot came from Doherty's address' Kirsty's eyes lit up as did the eyes of John Barrack and Shilpa Manov.

Mike Doherty was a known drug dealer in the area, the most aggressive she had come across and she would do anything to get him off the streets.

'Boss' John was rising out of his seat 'that's...'

'I know' Both Kirsty and John reached Tim at the same time, John taking the printed crime reference report from Tim and looking through it with Kirsty.

'That's great. Anything else?'

'Not much really, we know who made the call due to call recognition and it is noted in the anonymous section of the crime report on the system but not on the report you have there. It was reported by the direct neighbour. She said that hadn't wanted to say anything because he isn't really the type of man to mess with. Funnily enough it was the priest at her church yesterday evening that asked her to ensure it was reported.' Tim finished with a smile and turned to walk away. Kirsty and John hadn't noticed.

'Thank you Tim.' Shilpa said loudly so they would notice.

'Thanks Tim' John said 'Speak to you later'.

'Thanks Dad, that's great, but knock next time' Kirsty said to her father. He turned back and looked at the rest of the room.

'I spend my life telling her to close doors behind her and knock before and entering and look where that gets me' Tim closed the door behind him.

'Boss, this could tie in to a bit of information I got from an informant over the weekend.

Apparently Tony Cash is known to be on our patch as of yesterday afternoon' John said looking at Shilpa.

'I was going to mention it after the meeting ma'am' Shilpa said to Kirsty 'I got the info through about an hour ago, sounds pretty legit.'

'Hang on, hang on' Jack Daniels butted in, 'what on earth is all this about? We are here to get a case sorted for this 'Queer bashing' and you're talking about gunshots and someone who is on the patch. What's going on?' Kirsty's blood boiled again, his voice went through her and the language he used grated, she boiled over.

'Detective inspector it is a mystery to me how you have gone so far in this police force without an ounce of humility, common sense and the least bit of political correctness. This is a hate crime and I will thank you to be more sensitive to everyone around you, including the deceased. However, you are right this is not what we are here to discuss. Just to let everyone in on this, as you can gather a gun has be fired and it just so happens to be in the home of a known drug dealer on our patch. This dealer is quite far up the chain in the London drug scene. Someone we have had our eye on for quite a while and looking for a way to get him and hopefully the rest of his chain. It is understood that the next step up from him is Anthony 'Tony' Cash, a self-proclaimed drugs baron who lives up in Manchester. If Cash is on the scene then something is happening.' She looked at Shilpa 'I want this confirmed if he is on scene and I want to know where he is and everything he does. The murder case is being handed over to homicide team now anyway so you can get back to your day job and track him down. How can we confirm?'

'He has a brother who lives in London, would he visit?' John said.

'As far as I'm aware they are no longer in contact' Shilpa replied. 'Mark Cash, the brother works at a marketing company in Fred.'

'We need to send someone over' Kirsty thought in her head, she didn't want to send her best officers, mostly because they were known to both Mark and his slime brother. She needed someone who knew nothing about this and wouldn't spill anything. It pained her to do this but Jack Daniels was the best hope.

'Detective Inspector Jack Daniels' she looked at him. 'Would it be ok if I took you off the current case and moved you over to an ongoing investigation?' Without allowing him time to reply as he looked up at her. 'Shilpa will give you the details and direction over what is needed, in short can you go to the office of Mark Cash and find out what he knows about his brothers whereabouts? Thank you.'

'Yes' Jack was taken by surprise 'erm, Yes Ma'am.' Jack stood up and looked at Alan 'Come on you, proper policing to be done.' Alan stood up and followed him out the room. Kirsty gave Shilpa a nod and she followed them out of the room.

'Now then' Kirsty started 'Sorry for the distraction, back to this poor victim in the canal on Saturday. I want to find this perp fast and get them up in front of a judge as soon as possible. She looked at the now smaller team. 'What do we know?' John was looking at her, still stood with the crime report in hand. 'Go on John, off you go and get on with that.' Andy Grey stood up and took over from Kirsty and started to present the information they had on the case. Kirsty sat down. She would stay for this meeting and then expect progress reports from Andy.

30

Mark arrived at the offices of HBM at eight having stopped off for a coffee, grabbed a bite to eat and was fresh and ready for the day, ahead of his normal office hours of eight thirty. Several times along the way he had stopped to look at himself in the window of shops and while he was waiting for his coffee at Starbucks stood admiring the suit he was wearing. Whilst being stood in the elevator to the eleventh floor he was looking at the suit again and thinking about what had happened over the weekend and how he had ended up stood here right now. He thought about the sex he and Stuart had for the majority of Sunday. As he stood there admiring himself, he realised he had a full erection. Giving a cheeky smile, he adjusted himself so that it didn't show, he then checked himself in the mirror. He stepped out of the elevator and into the reception area of HBM. Hayden & Brown Marketing's impressive reception was clean and crisp. Everything was white.

The leather sofa's that had been shipped from Milan had the softest white leather and egg shaped receptionist desk made out of plaster by one of the partners Mr Hayden sat perfectly in the centre of the room. The only colour in the room stood out from behind the egg in an electric blue blouse and matching skirt with a mess of dark chocolate hair and bright blue eyes looking out over the rim of a spectacular pair of red or dead glasses was Vonda.

Vonda was a forty something American who tried to look like she was a twenty something and dressed like she was a teenager. She brought no real value to the company apart from the fact that clients loved her and she knew everything that was happening with everyone in the business.

'WOW!' she shouted across the reception. 'That is a mighty impressive suit you have there Mr. What's the occasion?' without even waiting for an answer she continued 'you expecting a promotion? Dress just likes the boss and soon you will be one?'

'Morning Vonda' Mark was still full of the confidence of the last twenty-four hours. The suit helped, Vonda was almost right, dressing like the boss might help.

'This Suit, surely you've seen this before' knowing that Vonda knew everything and this suit stood out as something new, he expected a smart reply.

'Erm…. I don't think so.' Mark waited for more, but Vonda's mood then changed. 'Mark, there are two police officers here to see you. They said it was a personal matter and wouldn't tell me anything else. I said you are normally in for nine am so they said they would wait. I put them in the board room. I figured you would want to go in your office first.'

Mark's confidence dropped a little and confusion set in, what would the police want with him. The most illegal thing he had ever done was take a few pills on a weekend and he really couldn't see the police coming after him when they want the dealers. Beginning to feel slightly nervous, Mark walked towards the double glass doors in the middle of reception to the left of the Vonda's egg desk, the doors led to the offices along a long thin corridor with a great glass walled board room at the far end.

'What time did they get here?' Mark asked quizzically.

'About ten minutes ago. They said they had been trying to contact you at home and got no reply so came here. I've made them coffee and they aren't expecting you until nine anyway. You got time to go to your office first.' Vonda spoke like Mark needed time to get himself together, turning this in to some big drama. Mark wanted the time to be able to get himself together and walked in the direction of his office about half way along the corridor towards the board room. He pushed open the large glass door to his office finding it empty. He shared the office with two others. Mary and Claire were currently away, Mary on a photo-shoot in New York for a fashion client and Claire running a press event in Manchester for the same client. He was glad they weren't about for this police intrusion, the two of them combined with Vonda ran the gossip network across the whole of the business, and nothing was a secret.

Mark dropped his iPhone into the charger on his desk and sat down turning his iMac on at the same time. The two devices sprang in to action, one charging and the other opening up programmes that he had been working on before the weekend. The RSS news feed set to deliver up to date news from BBC beginning to start pinging. A weekend full of news updates in one hit. Mark scanned past a few of them, accidents, pub brawls, a body found in the canal near Little Venice. That was near Sam's place he thought as he paid more attention to work. Nothing stood out to relate to any of his client list and nothing was in the tagged list showing up anything for his clients, so his switched to his email to see if anything urgent had happened during the 24 hours he had not been attached to his email and out of sync with the world. Being the Public Relations Manager for several major clients meant that he needed to be in constant contact in case anything should happen that needed immediate attention. Recently the son of the owner of a major fashion business had decided to go off the rails and it would be Mark's job to cover up anything he had done over the weekend. Luckily Mark knew that he was on holiday with the whole family so there was someone else to keep him in check and Mark could relax and go off the rails slightly himself. There was a loud beep and then several chimes. Mark jumped at the beep, his phone had enough battery power to turn itself back on and the beep signified he had an answer phone message. The chimes were text messages. The beep and chimes continued for a about another 30 seconds which got Mark's immediate attention. What had happened? Were they messages from the family holiday and something had happened? Was that why the police were here? Oh Shit thought Mark, how could he have been so reckless and allowed his phone to be out of action for so long. His afternoon and night of passion with Stuart was beginning to feel a little stupid. Looking at his phone he saw that he had 43 text message and 12 answer phone messages.

'What the fuck' he said out loud. In seconds Vonda was in the room.

'What is it, what's happened?' She said as she marched across the office to his desk in the corner.

'Vonda, it's nothing. I've had my phone switched off and had quite a few messages' Mark replied wanting her out of the way. The last thing he needed was word getting out that he had had his phone off for 24 hours. 'How are the police officers doing? Do they know I have arrived in the office?'

'No. I haven't told them. What do you want me to do? I can hold them off for an hour if you want?' Vonda was relishing the drama.

'I'd leave them for a few minutes. I will make my way down when I have gone through these messages' Mark tried to sound like it didn't matter but he was beginning to feel worried.

'Ok, whatever you need. Remember, I'm here for you.' With this Vonda left the room. Probably just to stand outside and listen Mark thought. He picked the phone up and read the first message. It was a list of text messages from Tom.

Tom - Sent Sunday 12.13 'Where you off to? Who was that bloke?'

Tom - Sent Sunday 16.23 'You still with that bloke?'

Tom - Sent Sunday 17.06 'you home yet?'

Tom - Sent Sunday 18.12 'Did you get my answer phone message? CALL ME!!'

Tom - Sent Sunday 19.28 'I'm nearly back at Sam's where are you? CALL ME'

Tom - Sent Sunday 19.48 'CALL ME'

Tom - Sent Sunday 19.52 'Answer your fucking phone'

Tom - Sent Sunday 20.10 'mate your phone must be switched off. Listen to your answer phone messages. I have Dean with me now and heading back to my place'

Mark read the messages wondering what was going on. Tom was never this bothered about him being out with some bloke. He had his own bloke he went back with. The rest of the text messages were answer phone reports and then five messages from Sam following a similar line to those from Tom, asking him to call and something about Dean. What had Dean done now? Probably upset Sam in some drugs related conversation. He flicked to the answer phone and heard that he had 12 messages. The most recent he played first.

Message received on Monday at 12.18am

'Bit worried about you mate. Dean is ok now. Got him to go to bed. Can you call me? Doesn't matter what time. Just call.'

He was cut off from listening to the message from a loud knocking on the door, it was Vonda.

'The officers are in the meeting room' Mark looked up at Vonda.

'Right I will be there in a minute.'

'What do you think they are here for sweetie?'

'I don't know until I get in there, but don't worry I will tell you everything when I get out.'

'Oh good, good, good. I'll make them coffee, they look ever so tired. But then all police look tired don't they?' She waited for a reply from Mark who seemed more interested in his phone. She left the room without him even noticing. Mark picked his phone up and decided to send a quick message to Tom.

'Got all your messages, sorry phone battery had died. Was with Stuart all day and night.

Will call you shortly. Not sure why but the police are here so gotta go to meet them. See ya in a bit.

Mark pressed send and walked out of the office. Seconds later a reply came from Tom in capital letters.

'FUCK DON'T TALK TO THE POLICE.'

Directly after the message was delivered Mark's phone began to ring. Mark was half way down the hallway to the meeting room. He was about 5 steps away from the meeting room looking towards the reception and seeing Vonda step out from behind her desk with her hand on her mouth, she turned and looked at Mark and back at what was shocking her in reception. Mark looked puzzled.

He put his head round the door of the meeting room, looking at the two police officers who were still stood waiting.

'Sorry gents, I will just be two minutes more. It seems something is happening in reception that needs my attention.' The two police officers nodded. Mark turned back from the door and continued to walk to reception and then stopped dead in his tracks. Stood next to the reception desk talking to Vonda was his brother, his brother that he had not seen in at least ten years. Vonda looked like she was flirting with him.

31

'Mark, Mark, Shit Don't talk to the police. Don't tell them anything. This is a right shite mess and... actually, you don't know anything. What are the police doing with you when you don't know anything? Call me back!' Tom hung up the phone and looked at Gavin who had just woken up hearing Tom in a panic.

'What's happening?' Gavin asked.

'Really strange, Mark just text to say his battery had died and he was with Stuart all weekend. I'm guessing he is now at work but the police are there. Why would the police be with him? He doesn't even know what's happened and it isn't even related to Dean?'

'Maybe they are there about something else?'

'Maybe' Tom said as he lay down and kissed Gavin. 'What has our Mark been up to then in his absence?' The two men continued to kiss with the duvet wrapped around them.

'I'm going to have to go to work soon' Gavin said.

'You mean you're not staying in here with me all day? I booked today off work knowing it was going to be a big weekend.'

'Nice offer.'

'What do you do?'

'I'm a police officer and I work on the drugs team' Tom took a deep breath,

'erm....'

'Ha Ha, I'm kidding. I leave the policing to my brother'

'Twat' Tom lightly punched him in the arm and moved in a bit closer after.

'I'm sorry' he smiled at Tom, a lovely big smile and stared in to his eyes 'However I do have to go, the sick and wounded need me'

'What?'

'I work in casualty'

'A nurse?'

'A doctor.'

'Impressive' Tom sunk another kiss on Gavin. Gavin pulled him round and on top of him and continued to kiss him.

32

'Alright our kid,' the man in reception said as he looked over at Mark. 'See young lady, I told you he would be excited to see me. That's excitement on our Mark's face.'

Vonda was still looking shocked at the presence of the man in reception. Anthony Cash was Mark's elder brother, born just 14 minutes before Mark they were identical twins. The years since they were born had served them differently. Mark was always the weaker of the two, or at least the elder twin had made Mark feel that way. Part of the reason why he had left home just as soon as could was to create some space between the twins. Always more academic than his brutish brother, Mark had fled to university and never been back since. Anthony had become Tony, shortening his name and making it bigger as he did. Dealing in petty crime from a young age and moving in to the more profitable dealing of drugs around the same time Mark left. Being identical twins it was obvious they looked the same. They looked the same facially, apart from a scar on Tony's left cheek from a previous encounter with someone senior on a patch he was trying to take over. Having got in quick and made the scar to Tony's face, Tony had quickly turned and one punch to the man's face knocked him cleanout on the ground. He could have left it there but the rage at seeing his own blood drop from his cheek, Tony had decided to make him pay. After spending 3 weeks on life support the man's family had decided to turn the machine off and let him pass. They didn't however, let it pass with Tony.

After a long year of territory wars with other casualties on both Tony's side but mainly on the opposing side Tony, was crowned the victor and ran the scene for the whole of the North West. Slowly over the years he had taken more areas and was now feared by many. Never far from his large black Range Rover with blacked out windows, he had become savvy to the police following him and began to court them. His Range Rover always full of minders ensuring no one could get near Tony himself and also full of whatever the local police's favourite tipple was.

This was his way of poking fun at the establishment. Tony knew that most people can be bought and those that couldn't could just as easily be shut up.

The two boys had always looked the same growing up. Their mother thinking it great to dress them the same and drag them to whatever event they were attending, mostly for their local catholic church and had numerous people asking 'Now which one are you?' and then Mark seeing their face change when he told them who he was and getting the reply; 'Oh, the quiet one' and they would soon turn their attention to the louder look-a-like. As they continued to grow up Mark would try desperately to look different to his brother. It wasn't hard, as the boys moved in to their teenage years their characters had become very different.

Tony becoming the brutish thug he later turned out to be and Mark, paying more attention to grooming and looking neat and tidy. The comments from the ladies at the church group most of the time seemed to go over their mother's head. One day however, around the age of 12 or 13, Mark had overhead two older ladies talking and as he walked passed they looked and said; 'It just shines out of some boys doesn't it?' Mark, taking this as a compliment had smiled and walked on as the two giggled at each other before catching the annoyed eye of Mrs Cash and the eye of the identical face but with an angry snarl of Tony. Mark had known this wasn't going to be a great place for him after that. The church had never liked anything they didn't understand or were able to control and this was the same in the closed minds of the people around him. Yet his relationship with his brother had always been an interesting one over the years. Never acknowledging the difference in Mark but always there to protect him. The next five years had been a repetitive story of people trying to bully Mark or make fun of him and spread rumours about his being gay. Mark never denied it. Tony stepped in and put a stop to anyone saying anything. No one ever placed a finger on Mark and Mark never had to deal with coming out, he had no choice he was always put back in before he could.

'You not even gonna say hello?' His strong Mancunian accent stood out more than it had ever done before. Maybe it was because Mark had lost the nasal accent a few years ago having lived away from Manchester for the best part of twenty years. The last time Mark had seen his brother was ten years ago when their father had taken ill and he had been called back to Manchester to say goodbye. Mark had always liked his father and had a much better relationship with him, he had gone back to say goodbye and met with his mother and brother at the hospital.

His mother praying next to the bed had jumped up and hugged him and brought him to his father. He hadn't lasted long after that, the following day Mark returned to London. He attended the funeral the week after and was shocked to see what had happened to his family over the years he had been away. His brother was now wearing expensive suits and driving ugly expensive cars. Houses several times bigger than the council house they had grown up in. Mark had spent the last week understanding and knowing that he had moved away to be able to be himself and now the realisation that he had moved away so not to be part of the culture his family now lived in.

'What happened? Why are you here? Is it Mum?' Mark sounded shocked as he spoke.

'Don't be stupid little bro, I'm here to see you. Thought I would pay my little bro a visit while I'm in town' Tony said to his brother. Mark still felt the cut of the words when he called him his little bro. All these years and the words still dug deep. 'Oh' Mark was still shocked to see him. Vonda was looking on at the two men. Mesmerised by the fact that they looked so similar, she was looking at every bit of them. They both wore black suits, but that wasn't normal as Mark would wear jeans and a shirt to work normally. She still needed to get to the bottom of him why he was wearing such and expensive suit, maybe he had known his brother was coming, who obviously always wore suits like this. But how could he, he looked really shocked to see him. They had different hair styles. Mark's was very trendy grown long on top and short on the sides sweptback creating a flick of hair. His brother had a shaved head. The only other difference was a scar on the brother's cheek, she suspected from some childhood accident from when these two had played so much. She found herself daydreaming whilst watching the interaction. Wondering what life must have been like growing up with an identical bother. Then she wondered why Mark had never mentioned his brother. She soon realised that although Mark would quite happily talk about his friends, even introduce her to most of them, he never; she thought for a minute, no, he had never mentioned his family.

'Mark, you never mentioned you had a handsome twin brother to introduce me to' Vonda added looking at the brother. 'If I had known I might had asked for introductions, I might be in with a chance with one brother' Mark blushed as he looked at Vonda. Slightly taken aback and lost for words.

'Don't you worry little lady, you would be in with a chance. We all know you're barking up the wrong tree with my little bro' Tony leant forward with his hands on the desk Vonda was now curling over.

'As wonderful as this visit is.' Mark looked at Tony 'I actually have two police officers waiting for me in a room two doors down this corridor' Mark looked at his brother giving him as a best a warning of what lay down the hallway as he could. Tony looked puzzled.

'What have you been up to little bro?' He quizzed looking slightly confused.

'I'm not sure yet, doubt it would have much to do with me anyway.' Mark was throwing this back at his brother wondering if his visit had anything to do with the police arrival. 'Maybe Vonda could show you down the hall to our kitchen and get you drink while I go see?' He held his hand out to the other door whilst looking at Vonda who was now standing up with a beaming smile. The prospect of spending time with Mark's brother was appealing, not only that, she could quiz him all about Mark but also she was very much attracted to him.

'That won't matter, I will make my way. I have business to attend to. I will see you at your place this afternoon?' Tony was already walking out the door.

'But you don't know where...' Mark was interrupted before he could finish. This was another thing that he hated, growing up with him as a brother.

'Yes I do!' Tony cut in 'Maybe I will see you again, the lovely Vonda.'

'Yes, Yes that would be fantastic' Vonda looked at Mark and made a slight school girl giggle, then she shouted after Tony, 'I will get Mark to pass my details on' She then turned to Mark who was now stood just staring at the place his brother had previously been.

'Mark.' Vonda walked to him 'Mark, don't keep the police waiting.'

33

Ben jumped off the DLR at Canary Wharf and made his way over to 1 Canada Square into the office building where he had worked at for the last five years. Starting out at the bank and working his way up the ladder in five years was pretty easy, the work was easy and the bank had a great development programme for those that are eager to grow and develop. It wasn't that he was really ready to grow and develop it was more that he saw the big money was in the senior roles.

Personal banking paid a low wage and living in London wasn't cheap. He lived beyond his means. Keeping up with his University chums was a must. They all worked in the area in high powered trading jobs working until all hours. Ben had managed to get a senior role in the personal banking section and now managed a team of about 50 people with a few layers of management. The higher you are the less you do and he aimed to prove the fact. The last year hadn't been good, the banks were under the spotlight and there had been little to no bonus.

It was on his way in to work today that Ben was remembering the previous Manager he reported in to just seven months ago before he retired and Ben took on his role. His wisdom was good, don't do anything that you wouldn't do yourself and only ever do it once yourself from then on, that's what staff are for. He was pretty old school in his thinking but it was good wisdom, Ben could sit back in his office now safe in the knowledge that everything would get done by his impressive team. The best lesson he was taught by Derek, his previous manager, was that if in doubt, look after yourself. Today was a day for looking after himself. He'd had a brilliant weekend, apart from the one strange bloke who didn't even want sex. He had caught up with friends had a great night out and even met up with a guy had been trying to shag for ages and they had spent all of Sunday evening at it. 'It' didn't come cheap, he had to buy the guy dinner and that on top of Saturday night out and the rent being due he had totally wiped out his wages that had been paid last week. Time for an overdraft increase he thought.

He walked through the office saying hello to the majority of people who were already at their desks having started some 30 minutes before Ben had arrived. He stopped to speak with the newest member of the team, a young man called Jeremy who had been transferred from the HR team to work on a project with one of the more experienced managers in the department.

'Hi Jeremy, how was your weekend?' Ben was still trying to work out if he was gay or not.

'Great thanks, spent with the family. What about yours?' Jeremy smiled at Ben and leaned back in his chair. He was a tall guy of about 6ft with jet black hair, a little stubble and generally good looking. He was the type of guy that was good looking but didn't really know how good looking.

'It was excellent, out with friends and dinner last night. We went to this really great place near Clapham Common' Ben smiled back, maybe he was getting somewhere.

'Great, the wife works over that way you should let me know the name' Ben lost interest immediately.

'Yeah I will' He continued walking leaving Jeremy with a knowing look on his face. He watched Ben walk away and in to his office. He knew his type. He'd had guys come on to him before and knew plenty of gay guys to drill this one in to a category. All he wanted was to chase men around, as Jeremy had just proved by mentioning his boyfriend as the wife, if Ben thought it was a woman that was up to him. Ben turned once and looked as Jeremy leaned forward in to his computer. His loss anyway he thought as he hung his coat and sat down at his desk. He flicked the mouse to wake up the computer and logged in to the bank's main system. Knowing his banking codes by heart he tapped them in and went directly to the lending pages where he increased his overdraft by another thousand pounds. That should see him through until pay day. Then he continued to get on with his day's work.

34

'Officers' Mark walked in to the meeting room looking at the two police officers. One was dressed in a full suit with a strange little moustache. He was older than his colleague who was wearing police uniform complete with bullet proof vest and Walkie-Talkies. Mark wondered if all police officers wore bullet proof vests or just the ones that knew they were going to be in the same building as his insane brother. A cold chill crept over Mark as he began to realise his life was about to get way more complicated that he had ever expected.

'Sorry to have kept you waiting, we have an over dramatic receptionist. Have you been offered tea or coffee?' Mark moved towards the two officers who were stood by the window looking out on a view of the London skyline. 'Would you like to take a seat?' Mark became more nervous. It was the suited office that spoke first.

'Thank you, we have been adequately refreshed. It was a very reasonable cup of coffee indeed, let's take a seat.' He sat down and Mark took a seat on the other side of the table to him. The uniformed officer stayed stood, now with a notebook and pen in his hand. 'I am Detective Inspector Jack Daniels and his is my colleague' He turned his head in the uniformed officer's direction. 'Officer Alan Jones.'

'Detective Sergeant Alan Jones' the uniformed officer said. Mark couldn't be sure but he thought he saw the moustached Inspector roll his eyes.

'Well, good morning to you both' Mark tried not to sound nervous but came across as a wooden character actor instead. 'What can I do for you officers?'

'Can you confirm you are Mark Alfred Cash, of Vassal Road, Oval?'

'Yes that's me, can I' Mark was cut off before he could ask a question.

'Could you please confirm your date of birth Mr Cash?' DS Alan Jones was now behind DI Daniels, he had a softer voice, less questioning and more supportive, there was also an Irish accent coming through.

'Sorry, could you tell me what this is about?'

'Your Date of Birth Mr Cash?' He asked again

'June 3rd '77'

'Thank you, we have to be sure we're talking with the right person'

'You seem to already know a lot about me' Mark quizzed; now his nervousness had resided he wanted answers. It was the DI's turn to speak now and it was back to his harsh questioning.

'Are you the same Mark Alfred Cash that is the identical sibling to that of Anthony Alfred Cash?' Mark listening to what the DI had asked and like he had heard it for the first time was thinking about being an identical twin with an identical middle name.

'Yes. Is this about my family? Has something happened?'

'When was the last time you saw your identical twin brother Mr Cash?' The DI continued.

From this question alone Mark knew that they were looking for his brother. He himself was squeaky clean and this line of questioning combined with his brother being outside moments ago, could only mean one thing. Trouble.

'I don't have anything to do with my family and haven't done for nearly 15 years' Mark said, at the moment knowing that he had not lied to the police. Could he get away with not lying and also not telling them that their suspect was right outside moments before?

'So you haven't seen Mr Anthony Alfred Cash in 15 years. Can you be more specific about which year it was when you last saw him?' The DI asked and then starred at Mark.

'Actually, it has been 10 years. I moved away from them 15 years ago to go to University and went back about 10 years ago in 2000 to visit my father who died and I went to his funeral. I saw Tony.' Mark corrected himself 'I saw Anthony then, we were pleasant to each other. I returned to London and haven't heard from him since' Mark realised he had just told his first lie. How many more was he going to tell and why was he lying? He didn't even know his brother so why lie for him?

'Have you had any contact with him or anyone known to him in the last ten years since 2000, which is actually 9 years Mr Cash?' The DI asked keeping his formality.

'I get Christmas and Birthday cards, to and from my mother and a great aunt. Although I suspect the great aunt may had died as I didn't receive anything last year.'

'And you haven't bothered to check?'

'As I said, I don't have anything to do with the family.' Mark took a deep breath feeling like the DI knew he had lied and was going to interrogate more. 'Can I ask why you need to know about my relationship with Tony? Has something happened to him or my Mum?' He showed real concern about his mother. Maybe that's why Tony had been here. 'Is my mother ok?' DS Alan Jones now took a seat next to the DI and looked directly at Mark.

'Mark' His Irish accent sounding quite soothing 'May I call you Mark?' He asked.

'Yes.'

'Mark, we are following some routine inquires as to the whereabouts of your brother. I assume you are aware of your brother's line of work?' He smiled at Mark, hoping his was building a relationship where DI Daniels really couldn't. Having decided just before he sat down that Mark probably knew where his brother was and had some misguided loyalty to him, it was better to have him on their side and be able to give them information when he was ready.

'I know enough to stay away.' Mark replied trying not to give anything away. In fact he knew all too much about his brother's activities. The long letters his Great Aunt used to send him were like chapters from a best-selling crime novel. Most of which he didn't want to know but found them compelling reading. Pages and pages of A4 handwritten notes sent to him four or five times a year.

It was only now that he was realising it had been about seven or so months since the last letter and she had said she had been feeling old and unwell. Mark began to wish that he had paid more attention to the letters and got back in touch with her after the last one. Instead he sat here now feeling the loss of a loved one knowing that he would not be able to find out. A question he may be able to ask his brother this evening whom was going to be at his place.

'Are you ok Mark?' DS Alan Jones asked 'You drifted away a little there.'

'Sorry, I'm sorry. I got to thinking about my Great Aunt and wondered why I hadn't received a card from her at Christmas' Mark replied.

'Ok, sorry sir, if you like I could make a few enquiries with colleagues, local to where she may have lived and find out how she is, unless of course, you have a way to contact her yourself?'

An indirect way to find out more information often helped in these cases and this was a great avenue to explore.

'I have her address' Mark thought best to keep the no contact with family line as long as he could. 'We wrote to each other a few times a year. I could write to her.' Mark thought for a minute.

'Are you allowed to get someone to look in on her to see if she is ok? It would get a quicker response.'

'Consider it done Mark. Let me have that address and I will see what we can uncover.

The big question was almost ready 'Anthony, Tony I think you called him' He looked down at his notepad not to read it as all the information was in his head.

'Yes.'

'Tony, if he was to make contact with you how do you think he would do that?' DI Daniels was watching the interaction and making some kind of notes in his notebook. He was also obviously upset that DS Jones had taken over the conversation.

'They have my mobile number. I haven't changed it since I got it 15 years ago. That's how they contacted me for the funeral.' Mark had moved away from the thoughts of his aunt and was back talking to the officers. 'I guess someone would call me if they needed me.'

'And that's the only way they would ever make contact with you?' DI Daniels had decided he was back in the conversation.

'As I say, I haven't been in contact with any of them for a number of years. They have my number and my Great Aunt and I wrote to each other. I don't know them so couldn't comment on how they would go about getting in touch'

'OK, well if you do hear from Mr Anthony Alfred Cash then you must call us at once and notify us of the interaction' DI Daniels said in a matter of fact voice that made Mark want to argue with him about what he did and did not need to do. He held off and decided he could save that argument for another time when he wasn't lying.

'What DI Daniels is trying to say, is we would be grateful that if you did hear from your brother, that you would keep us informed. As much for you, as it is for us.' D.S Jones stated.

'Really?... Should I be worried?' Mark asked nervously.

'Not at all Mark. We have reason to believe that your brother is in and around the London area and given his activities up north we would just like to keep a check on him and the nature of his visit.' DS Jones said this so dismissively that Mark actually began to believe what they were saying. He knew different, there is no way that any police force in the UK would want Tony Cash on their patch, just as much as he wanted him as many miles away from him as he possibly could be.

35

Sam lay still in bed. He hadn't slept, spending the majority of the night either staring at the tiny hairline crack in the ceiling or getting up and walking round the flat. Constantly looking out the window to see what was going on in the street below. The flat was silent all night and then slowly around 5am the world outside had begun to wake up. The buzz of a rubbish truck reversing to collect waste from the streets below, the marching of someone's feet as they went for an early morning run. Noises he had never noticed before until now when time seemed to be stretching too far. He looked at his clock and it was 10.49am. He had spent the night worrying about the events of the weekend, annoyed that he had now become involved in this. That little shit James bringing trouble to his doorstep. Sam picked up his mobile phone, opened the text message function and added in the names. Mark, Tom, Dean, James, Fred. He typed the text message and pressed send.

After getting rid of everyone from his flat yesterday he'd had to go to work. As always he was running late and flew down the stairs passed Mrs Potts, whose door was wide open.

'Evening Mrs Potts, you know you really should keep this door closed' He shouted putting his head around the door.

'Yes dear, I know. But's it's good for ventilation' the elderly voice travelled along the hall of her ground floor flat. Yes he thought, good for ventilation and being able to sit back and watch the comings and goings of everyone's business. 'You'll join me for birthday drinks won't you dear?'

'Yes, see you later. I'm off to work. Do you need anything bringing home?' He hadn't waited for an answer and was out the door running with his huge carry all bag over his shoulder. Sam liked Mrs Potts a lot. When he had time he enjoyed going down to her flat and listening to her tell stories about her days in front of the camera. Her walls were covered pictures of her as a young actress with various leading men. Mostly black and white pictures, the colour pictures beginning to show her as she aged and became fewer as she got older. She would often tell him about how she never leaves the flat anymore. He knew this not to be true as he had seen her a few times a week getting her hair set at the boutique further down the road where several of the older ladies of the area went to meet and chat. As he half ran half fast walked down the road, he went through the checklist in his head making sure he had put everything he needed in his bag to have a quick turnaround and be on stage in time for his act.

Sam had arrived in London as fresh faced 18 year old boy who liked to dress as a woman. He was now a not so fresh faced forty four year old man who loved to dress as a woman. His journey hadn't taken long, having left his parents and his life as the saviour of mankind and walked, in six inch stilettos and a red dress, to the train station. People stopped and stared at him in the street; the train conductor didn't know if he should check his ticket or chuck him from the train. Sam had gone to the toilet and changed back to jeans and a t-shirt and cleaned the make up from his face. Wanting to keep his killer heels on but realising he would be crippled if he walked any further in them, he opted for trainers. Now looking every bit the 18 year old gay boy about to start a life in the big city he arrived at Paddington Station, stepped off the train and realised the city was way bigger than he had expected and he didn't have a clue what to do about it. Within a few weeks he was working at The Black Cap and fast becoming a very popular barman. He spent his time chatting to everyone who came through the door, making friends and being mesmerised by the drag queens and their cabaret. It didn't take him long to get in the dressing room and begin to learn his trade. Born to perform he knew the stage would be his. Four years later and he was the headline act mixing comedy with cabaret, pulling in huge crowds every time he performed. He was a quick learner too and realised that it wasn't all lipstick and glitter balls. Sam had always known how to look after himself. At a young age he had realised he needed a thick skin to get through life, in his late teens realising he needed strong fists to get through the day sometimes. Constantly attacked by the people around him for the choices he made about his life he had grown up fast and knew how to look after himself. Haters are going to hate and he knew how to handle them. A few sassy words could get most people to walk away and if not the shock of a fight with a drag queen would see most others off. This time, he knew it was different. Moving in the right circles and mixing with the right crowds allowed you to know who was who in any party scene. It also helped you understand who did what on the darker side of any scene.

Drug dealers and pimps had always run certain clubs and bars. The protection rackets were governed by psychos who didn't take the time to find the truth. They act first and ask questions later, if there ever was a later. Mike Doherty, or Manic Mike as he was affectionally known throughout the area, was one of those psychos. Sam had heard all kinds of stories told about him, the fact that he had hospitalised a rent boy for nearly four weeks because the boy had told people he had had sex with him. Manic Mike was definitely someone not to be messed with and Sam had no intention of pissing him off. He had stood in Sam's flat this afternoon in a rage over what James and Dean had done, it looked to Sam that James was going to end up in the same place the rent boy had.

Fred had calmed the situation down and now James, Dean, Fred and Sam were in the debt of Manic Mike. For the twenty years Sam had been in London he had always known who and what Manic Mike was. He had watched him be a younger arrogant aggressive small time dealer and grow in to an older aggressive arrogant dealer. Sam's impression was that Mike thought he was bigger than he actually was, but after a year of bragging, he had created the legend he wanted to be and was now feared by most. Sam had always stayed away from him, never quite crossing his path and never quite getting anywhere close to his business, that's the way Sam liked it. Stay away from trouble and trouble would stay away from you. But not this time, it had come right to his door and almost kicked it down. He sat back in the chair of his dressing room back stage at The Black Cap, this was his home. He had been comfortable here for many years now.

His name was bigger than the pub itself. Well, his stage name that is, Rocky Star. He looked at himself in the mirror and saw the familiar face. At 6ft Sam was tall, had broad shoulders and looked after himself. His muscular chest worked well for him, pushing his pecs in to a bra created a great cleavage. He had never needed the chicken fillets the others had used to get breasts. His pecs and a bit of clever shading from his makeup bag always did the job. He began to add make up to his square chiselled face, his short spikey black hair now gelled back ready for his wig, a few grey bits showing through.

'Not bad for forty four year old wreck' Sam said to himself.

'Forty Four, fuck you're well old' the high pitched, Mancunian, squeal came from the door. Jonathan, or Jonah, as he now liked to be called stood looking in at him.

'Fuck off child' Sam smiled back at him. He like Jonathan... Jonah... He reminded him of himself all those years ago.

'I'm 20 next week. Wanna shag me for my birthday?' Jonah grabbed his dick in his loose fitting pants and thrusted it in Sam's direction.

'I bloody well do not want to go anywhere near that. God knows where it's been.'

'Your loss' and Jonah walked out the door. 'Oh' he shouted down the corridor 'That guy you're always hiding from is in again with his girlfriend.' Jonah's voice drifted off down the corridor towards the bar. The music got louder as the door opened and then faded out again as it closed.

Jonah went back to collecting glasses and flirting with everyone. Sam sat starring at himself in the mirror. He suddenly didn't see a not bad for forty four version of himself, he saw the scared little boy who had fallen in love and had his heart broken.

He had first met Dave on a rare night out, when he was on the other side of the bar celebrating Mark's birthday. His thick Glaswegian accent had been the biggest aphrodisiac for Sam and he had instantly melted into his arms. Spending the whole night buying him drinks and listening to his stories of when he was in the army. That was nearly ten years ago and for the following five years they'd had a loose relationship resulting in Sam falling head of heels in love with his Scottish army man. He was older than Sam by eight years and as tall as him and was built even stronger, there were muscles on the muscles and he spent a lot of time at the gym making sure they stayed looking good. The relationship itself had been great right up until about four years later when Dave had left the army and began to treat Sam badly. Going away for weeks at a time and not being in contact, when he was around treating Sam's flat like a hotel and coming and going as he pleased. Generally turning up in the bar at the end of the night drunk, with a bunch of different people, none of which Sam had ever met before. But still Sam loved him and put most of it down to his leaving the army and not getting any permanent job. This lasted for around a year until one night a small blonde woman in her mid-forties, quite petit, wearing a twin set and pearls, every bit the stereotypical housewife appeared in the club. Sam was on stage, belting out show tunes to a packed Black Cap audience. He finished his last number and thanked everyone for coming along. The audience cheered and Sam took his final bow before moving to climb down from the stage and head to the bar. As he leant on the edge of the bar the woman moved in, standing in his shadow she was dwarfed by Sam in his heels.

'Are you Sam Rockwell?' Her Scottish accent was strong but just as timid as she looked.

'Yes dear' Sam said looking down at her 'You look a bit out of place here love, is there anything I can help with?' Sam looked at her puzzled.

'I'm Helen' She replied, Sam was even more puzzled.

'Hi Helen.'

'You don't know who I am do you?' Still every bit the mild mannered housewife stereotype Sam was looking at.

'Have we met?' Sam asked becoming even more puzzled.

'I'm his wife you dirty fucking queer!'

Sam didn't know if it was the fact that she had gone from mild mannered housewife to swearing homophobe in a matter of seconds or if it was the realisation that she was in fact talking about Dave and that this was in fact his wife. He had a wife.

'Excuse me dear' he was reacting to the comments. 'I may be a fucking queer but there is nothing dirty about me. Now which of these is your husband?' Sam knew the answer but was too far gone to stop reacting, his mouth worked way faster than his brain. He looked around, wanting to close his eyes and disappear, his heart was being ripped out of his chest and there was nothing he could do to stop it. People where now looking at the pair stood at the end of the bar, the music hadn't kicked back in yet and for a small lady she was making a lot of noise. As Sam stood there looking around, unable to make eye contact with her, his eyes met Dave's, stood about four people away from them. They started at each other.

'His' she replied to Sam's question, but Sam couldn't hear her. All Sam could see was Dave mouthing the words I'm sorry. That was five years ago and he had never really gotten over it. Never felt like loving again and certainly never felt like trusting someone again. He hadn't seen Dave from that night when he had dragged his wife from the bar, the tiny lady shouting and crying and calling Sam every name under the sun. Eighteen long months later, he had turned up in the bar having a drink with a young red haired lady. She could have been his wife with different hair, they were obviously together. Sam had to check if it was in fact his wife and realised it wasn't, Dave obviously had a type for the woman he dated. Every few weeks he would be back in again, sometimes when Sam was behind the bar and most times when he was on stage. Dave would smile at Sam and he would put on a brave face and smile back, when actually inside he was having his heart ripped out again and again. He stood in the corner watching him with her, this time a different woman than he had seen him with before. As he stared at him, he wondered why. Why would he keep coming here to watch the show? He must know what he had done to him. Was this his idea of torture? Sam wanted to have him thrown out, but he never would as that would mean he could never see him again, and as much as he didn't want to believe it, he knew it was the truth. Sam finished the nights show and crept out the back door of the bar, down the alley and in to the night. As he peeled his fake eye lashes off and tripped a little on the unloved street a tear rolled down his cheek. He stood still.

'Right, none of this' he said out loud to himself, 'there are worse things going on right now you have to get sorted.'

'Stop talking to yourself you sad old queen' Jonah shouted after Sam from the back door of the pub. Sam turned, smiled at Jonah and did a curtsy. He disappeared back in to the pub and Sam thought about the events on the day. He needed this shit even less than he needed Dave turning up all the time. He pressed send on the text message.

36

'My place tonight, 7pm. We need to sort this shit out.' Tom read the text message again lay in bed warm and cosy, he had been drifting in and out of sleep for the best part of the morning. Gavin had left in the early hours to go to work and Tom had rolled over and slept. Still enjoying the warm of the bed, imagining where Gavin had been and thinking about the fun they'd had. He read the text message again wondering why he was now involved in this, all he had done was go and collect Dean. But then family is family and Dean was in his care. Well almost. He was old enough to look after himself. He climbed out of bed and pulled on a pair of pants from the floor grabbing a t-shirt as he walked towards the door. He stopped and looked at himself in the mirror, his blonde messed up spikes hair ruffled from being in bed looked actually looked pretty cool. Why doesn't it look that cool when I do it myself? He could hear the TV was on and walked towards the kitchen and living room to find Dean making food and the news was on.

'Morning' he said as he walked in yawning and sitting on a tall stool in front of the kitchen worktop. 'How you doing?' he asked Dean. Dean turned and looked at Tom. His eyes were swollen with deep dark bags under them. He looked as if he had not slept for weeks. 'Bloody hell, not good by the looks of you.'

'Not good, I'm awful. I haven't slept all night. I wanted to call James but was worried.'

'What you worried about calling him for?' Tom was puzzled by the comment.

'You know, in case someone has like bugged his phone or something.' Dean had been moving about the kitchen and came to a stop in front of the worktop in front of Tom. As he spoke he placed a large plate with two large sandwiches on it down.

'Not lost your appetite then' he joked.

'What?' Dean was now puzzled, he looked down at the sandwich 'Oh, right, yeah' and sat down taking a bite.

'Why would anyone be tapping phones? Seriously, it's a misunderstanding between a drug dealer and you boys and it will all get sorted soon.'

'You didn't see what he was like, he scared the hell out of me' Dean continued to eat. Tom watched amazed that someone could eat so much when they were so worried.

'Drug dealers don't tap phones. And you think you were scared, think about how he felt when a gun was shot.'

'Sam wasn't happy that we went to his house. He just sent a text message' Dean held up his phone to show Tom.

'I know, I've seen it' Tom replied.

'Tell me again what happened' Dean spent the next 20 minutes explaining to Tom, in great detail what had happened leading up to Tom having to go and collect him. Tom sat back and listened still amazed that even though Dean was so scared he was managing to explain in great detail what had happened and continue to eat the two impressively large sandwiches. By the time the story had finished there were just crumbs left on the plate. Dean got up and moved the plate to the sink turned back to Tom and said 'What are we going to do?'

'We?'

'Well, yeah, you know us. What are we going to do? You have to have an idea' Dean pleaded with Tom.

'Truthfully, I have nothing to do with this.' Dean tried to speak but Tom cut him down 'You have gotten yourself in a whole heap of trouble. What were you thinking trying to get rid of drugs in someone else's flat that you didn't know?'

'I... erm..' Dean looked sheepish and his whole body seemed to get smaller as he thought 'I thought James was going to get in to loads of trouble with his new boyfriend and I didn't want him to. You know I don't like you all taking drugs.'

'You don't like it then stop hanging around everyone. You seem to be really good friends with James but he is worst of all of us for taking stuff. Now look at what's happened. You either deal with the fact that this group of friends take drugs or you start to hang around with friends who like the stuff you like. Don't you have any uni friends?' Dean's eyes filled with tears. 'Hey, don't go getting upset. I don't mean it. We like you hanging around with us. But, you got to get around the fact that it is something that we do.'

'I know, I know and I'm cool with it. I just wasn't cool with James becoming a drug dealer.'

Dean held back the tears and continued to speak 'What do we do now?'

'I don't know mate, will have to have a chat with Sam later and see what the situation is. He knows who this guy is and will be able to tell us the best option.' Tom stood and walked to the door. 'I'm off for a shower, just speak to James; I guarantee no one has bugged your phone.'

37

'My place tonight, 7pm. We need to sort this shit out.' James looked down at the text message briefly and then looked up to Vonda and continued what he was saying.

'So then he took me back to his place, and it was totally lush, like really nicely decorated and he has this great walk in shower. We had a shower together once we got back, it was amazing and then we went to bed.' He winked at Vonda who peered over her thick rimmed glasses. Still pretending to type out the email she had been working on when James had arrived in reception 10 minutes earlier to tell her all about his weekend. She was wondering to herself, as she often did when James came to tell her about the new man he had met and how much in love he was, how much was actually true and how much he had made up in his head. Never for one moment did she think that he was lying and the events he described to her had in fact not happened, it was just that James seemed to operate from a different perception of reality to everyone else. 'By then we were running down the street and Dean was terrified.' Vonda stopped typing realising she had missed a chunk of the story and it had taken an unexpected turn. 'I was ok; it was Dean that was scared.'

'Hold on, stop, stop' Vonda cut in. It took James a second to realise she had spoken before he stopped speaking. 'What the, I think I missed a bit. How did we get from the shower and the sex to Dean being scared and running away?'

'O M G Vonda, are you even listening to me?'

'Yes of course darling, I was doing two things at once. I'm sorry. You have me now, tell me all about it.' Given the change in direction of this recount, Vonda had suddenly become very interested. James went on to explain from the point where Dean arrived to make their way back to Sam's. In some parts his version of events were very different to the actual events and in some parts Vonda wondered if this was in fact the plot for a film he had been to see not the weekend. 'How much drugs did you have on the weekend honey? Are you sure all of this happened?'

'Yes' James's voice changed and he began to sound offended. 'Of course it did. Why don't you believe me?

'Honey of course I believe you, you're telling me what happened and I believe you. It just sounds so much like a movie' She tried to pull him back on side. She had realised that he had been out during the weekend with Mark and now things were beginning to fall in to place. He had arrived in work this wearing a very expensive suit, the police had been here asking lots of questions, information he was not sharing with her yet and now James with this story of drug dealers. No wonder the police had been here, what on earth had Mark done?

'I know, when you say it, it does sound like a movie. I wonder who would play moi?' James asked the question and began to think about Johnny Depp playing him. His phone vibrated again to tell him he had an unread message, looking down he read the message properly this time, it was Sam asking him to come to his place that evening. He thought back to the night before when Sam had gotten so mad at them for going to his house, like where else were they going to go?

'Honey, are you still with me?' Vonda asked James as he was now focused on his phone rather than the conversation. 'And you had a go at me for not paying attention.'

'Sorry, what did you say?' James's tone was now different one again. He was now much slower paced, the energy of the story now gone and the realisation of the situation flooded back to him.

'I asked you where Mark was during all of this, was he with you?' Vonda wanted the main information about her boss and to try and get to work out why the police were so interested in him.

'Mark?' James asked 'Erm, Mark wasn't there. In fact, I don't think I saw Mark again all weekend.' James looked down at Vonda, both of them jumped when a voice spoke out from the other side of the reception room.

'Did somebody mention my name?' Mark stood in the glass doorway that led to the corridor and offices, he was looking at Vonda and James who was stood with his phone in his hand held out in front of him.

38

'My place tonight, 7pm. We need to sort this shit out.' Dean read the message he had received 20 minutes ago. He had read it several times and still wondered what to do about it. He closed the messages on his phone and searched through his address book for James's number.

His thumb hovered over the call button. He put the phone down and paced around the room instead. What did Tom know about this? He hadn't been in the house and James's new boyfriend had a gun. The police were watching people who had guns. They were probably watching what was going on right now just because he had been in the flat. He wished Mark had been home. Mark always knew what to do. He opened the door to his bedroom and walked in to the hall between the rooms of the flat, he could hear Tom in the shower, music played in his room Tom and was singing along to it. What did he have to be so happy about? Maybe the new bloke he had brought home with him. The Irish guy, he did seem quite nice. Dean stopped for a minute and thought about Tom's last boyfriend, Paul, he had hated him. They had split up about a year ago. Paul would spend most of his time teasing Dean about being gay but never having actually been gay. He made sure that everyone had the same thought; that he wasn't even gay.

He totally was gay; he knew this because of how much he fancied Mark and didn't like the fact that he was way too young for him. Having recently turned 19 and Mark being nearly twenty years older than him, he knew there was never going to be a chance, plus he was his cousins best friend and had been around since he was small so really didn't see him in that way, but that didn't stop Dean from fancying him. He liked everything about him, his dress sense, his hair cut and his really cool job. It was one of the main reasons he had decided to study in London, so that he could live with his cousin and be near Mark. Paul would tease him about this, before he had moved to London and even more when he had moved in to Tom's flat. Dean was studying Classical Ballet at the Royal Ballet School; Paul would tease him about this too telling everyone that not all dancers were gay and that Dean was probably just doing it to pull all the girls at school. It was true, he had never actually done anything with a man, not a single kiss, but then he knew that he wanted Mark to kiss him and that would be enough to prove it to everyone. Dean leant against the door frame listening to Tom sing and hoping that his choice in men was as good as his was and that the Irish guy would be nice to him. He seemed nice when he met him last night.

39

'My place tonight, 7pm. We need to sort this shit out.' Mark read the message again sat in his office, he reached over and took a sip of the coffee he had brought with him from the conference room after his meeting with the police officers, and it was now cold. He looked at the cup and put it down. Reading back through the messages and gathering his thoughts on the answerphone messages too. What had been going on? This was fast turning in to the strangest day he had had in a long time, if ever. Having spent the weekend locked up in a club that he never even knew existed to come in to work and find his brother, who he had not spoken to or heard from in years, waiting for him, to be then greeted by the police who wanted to know about his brother. And now this, Sam texting him to meet about whatever it was that had happened with Dean overnight. He assumed it was to do with the Dean situation because as far as he could remember Sam didn't even know he had a brother let alone know he was in town.

He listened to the last message from Tom which had been left when he went to meet the police officers. He laughed at Tom, he quite often left messages where he was actually having a conversation with himself and answered his own question. This time it was almost that, telling him not to say anything to the police and then saying he couldn't as he didn't know anything. James! Mark thought to himself, James would be in work by now and he could ask him what has been happening and why he has been summoned to Sam's place tonight. He looked at the message again and saw that the group of people it had been sent to included Tom, Dean, Fred and James. As he stood up and walked to the door he saw himself in the glass wall and noticed the suit he was still wearing.

He couldn't help but smile a great big grin as he recalled his day spent with Stuart, getting the suit, the sex party, the room. Then he thought about waking up and finding Stuart had gone. He put his hand in to his pocket and found the hand written note and read it again. His grin still on his face imagining what it would be like next time he saw Stuart, then the realisation that he had no way of contacting him. He didn't give him his number and didn't even know his surname in fact, the only information he knew about him was the pub he had flirted with him in and the fact that he was a member of the I.o.G. What the hell was that place? He opened his phone again and did an internet search on Institute of Gentlemen and got no direct results, there were several hits for the Institute of Directors, a members club for directors of businesses in central London. He recognised these, as he had often been to client meetings at the grand location, but nothing for the Institute of Gentleman. He did a few more searches adding in club, gentlemen, and institute and finding no matches. He went to his computer and searched on a map the area he had been in. He couldn't quite recall the exact location he had left earlier that morning so looked around the whole area and nothing was showing. This day was becoming stranger and stranger. There was one thing he could get sorted quite fast and that was to get to the bottom of what had happened with Dean. He slid his phone in to the pocket of the suit and walked towards reception. He didn't need to ask if James was in work yet as he could hear him talking to Vonda.

Realising James was talking about the weekend and was quite animated he wondered who he would get a better recollection from, James or Vonda. He was stood in the doorway to the reception watching;

'Did somebody mention my name?' Mark held his phone out in front of him looking at James. James looked startled and Vonda turned to her computer screen and typed on the keyboard as if she had been in the middle of doing something. 'Are you busy James?' Mark asked 'Do you think I could have a quick word with you?' He looked at his phone 'About this?' James, with a puzzled look on his face walked towards Mark, who turned and walked in the direction of his office.

'Hang on, how do I know what you want to talk to me about if you are walking away from me?' James hurried after Mark and followed him in to the office.

'What's going on? What's this message from Sam about and what has been happening with Dean yesterday?' Mark demanded from James.

'You won't believe it if I told you.'

'Try me.'

40

'Well there is definitely something that Mr Mark Cash is not telling us.' DI Jack Daniels sat with his notebook open looking at the group around the large desk in the major incident room. Kirsty Brown was now intrigued. She has originally sent Jack off on a wild goose chase to get him out of her way while she continued to look in to the arrival of Tony Cash on her patch, the gunshot and also the apparent murder investigation. The gunshot was low priority for her and knowing that the murder should be the highest priority she couldn't help but give most of her focus to Tony Cash.

If she could bag him while he was here it would be a career changing moment as well as getting off the streets, one of the worst drug dealers she had ever come across. Six years ago, just before she had been promoted to the chief Super role, she had had the pleasure of meeting the low life scum Tony Cash. Part of a joint operation with the MET and Greater Manchester Police, Tony had been under surveillance as it was known that he was about to do a huge drug deal that would put hundreds of thousands of ecstasy pills on the streets of both Manchester and London. At the time it was part of a wider clean-up of the streets, the part that ate away at Kirsty was that a bunch of the pills were dirty and cut with some nasty ingredients, they had ended up on the streets of London. They didn't seem to have much effect when one or two were taken, a bad come down was reported from most people who had used them. Sadly, four teenagers, two girls and their boyfriends had gotten some and taken several in one night. Kirsty had been called to the emergency room when the second of the two boys had died. By the time she had arrived one of the girls had died. She wanted Tony Cash to go down for it and knew that there was never any way to link him to the deaths, but she knew he had pushed the drugs on to the streets and washed his hands of it. Scum, not even bothered to make sure his product was safe. They say there is honour among thieves, she saw this and knew several thieves that she could always tap up for information, but with dealers there was nothing but ego and money.

Back then, she had been given a tip off that Tony's brother Mark was living and working in London, she had spent weeks before and after the failed bust watching him. By the time she had given up on it, she had decided that Mark Cash had less to do with his brother than she did. The first time she had seen him it had freaked her out a little how much they looked like each other. Mark carried a little less weight than his brother and Tony carried the scar on his face. She wondered now if she had missed something and there was in fact a connection.

'What?' She looked at the outdated DI wondering if it hadn't in fact been a wild goose chase. He sat at the table with his notebook open. 'Where is DS Jones?'

'He will be along any minute. A call of nature I believe.' Jack read his notes whilst he answered and then looked up at his new boss.

'Tell me then! What do you believe Mark Cash is hiding?' Kirsty badly wanted the information.

'I wouldn't say he was hiding anything.' D.S Alan Jones had walked in to the room and looked at the interaction between his two senior ranking officers.

'What do you mean? Jack here was just about to tell me what Mark is hiding. Jack gave Alan a look of distant scorn and then turned back to Kirsty.

'I have been around the block enough to know when someone is hiding something. You just had to look at him' Kirsty raised her eyebrows at him. 'He was sat there is a very expensive suit desperate to get rid of us.' He looked up at Alan. 'I think that secretary knows a thing or two as well, she looks the type.' Alan looked at Kirsty not wanting to contradict his senior officer but also knowing he disagreed.

'I have an expensive looking suit sir, it doesn't mean I am hiding anything' Jack shot Alan another looked as if to tell him to shut up. Alan took the seat next to Jack and allowed him to carry on.

'We met with Mark Cash at his place of work, a marketing company called HBM, at eight thirty three this morning.' Kirsty had an inner sigh; the level of detail was going to kill her in this conversation. She didn't want to rub up Jack any further in the wrong direction. He was obviously upset with his Sergeant for not being in agreement with him. She looked at Alan, once again acknowledging that he was a fine officer and making a mental note to come back to him for his take on the situation once Jack was out of the way.

He wore a black expensive suit. We questioned him about his relationship with his brother Mr Anthony Cash also known as Tony Cash. Mr Mark Cash explained that he had nothing to do with his brother and or his family for' He stopped and looked at his notes 'for the past ten years since the death of his father when he attended the funeral and promptly left Manchester coming back to London. I have checked this information and it seems sound. His father did die at that time and was buried.' Jack looked up at Kirsty, still waiting for something more than facts.

'And from this you believe he is hiding something?' She asked.

'I believe he wasn't being totally honest sirrr..' He trailed off 'Ma'am.'

'Alan, do you have anything to add?' She tried to look at DS Alan Jones.

'Ma'am, he was a little cagey when we first questioned him, but nothing that would give me reason to believe he was lying. In fact I think he had realised a family member he cared about may have passed away and he wasn't aware?'

'What, who? The dad? I thought..'

'No Ma'am, A great aunt. I have done a little digging this afternoon and it seems the aunt of Mark and Anthony's mother who lived with the mother did pass away in June this year at the age of ninety three.'

'Wow, good innings.' Kirsty said 'and you say Mark wasn't aware of this? Had they been close?'

'Mark noted that they had written to each other several times a year and that he hadn't heard from her since Christmas I believe.'

'Well it all ties up with what Mark is saying. He still has no direct contact with his brother.'

Kirsty said to them both, Jack rolled his eyes and got up to leave the room. 'Where are you off too? She quizzed him.

'To type up my notes Ma'am'

'Good, get them over to me before you leave for the day.' Jack rolled his eyes again but no one saw this time as he was already walking out the door. As birthdays go he wasn't enjoying this one at all. But then again, he didn't really enjoy most days.

41

My place tonight, 7pm. We need to sort this shit out. Fred was typing her reply whilst sat at the departure gate of the British Airways 16.35 flight from London City airport to Paris Charles De Gaulle.

'Hon I'm on my way back to my babies and my babe. Let me know what happens. Call me when you spoke to the others. I'm worried.' The reply came back almost instantly.

Don't you go worrying one little bit. It'll get sorted. Give all your boys big kisses from me.' She replied with a single X and got up and walked to the gate that had just been called.

42

By 7pm Tom was sat on the sofa in Sam's apartment chatting to Caroline about her trip to Australia. 'You won't believe what happened on my way home.' His thick Manchester accent reminded him of Mark when they had first met all those years ago. Mark had lost the accent having been away from Manchester for so long but Caroline had never lost a single bit of it and had been away from Manchester for much longer. 'So I leave Alice Springs on this tiny little plane. It was like a self-propelled thing'

'Self-propelled? What?' Tom looked confused.

'Well not self-propelled but like, you know them old planes with propellers at the front.' Tom mimed an ok and Caroline continued 'So I gets off at Brisbane and needs to connect with my international flight, only I'm in domestic. So I followed the signs for international and goes through these double doors and there is this elderly lady following me too so I thought I must be going in the right direction. And then, you won't believe it.'

'Go on then, tell me' Tom had sat up to listen

'I walks through these double doors with international above them, they were like a fire exit type door, you know the one with the metal bar?'

'Get to the point' Tom cut in.

'Oh yeah right, well I walks through these doors and they open up on the other side and it looks like international departures and then this big bloke with a gun dives on me asking what I am doing and where I came from.'

'What the fuck' Tom wasn't expecting that

'Yeah, I know and the old woman behind screams and nearly faints and they catch her and I have to check her and they don't want me to check her cause they think something is going on and I'm shouting I'm a nurse I'm a nurse.' Tom looked at Caroline with a slight laugh and slight look of concern.

'What happened?'

'They dragged me off to a room and that was the last I saw of her.'

'Not to her, to you, what happened in the room?'

'They asked me loads of questions about where I had come from and How I got through that door and, well I think they got the wrong end of the stick as they thought I was her nurse and then I explained I wasn't and I was just saying it because she looked ill and needed help.'

'Are you telling that story again Caro?' Sam walked in through the front door listening to the story he had heard earlier that day. 'Hiya Love' He leant down and gave Tom a hello kiss on the cheek. 'Have you heard from Mark?'

'Yeah I spoke to him this afternoon' Tom had finally spoken to Mark at about three o'clock when Mark had called him to find out what was happening. He had already had a conversation with James and still didn't quite understand what was going on. Tom took him through the version of events as he had known them.

'So what has it all got to do with me?' Mark asked Tom on the phone.

'Nothing I don't think, I'm not sure why you got the message' Tom had replied.

'Well I can't come over to Sam's tonight anyway; I've got some stuff I need to sort out.'

Mark went on to tell Tom about his brother turning up at work this morning and then the strange meeting with the police quizzing him. 'You know when you walk passed the police in the street and have done nothing wrong and still feel like you have, well this time I had done something wrong and didn't know what to do.'

'Fuck, what's your brother doing in London? When was the last time you spoke to him?'

'Ten years ago at Dad's funeral.'

'Wow, and he knows where you work?'

'It seems so. Anyway, don't tell anyone any of this. I am meeting him tonight. I think he is coming round to my place. I'll tell you everything after I have seen him.'

'Right, well I'll be back home when I'm done at Sam's.'

'Cool, see you later.' Tom was about to hang up the phone when he realised he didn't know where Mark had spent his Sunday.

'Hang on, hang on' he shouted back down the phone. 'Where were you yesterday? And who was that guy you disappeared off with?'

'Oh bloody hell yeah, my brother is about half of the excitement of the weekend.' Mark went on to tell Tom all about Stuart, the club and how confused he has been about it since.

'Call him and ask him' Tom suggested.

'I can't I don't even have his number' Mark said at the same time he realised he had no way at all of contacting Stuart.

'That all sounds well dodgy. And you still have the suit?' Tom asked.

'Yeah, got it on right now.'

'You're some form of mistress or gangster's moll. You're a gangster mistress' Tom laughed.

'Go away Twat' Mark replied 'See you tonight.'

Dean knocked and buzzed the outside buzzer for Sam's flat and waited to hear the unlocking clink of the entrance door. He looked around the street to see if anyone was watching him. As the door clicked he pushed forward and was instantly greeted by Mrs Potts, she must have heard the buzzer.

'Hello dear' She said looking puzzled at Dean's arrival. 'You're the young one aren't you?

'How's the dancing going my dear?'

'Erm, hi, erm... yeah that's me. It's good.' Dean continued to climb the stairs.

Mrs Potts watched him disappear and thought to herself, as she often did when she saw the comings and goings of the people in and out of the three other flats in her building, that youth was most definitely wasted on the young. It was only when they got a little older that they did in fact get manners. Dean looked back over his shoulder and gave Mrs Potts an uncomfortable smile and walked up to the door of Sam's flat that was now open waiting for him to enter.

'She is a strange one that old woman downstairs isn't she?' Dean asked the group sat in the flat. He looked at his cousin Tom sat on the sofa with Caroline and then over to Sam who was in the kitchen making what looked like coffee. 'Where's Mark and James?' he asked openly to the room.

'Not here yet' Sam said from the open plan kitchen. 'Mark isn't coming' Dean looked puzzled and then angry.

'What? What do you mean he is not coming?' Tom stood up and walked over to Dean.

'Calm down. He's not coming because it's got nothing to do with him. Truthfully it's got nothing to do with me either' Tom looked over at Sam 'But you wanted me here.'

'Dear, he is in your care' Sam said almost laughing with a sarcastic tone to his voice.

'I am not, I can look after myself' Dean said stubbornly. Sam looked on, rolling his eyes.

'Thanks' Tom said and sat back down next to Caroline, now aiming his conversation back at her. 'How are the boys doing?'

Dean continued. 'And James, what about James?' he persisted

'On his way, I thought you were him actually.' Sam placed several mugs on a tray and carried them through to the dining table in the middle of the room. As he did so, James walked in through the still open door closing it behind him.

'Hiya,' he was quite cheery. 'Crazy downstairs let me in, she's great isn't she?' James looked over to Sam, seeing he was making drinks 'Oh, can I have a coffee please? I've not had a cup all day. It's been crazy busy at work.'

'Sit' Sam looked at James and then turned to Dean. 'You too,' as he did so Tom stood up leaving the conversation he was having with Caroline who also stood and walked to the other side of the flat and towards her room.

'See you in a bit boys' she said as she left.

Tom, Sam, Dean and James sat at the table while Sam poured coffee in to cups.

'Fred has headed back to Paris; she said she was worried about what's happening. I told her not to be.'

'Why? What's happening?' James looked the others.

'What the fuck James. This is serious' Sam looked annoyed at James and then turned to Tom for support.

'James' Dean was the one to speak 'Are you serious? This is really bad and you seem like it didn't even happen.'

'What? All this yesterday? Oh right. Well you know. I'm sure it will sort itself out.' James looked at the others. 'Is that what this meeting is all about?'

'You fucking little shit' Sam shouted jumping up from his chair 'Do you realise how fucking serious this? Do you even know who that fucking insane drug dealer is?'

'I think you're over reacting a little bit aren't you Rockers?' James stayed sat in his seat looking up at Sam.

'Don't you Rockers me.' Sam stood, took a deep breath and composed himself 'Well, you obviously don't know who he is so let me tell you.' Sam went on to tell James about the rent boy who was hospitalised and other stories he knew and explaining who in fact Manic Mike was. All the time, as he told James he could see the optimistic cheery face move slowly into disbelief and then from disbelief to shock and finally ending in what Sam thought was fear. He looked over and saw that Dean was crying.

'Sam.' Tom said getting Sam's attention 'I think you laid it on thick enough now.' Tom shook his head over to Dean. Sam looked down at Dean again and then took his seat back at the end of the table.

'So,' he sipped his coffee. 'What are you going to do about it?' He looked from James to Dean and back again. 'This bog ole mess we seem to be in.'

'I...I...' James was finding it hard to speak.

'Let me rephrase that for you James. Where are you going to find fifty grand in the next week to pay of the dealer that' he paused for dramatic affect 'will kill you, or at least seriously maim and hospitalise you, should you not deliver.' When Sam had finished, all that could be heard was the heavy breathing of Dean trying hard not to cry out loud.

'It's all my fault!' Dean blurted out 'It was me that did it. It's not James' Dean then continued to cry out loud.

'You both got us in this mess' Sam put his hand on Dean's arm 'You're too young to know any better.'

'That's not fair!' Dean had changed from crying in fear to anger at Sam.

'I got us in to this mess, I will get us out. I'm going to call my Dad.' Dean was reaching for his phone in his pocket.

Tom grabbed his hand quicker than he could think about it. There was no way he was letting Dean call his Dad, his uncle, and tell them anything that was happening.

'No you're not matey. We can get this sorted. Your Mum and Dad don't need to be dragged into this too.' Tom had Dean's phone now and put it at the end of the table away from his reach.

43

Mark stood in his bedroom looking at the suit he had taken off moments before, placed on a hanger and hung on the outside of his wardrobe. Still wearing the Calvin Klein's Stuart had given him he was thinking about his time at the Institute of Gentlemen. He thought about the gathering in the bar and then the men having sex in front of whole room and then about being back in the room with Stuart.

Pushing his hand down his pants he played with his now hard dick. As he thought about the day and about Stuart he sat back on his bed and got ready to have a wank. As he lay back on the bed he heard the door of his flat bang open. Fuck. He dived up fast. What was Tom doing back already? He was the only person who had a key to his flat so it must be him. He dived over towards the bedroom door pulling the pants back up and grabbing his jogging pants from the chair.

'Yo Bro, you in ere?' The unmistakable Mancunian voice of his brother shouted in to his flat. Mark stood still frozen to the spot. 'Bro?' the voice was getting closer.

'Yeah' Mark mustered his voice. 'Yeah, Yeah I'm right here.' He shouted back and stepped out of the doorway pulling up the jogging bottoms.

'Ha ha, there you are. Catch you tossing off did I? Just like old times.' Tony walked up to Mark and grabbed at the back of his head pushing him forward.

'Fuck off, no you didn't,' Mark lied embarrassed, then looked puzzled. 'How did you get in?' Tony finished his sentence. This annoyed Mark even more. For years when they had been growing up Tony had always answered for Mark, never letting him have his own opinion. Old emotions stirred and anger was the strongest. 'I have ways of getting in to where I want.' Tony was looking passed Mark in to the bedroom. 'Two bed place?

You got a flatmate? Some nancy boy living with you?' the words grated on Mark. Tony knew this and used them all the same.

'No. It's just me' Mark said dead pan to his brother. He was looking at him closer now.

Noting the differences in his twin, there weren't many, just the hair and the scar and maybe Tony was carrying a little more weight than him. Slightly bulkier which looked like it was muscles rather than fat.

'Is that door to the bathroom?' Mark gestured to the door at the end of the hall.

'I need to take a slash' Tony pushed open the door next to him. 'In here is it?' Mark watched his brother. Fucking liberties, who did he think he was turning up like this? Tony didn't close the door and used the toilet. Mark walked in to the living room and the open plan kitchen. The flat was exactly the same as Tom's flat over the landing, except in the opposite direction. It was decorated pretty much the same too, with white walls and a grey modern kitchen. His leather sofa that he often thought may in fact be older than him sat in the middle of the room looking at a large T.V that took up most of the corner of the room.

'I'll get you one of them flat screen TV's. That fucker's too big for in here.' Tony had finished in the bathroom and followed Mark through to the living room.

'I don't need one.' He said bold and direct to Tony 'Why are you here?'

'I have business to take care of and thought I would drop in on mi ole brother and see how he is doing.' Tony stood looking at Mark. 'You got a problem with that?'

'No' Mark didn't want to make small talk and really didn't know why his brother was here.

He must have been to London countless times over the last ten years, why was he here now.

'What did the police want you for this morning? What you been getting in trouble for?' Tony questioned.

'Actually' Mark opened the fridge and grabbed a bottle of coke. He waved it passed his brother, remembering that he only ever drank beer or coke. Tony nodded. 'They were looking for you. They knew you were in town and wanted to know if you had made contact with me.' He handed the glass of coke to his brother who moved across the room and sat in the leather sofa. He sank back and looked uncomfortable, adjusted himself and sank back even further which Mark found funny.

'Thought as much, follow me everywhere these days.'

'Why?' Mark was finding his confidence.

'Ha ha, never you mind little bro, you don't need to know why.' Mark felt the anger in him for being called little bro and then the disgust at his brother for being who he was.

'So this is a social visit then?'

'Sure is little bro.' Tony was being quite direct and Mark thought quite cagey too. He stood up from the sofa and walked to the window, standing to the side and moving the edge of the open curtain to look out to the street below. He was checking the street to see if there was anyone about, anyone who had followed him. 'So what did you tell them?' he asked looking down to the street.

'I told them I hadn't seen you since Dad's funeral' Mark watched his brother. Last time he had seen him he was full of confidence, his ego bigger than him and his notoriety allowed him to keep the ego. Over confident and cocky, everything Mark hated in people. He wondered if his hatred of the character type was due to his relationship and growing up with his brother, it was for sure. He had carried it round with him for long enough. Pip, would have a field day if he ever let her loose on his pent up anger about his family. She would NLP it out of him. Near Linguistic Programming was her thing and she was bloody good at helping and supporting people to get rid of the baggage they carry, well at least the stuff that wasn't good for them. He had never opened up to Pip about his family, in all the years he had known her. Keeping the emotions to himself, meant he never really had to deal with it. Maybe that was why he had never told anyone apart from Tom about his family. Did he actually like being mad at them?

'What happened to the fella you were with?' Tony asked, still looking out the window as if he was watching someone himself.

'What?' Mark was a bit taken aback by Tony's question. Why would he know anything about his life? 'What fella?'

'You know. That blonde bloke you have been with for years.' Tony turned and looked at him.

'Don't think I don't know what you have been up to little Marky.' He had a big grin on his face now. Mark was getting more irritated.

'Well your information isn't all that good. I've not been seeing anyone. Not for a long time.'

'Aww, Marky Mark, what's wrong? You not enjoying our little catch up?' He paused but only for a second not allowing Mark to answer 'Tom! That's his name, that's the fella'

'Tom is a friend' Mark was being more matter of fact.

'Oh. I thought all you puffs were at it with each other all the time.'

'Well you thought wrong.' Mark was done with the conversation now. His brother was reverting back to his true colours. 'Have you got somewhere to be? Business to take care of?'

'You want rid of me already do you?'

'Truthfully Tony, yes I do. We haven't seen each other in years and you turn up being exactly like you were all those years ago.' Confidence taking over Mark was ready to get rid of his brother.

'And how's that our Kid?'

'A self-righteous prick who thinks he can treat me like crap for being 15 minutes younger than him.' Maybe the pent up anger was making a move to break free and Tony was about to get it all.

'Howdya work that one out?' Tony looked shocked 'I treat you better than anyone else.'

'So being homophobic and a bit of a prick, is nice in comparison to what other people get is it?' Mark was shocked.

'Homophobic. Bleeding hell! You're all the same you gays. Everyone is bleeding homophobic just because you don't like what they are saying.

'Fuck off!' Mark shouted 'That's not true, you are fucking homophobic. You always have been. And it's not because I don't like what you say, it's because what you say is homophobic.'

'What the fuck have I said?' Tony sounded shocked

'Erm... I thought all you puffs were at it with each other all the time.' Mark repeated Tony's comments.

'Did I say that?' Tony smiled 'Sounds like something I'd say. Well if it makes you feel any better I ain't homophobic. I like you, you're my brother.'

'Oh right, heard that before. I'm allowed to say that as my brothers gay' Mark said sarcastically.

'Calm down precious. You were always like this, flying off the handle. Little Drama Queen.'

'I think your visit is done' Mark said looking at his brother. He was beginning to calm down a little now. It looked like Tony hadn't heard him or paid attention, as he was now looking around the room at Mark's things.

'It's one of your team I'm here to see actually.' Tony was bending down and looking at Mark's DVD collection on the shelf in the corner of the room, flicking his fingers through a few of them not really talking, more thinking out loud. 'Some batty boy dealer working down here who seems to think he can take shit load of my stuff and get away with it.'

'What?' Mark was shocked now that his brother was sharing this kind of information with him.

'What's that?' Tony stood up straight and looked at Mark.

'You were saying?'

'I was saying nothing,' Tony stared at Mark. 'Forget it, the less you know the better. Don't want Daniels and Jones asking you questions you know the answer to now do we?'

'How do you know their names?'

'As I said Mark, I know what I need to know and you know what you need to know.'

'You never said that.'

'Well I should have. Want to know anything about Mum? Know how she is doing? Or is this conversation going to be all about you?' Tony was now next to Mark.

'What?' Mark could feel himself getting angry again. He breathed deep. 'How is she?'

'She is good. I gotta go now. I will tell her you asked after her. I doubt she will be happy to know you're still a batty boy.' Tony screwed his face up 'Now that did sound homowhatever!' He smiled 'She is the one who doesn't deal well with you being a gay.'

Mark watched his brother walk from the living room and into the hall way, he followed him. They arrived at the front together and Mark closed it behind his brother. They didn't speak again as he left. Mark stood looking at the door to the flat wondering how his brother had managed to get in, there was no damage to the Yale lock, the main bolt was not locked as it never was when Mark was in the flat. He thought to himself that he would need to start locking that too.

44

'I'd quite like realistic suggestions please Dean.' Sam said. Dean had moments before made a suggestion about a talent contest being held at G.A.Y at the weekend and that they could enter.

'The prize is twenty grand' Dean continued, he was reading the information from one of the free gay magazines that Sam had. Dean had found it just before he had started to rave about it being the answer.

'Where do you suppose you get the other thirty from?' Sam looked at Dean. It made him feel good that Dean thought he had enough talent to go ahead and win the big prize. He was also nearing desperation trying to work out where the money was going come from. Several suggestions had been made, the most realistic had been robbing a bank, which was quite possibly the worst suggestion James had come up with. Tom and Sam had been having a private conversation in the kitchen about 30 minutes previously.

'Even if we manage to sell them at about five pound each that's what?' Tom whispered and looked at the bag 'How many you reckon are in there?

About two thousand? So at about £5 each..

'That's about ten grand' Tom screwed the corner of his mouth at Sam. 'What's the crack with it being fifty grand they owe the guy?'

'Manic Mike said they had either flushed or ruined the rest. This is what James had grabbed and ran off with.' Sam said, counting a few of the pills in his head.

'So they grabbed these? Do you think the shit would've hit the fan if they had just left?'

'Probably not as bad as this, they could've just gone in to hiding and not have a psycho after them. As it was they got followed back here and now I have a psycho after me too.' Sam leaned back against the worktop and looked at the two boys sat at the table, Dean by now had started to look through the magazine and James was just staring at him.

'The other problem is my love, where the hell are we going to off load nearly two thousand pills?' Sam and Tom were still whispering to each other. 'Like, I could take a few for stock and I'm sure the inner circle would but that's only going to be about a hundred or so. How do you sell the rest?

'And that is if we can get street value. Bulk selling we are not going to get five pound each' Sam turned back to the bag. 'We ain't dealers Tom; we don't even know where to start'

'You're right, where do you start to try and sell this stuff. I'm bloody crap at buying it. I always leave it to you or Mark' Tom looked helpless at Sam.

'And family isn't an option?'

'What? Sell my family a load of pills?'

'No dickhead, like is there any money these two could get their hands on with family?' Sam was still whispering and mentally counting the pills.

'I know what you mean,' Tom smiled for the first time since finishing his conversation with Caroline earlier. 'And no! There is no way I want any of my family involved in this. Bleeding hell can you imagine what my parents, his parents would say?' Tom nodded towards Dean 'They'd freak if they even knew we took drugs never mind got involved in something like this.'

'I forget what family life can be like.' Sam smiled at Tom. The two of them had walked back to the other two sat at the table and Dean had given them the rundown of the G.A.Y talent contest.

'It is a serious suggestion. It says here that the top prize is twenty thousand and it is to celebrate the closing of the Astoria.' Dean was getting more animated as he explained.

'They're closing the Astoria?' James asked sounding upset. 'What will happen to G A Y?'

'It's being pulled down in the New Year, Tottenham Court road station is being made bigger for Cross Rail' Sam said dismissively.

'Aww, I really like it there' James was still upset at the news.

'G.A.Y will still be going, round the corner I think.' Sam directed his comment at James and then back to Dean.

'Realistically though Dean, it's a slim chance of one of us winning and then we still have to focus on the rest of the cash.'

'Ok, but it is a good idea. You should totally enter it Rockers.' Dean said enthusiastically.

'Thank you lovely, maybe when I'm not about to be killed by the London mafia, I might think about entering the talent show and making it big in the music industry. But for now...' Sam ended the conversation with a wry smile.

'Oh my God!' Caroline's voice carried across the room. 'That sounds excellent you should totally enter. Do you know that Mel C is the presenter judge there? Oh My God I could actually meet her.' Caroline had walked over to the table and grabbed the magazine from Dean. 'I totally love her, best Spice Girl by far.' She looked down at the boys sat around the table. Sam looked up at her and smiled.

'I think we could totally be friends.' Caroline said looking down she scanned pages through pages of the magazine.

'Perhaps, not now.' He attempted to stop her taking over the conversation, giving her a wink.

'I think she is class. I love her. She has an excellent voice. I have just bought her last album.'

'She's still releasing albums?' Tom asked.

'It's an old one.' Caroline replied. 'Oh fucking hell have you seen this, G A Y is closing down' She was now reading the article about the talent show.

'Caro, the Astoria is closing down. I was just saying.' Sam was desperately trying to get the conversation back on track.

'Oh right, aww gutted, it's such a great venue. I've had plenty of good nights in there. Do you remember that girl who worked on the door? What was her name, Jen?' Caroline thought for a minute. 'No, it was Paula. Yeah I used to really fancy her. I wonder if she still works there. It says here that it will be closing down in the New Year. I bet that's so they can make loads of money over Christmas before they close it down.'

'Yeah most probably' Sam said. 'Boys, more ideas. Come on' Caroline seemed distracted now by the article.

'I've got nothing' Tom said now leaning his head on his hand.

'Me neither, apart from the bank job, you see it happen in films all the time.' James offered nothing better than his previous comments. Caroline was the next person to speak, as if the conversation hadn't moved on from where she had left off.

'It says on here that on a good night, like the talent show night, G A Y could take up to fifty thousand in cash on the door alone' James looked up at Sam, Tom sat up and also and looked at Sam.

'Maybe not a bank job' James said. The boys sat looking at each other. Sam's heart began to sink. There were no actual ideas. In the face of adversity they were now looking at insane ideas.

'It doesn't say anything in the article that she is the judge. Just that there is a special guest judge slash host for the night. That must be her and they have decided to announce it later for a big dramatic effect'. Caroline flipped the magazine to the front page and looked at the publish date. 'Yeah that's it, this was published a month ago' She looked up at the boys all staring at each other and Sam looking like he was about to be sick 'What?' She looked at him and questioned having missed their reactions moments ago.

45

'Ma'am.'

The man with his head round the door was trying to get the attention of the Chief Superintendent. He had slowly pushed open the door enough to fit his head through a few minutes ago and had been whispering 'ma'am' a few times. It was Wednesday morning and everyone had been working away on the murder case, following leads and putting together the case file. At the moment they had nothing to go on. Detective Inspector Jack Daniels had noticed him first but decided to ignore him. He knew that the man poking through the door was one of the pathologists and he hadn't cared to remember his name. Thinking to himself if the man can't come in a room and announce himself, then he surely wouldn't be doing it for him, Jack continued to read through the notes he had made in order to be ready for the briefing that was due to start. Chief Superintendent Kirsty Brown was deep in a conversation with DS Alan Jones, Jack found himself wondering about this too. What did they have to talk about so much? A Sergeant should report through his Inspector and not be jumping rank like this. He made a mental note to follow up on this with him after the meeting. 'Ma'am' the voice came again, Jack was now staring at him.

'Detective Inspector Jack Daniels,' Kirsty's voice was loud and stern. Jack jumped from his gaze to look at her, catching her eye in the death stare, as he now called it 'You can see that I am busy in conversation and that the gentleman at the door is trying to get my attention.' She continued to look at him. 'Polite people would normally ask if they can be of any help'.

'He is asking for you, not me' Jack replied curtly.

Kirsty rolled her eyes and turned to Alan. 'Give me a moment. I'm sorry' she turned from Alan looking at Jack as she walked to the door. 'Johnny, what can I do for you?' She asked him as she neared the door. Jack watched as he stepped inside the door. He was wearing green scrubs and had dark tanned skin as if he had just got back from holiday. His hair was sun kissed blonde and he spoke with a Birmingham accent.

Jack watched as they spoke to each other in hushed voices and then the man in scrubs handed over a folder. Kirsty obviously knew what she was looking for as flicked through the papers in the file quickly until she landed on the page she wanted. He couldn't quite hear what was being said but Kirsty looked at first shocked and then unhappy.

'And you are sure?' She said loudly as they both looked at the page.

'Yes. Ma'am. It's very straight forward. There's a note.' He leaned in and turned the page.

Kirsty scanned the page quickly and then slapped the file closed.

'Right, that's it then, thank you for letting me know. Can I keep this file for now?'

'Yes, it will need to be returned to complete final details but I can come by and collect it later.'

'Thanks Johnny, that's a real help.' Kirsty turned and walked to Andy Grey who was sat at a computer terminal on the other side of the room. Jack continued to watch, wanting to know what was going on. Kirsty leaned down and had a similar hushed conversation with Andy. She crouched next to him bringing her head just below his where he was sat in a chair. They both looked at the file and the details on the page she had been reading just before slamming the page shut. Both of them looked unhappy.

'And you think it is correct?' Andy asked her.

'It's all we have to go on and the coroner has agreed it' Kirsty said. 'Do you want to announce it so we can move on?'

'Yeah, I will do. Do you want me to go through the full details or just close it off?' Andy asked his boss.

'Let's do it properly and give all the details leading up to the time of death.' Kirsty smiled at him, stood up, walked to the main boardroom table and started to speak. 'Everyone, we have some further information about the murder enquiry we have been working. Please can you all join us here and Andy will take you through it. Jack was already sat at the table, sitting up straight and thinking to himself that they were finally going to get to the point. Listening to whispers wasn't good for this job.

Detective Inspector Andy Grey stood at the head of the table, Kirsty took a seat to his left and everyone else in the team who had been milling around the office deep involved in the work they were doing as part of ongoing investigations, now had taken their seats around the table too. Andy looked at the group and noticed that everyone had sat in the same seats they always did. It was something he noticed every time they called a meeting, people had a tendency to own a seat and make it theirs. Their minds sticking to the sameness of the situation in order for them to not have to think about where to sit along with the number of other things they had to think about during these meetings. Sameness was good for a meeting and would keep everybody on track. The main thing that Andy noticed from this team was that one of the new members, Jack Daniels, did not follow this normative pattern. Whenever a meeting started his would spend time chasing a seat or, in this case already be in a seat that happened to be the seat of someone else in the team. Right now Andy was watching as Shilpa was making a decision about where to sit, helping this Andy stood aside and allowed her to take the seat he would normally be sat in. He wondered if this was some form of power play from Jack who had been upset earlier that week that a lower ranking officer, Shilpa, had been the person to brief him on his task to interview Mark Cash. Across the room Jack Daniels sat watching Andy as he stepped aside for Shilpa to allow her to take a seat. He wondered why she was finding it so hard to decide where to sit, completely oblivious of his faux pas and to any of the normative states of the group.

'Good afternoon. This meeting is in relation to the murder that took place over the weekend, it was suggested that it was a hate crime against a homosexual male. We have now received the Coroner's report and it details that the incident was not a murder and was a suicide. I am now formally standing down the investigation.' Everyone on the team looked perplexed. Andy knew that the people he had worked with for so long would be upset about the suicide, not for the fact that it removed the investigation that they had been working on but for the fact they now knew that someone had taken their own life, and none of them liked that.

'So it wasn't The Pusher' Shilpa questioned.

'On Saturday night Paul Jones, the name we now know, was in an altercation at Black Cap club and was ejected by the bouncers. The police were called and he was moved on, no arrest was made and he was given a warning. We have information from a witness away from the crime scene who has identified Paul Jones being in a further altercation, described as quite an aggressive fight. This took place on the West side of Regents park around an hour after Paul exited The Back Cap. The next time we have any information on Paul is when his body was found.'

'Excuse me sir' Shilpa asked sounding upset 'Why do we believe this to be a suicide. I saw the details of the body and it looked like murder to me.'

'Thank you Shilpa. There is a note in his jeans pocket explaining.' Andy opened the file and passed around a plastic bag with the note for the team to see, it detailed that he no longer could live with his secret and drinking didn't help any more. He knew of a better way. Everyone took a moment to read the note as it was passed around, Andy allowed everyone to read it before he continued. 'The way he did this was particularly gruesome, drowning yourself is no way to go.' Andy looked over at Shilpa and then to the rest of the team. 'I am now formally standing down the investigation and handing over the enquiry to the local community policing team to contact the family. The Coroner's office will handle it from there on. Thank you to everyone for their care in their part of the investigation, if there is nothing else I will hand back to the DCI to continue to talk about other investigations.' He looked around at the team to check if there was anything else and then sat in his chair at the head of the table, physically looking unhappy and upset about the news he had just delivered.

'Thank you Andy.' Kirsty now stood next to his chair with her hand on his shoulder. 'Hearing about suicides or murders is never good. A life has been lost and in this case there is nothing we can do to help. Why don't you all take five to gather your thoughts and we can continue with the rest of the meeting then.' Kirsty smiled at her team and then turned to walk to her office at the end of the long open plan room.

'Detective Inspector Jack Daniels' She looked him directly in the eye as he stood up from the table. 'I believe you can take this forward with community policing and inform the family' She was delighted to putting him back in his place "there is no longer a need for you to be part of this team'.

46

'Ok, so explain this to me. You're a bloke and you are on a gay sex site looking for other blokes to have a wank with... BUT..' Ben shouted the but. 'You don't want to actually have sex, just wank and watch gay..' The gay was high pitched too '...Porn!'

Ben sat on the worktop in Tom's flat talking to Mark who was making coffee in the kitchen.

'Hang on, hang on' Mark turned to Ben with the kettle in his hand having just filled it with water 'You've lost me. When was this?'

'Sunday morning.'

'And the guy didn't want sex, he actually said that?'

'Well, what he actually said was that he had a girlfriend and that he just wanted naked beers.'

'Right, and we know where that leads. And this was on Gaydar?'

'Exactly, so he comes over and we watch porn and we are wanking and' Ben stopped talking; when Mark realised he turned and looked at Ben.

'And?'

'That's it, the guy just wanted to watch me wank and watch porn and not even touch.' Mark was a having a little laugh at Ben. 'It ain't funny; I'd shaved my balls and everything.'

'Everything?' Mark looked shocked as he questioned.

'Well, sack and crack.'

'Nice.' Mark placed a coffee cup in front of Ben 'Thanks for that. So what did you do?'

'I got right back on Gaydar and sorted out shagging the guy from Thursday night.'

'So you still got a shag then?'

'I fucking needed it. You should have seen the straight German Americans cock. I was desperate for it the bleeding prick tease.'

'What was his name?'

'Dunno.' The kettle boiled and Mark walked back over to pour hot water in to the coffee pot.

'What did you get up to then? Did you stay to the end?'

'Yeah we stayed. Then we headed back over to Sam's with the girls. Sam had left earlier so we went back, which is when we saw you. So all this had happened by the time we saw you Sunday morning?'

'Yeah, I shagged Thursday night guy on the way over to Sam's. I thought everyone was going out for lunch, not still be wrecked and still going from Saturday night. You left soon after I got there. Was that guy with Tom?'

'Yeah, I was pretty wasted. Tom and...' Mark thought for a minute 'I want to say Gavin' he thought more. 'We had named him sexy Irish guy with muscles and tattoos for the majority of the night.'

'You two need to get out more' Ben laughed 'Actually no, you two need to stay in more.'

Both men laughed and began to drink the coffee that Mark had poured.

'So at what point did you end up in the Canal with a dead body?' Mark asked making reference to the start of the conversation from when Ben had first arrived.

'Oh yeah, I almost forgot. So after Sam's I headed over to meet a guy I know who lives round the corner, I had to walk along the canal to get to his and about half way over, there it was. A guy, face down in the canal. There was a guy out walking his dog who looked like he was also about to die stood right there, so I calmed him down and called the police.'

'Fuck. That's….' Mark paused looking at Ben 'That's scary. Are you ok?'

'Me love? I'm fine.'

'That's a bit out of character for you, caring about some dog walker.'

'He was cute.'

'Figures.'

'So yeah, a pretty eventful Sunday. Top that Mark.'

'Ha Ha' Mark smiled to himself.

'What? What did you get up to?' Ben was now interested, looking at the knowing look on Mark's face. 'Have you finally had sex with Tom and had a threesome with tattoo guy?'

'Ha Ha, not at all, but I can definitely top anything you've ever done.' Mark sat down next to Ben and told him all about meeting Stuart and the Institute of Gentlemen, when he was finished he looked at Ben to see what he was going to say.

'You've got me hard' Ben said looking directly at Mark 'That's fucking horny, where the fuck is it? I want to go.'

'Hard? Fuck Ben you just got hard over me?' He reached over and prodded Ben's pants. He was in fact hard. 'You can keep that away from me, I'm not going there again' he laughed.

 'Now, this is the strange thing. It's over near your place but I can't quite remember where, as I was in a mad rush when I realised I had been there for so long and ran off to work.'

'Right so we go for a walk and find it.'

'I tried that after work tonight and can't find it. Think I took a wrong turn and I ended up back at the tube station.'

'We have to find it, I want to join.'

'Ha ha, I want to find Stuart again. It was so fucking horny!' Mark had the smile on his face again that he had had when he admired the suit on Monday night. The suit that was still hanging on the door of his wardrobe in his apartment across the hall, it had been there for the last 48 hours and he had spent the last evening looking at it and getting horny again. Tuesday had been a worse day at work for Mark, his come down hangover had kicked in as well as the world's press going crazy over one of his company's clients, which had meant he was on damage limitation all day.

Today had been much better and at the end of the day he had made his way over to Fred to see if he could find Stuart and the Institute of Gentlemen. Whilst wandering around he had remembered that Ben was coming over after work so headed back to meet him and planned to return the following night.

'Oh my God, I am obviously losing my touch. Since when did everyone else start having a better sex life than me?' Ben said, as he did so the door to the flat opened and Tom walked in.

'I can hear you two out on the landing. What's wrong with your sex life Ben?' Tom asked as he walked over and gave both men a kiss on the cheek. He walked in to the kitchen and grabbed a mug from the sink placed it on the worktop and poured himself a coffee. He then looked down at the coffee, 'Why are you two sat in my flat drinking my coffee?' Ben looked at Mark.

'No coffee at mine' Mark smiled at Tom.

'Oh right' Tom smiled back 'so, who was the dead body and has he told you about his new suit?' Tom asked Ben.

'He has told me everything and I am now his number one fan and want to join his secret club.'

'Good me too' Tom replied

'And you? You got sex this weekend too?' Ben stood up and moved round towards Tom.

'Actually I didn't. Well we didn't actually have the sex, just lots of naked kissing.'

'Fuck, what is it with guys these days who don't want the sex? Are you a bloody lesbian?' Ben said with real shock in his voice.

'What's got in to you?' Tom asked

'It's more what hasn't got in to him' Mark laughed at Ben. Ben told Tom the story of the guy that had come round and only wanted to watch him wank. This time it seemed to be more dramatic than the first time he had told Mark.

'So it is a case of what hasn't got in to you' Tom teased Ben.

'Ha ha, very funny I got it sorted in the end. I bet you fall in love with him.' Ben looked at Tom 'It's always the way. I have lost so many good friends to relationships with people who they didn't shag the first time they met.'

'So if you shag then you can't have a relationship?' Tom asked

'Yes!' Ben replied

'That's why you will be single forever then?' Tom threw back his reply.

'Of course' Ben said.

The three friends sat and continued the conversation which soon led to Tom giving Mark and Ben an update of the meeting on Monday night where he explained the two ideas of Sam entering G.A.Y Idol and winning the money to help pay off the drug dealer and then the even more ridiculous plan to rob the takings from the door of the Astoria on the night instead. Tom explained that it had started out as a stupid rush of inspiration and then had moved on to actually making plans to do it.

'It was a bit like the planning part of Ocean's eleven.'

'Ok Brad Pitt.' Ben quizzed Tom 'So you have this rough idea of robbing fifty grand from one of the biggest clubs in London on one of the biggest nights of the year in order to pay a drug dealer that that little twat James has got you in trouble with?'

'Yeah!'

'Fucking losers!' Ben continued. 'That little shit James is always doing something stupid.

'Truthfully, it isn't all his fault. Our Dean is more mixed up in it and it turns out it was his idea to run to Sam's place. Apparently he thought we were still there.'

'Still, it's that bloody James that's got Dean in to it.' Ben had never liked James. He had met him about five years ago when on his way home from work one day. James bumped into him heading to the underground station. James had cruised him for a while and got him interested and then made sure he had followed him out of station and towards Ben's flat. Knowing James was following; Ben stepped in his front door then looked back at James.

'Come on then'. They had pretty good sex for a few hours and then Ben had politely, as he always did, asked him to leave. The next day he had arrived home from work and heard the buzzer, thinking it was the guy he had planned to meet that night, he buzzed him in and waited at the door to his flat. He was shocked to see James walk up the stairs and shout hello. 'What the fuck are you....' Ben said and was cut down by James speaking over him.

'Hiya, I realised I didn't have your number so I thought I would just pop over on my way home from work and get it and see if you wanted to, well, go for dinner or something?' James said to Ben. As he did so the guy Ben had planned to meet had walked up the stairs behind him, stopped and leant against the wall smiling at Ben. Ben smiled back.

'Listen mate, I'm a little busy tonight' Ben gestured to the man behind him, the man waved when James looked at him.

'But I thought we were like...' James looked upset and confused.

'You thought wrong. Come on.' He put his arm around his shoulder and ushered him to the stairs, passed the man waiting and watched him walk out. It was about a year after meeting him that Ben was on a night out with Mark and Tom when James had come over speaking to them. Ben realised that James had started working at the company Mark worked at and to his bewilderment, James had become a regular part of nights out with the small group of friends. Ben spent his time avoiding James and James never quite understood why Ben never paid him any attention.

'So why is Sam sorting all his out?' Ben said to Tom.

'Because the dealer turned up at his flat looking for them and got him involved' Tom said now sat on the sofa drinking his coffee.

'But seriously?' Ben looked to Mark and then to Tom 'Robbing the money from the Astoria isn't a serious plan is it?'

'As I said, it wasn't and the more we talk about it the more serious it becomes. The whole situation is really fucking serious and we only have four days to get it sorted or Sam, James and Dean will get wasted.' Tom's mood had changed and he had gone from joke to serious in seconds. His face had greyed, it was as if saying it out loud had confirmed to him the severity of the situation and the fact that they we going to have to get the money, most likely from stealing it, to pay off the dealer.

47

The major incident room had become a cold and emotionless place since the news earlier in the week of the suicide. Detective Inspector Andy Grey had taken it particularly badly, not just that it was suicide; no one ever liked dealing with such a sad loss of life. It was Andy's first major crime that he was to head up and it had come to an abrupt stop. Quite often in such cases you are running at a hundred miles an hour and then all of a sudden you stop and have no finish line.

Earlier today he had met with the parents and family of the deceased and handed over and personal belongings, closure of sorts but he still felt there was more to be done yet he had nothing to do. Everyone on the team had busied themselves for the last few days with admin and continuing investigations into the appearance of Tony Cash in and around the London area. Rumours were coming in thick and fast and Shilpa had spent most of the day taking calls from police officers out on the beat who had been gathering information from any informants they had.

'Boss' Shilpa said walking over to where Andy sat, her head down reading a pile of papers and reordering them, not even looking up to see if he had responded. 'Take a look at these; I think we might have something here.' She finally looked up at Andy and realised she had now walked quite close, took a step back, and laid the paperwork on the table in front of him. 'Sorry, do you have a minute?' Andy laughed looking up at her.

'It looks like I have.' They both smiled at each other and looked down the paperwork

'What have you got?'

'Well, it may be nothing but' She pushed a printed report forward 'I took a call from PC Roth this morning with some information he had from an informant of his. He had originally passed it off as him trying to get some free fags.'

'Fags?'

'How he pays him for info.'

'Cheap' Andy mused to himself.

'Not that cheap anymore boss, have you seen the price of fags. I'd be handing out cash these days if I was still on the beat' they both laughed. On the other side of the office Jack Daniels watched the conversation. He noticed the way the two of them interacted and thought he would have a word with Andy about how to behave with lower ranking officers. If he ever wanted to get anywhere in the police force he would need to draw a clear line between him and them. Something he prided himself on being able to do to. He had seen some of it in his direct superior Chief Superintendent Kirsty Brown, but still he knew she spoke to the rest of the team as if she was still on the beat with them. To get the best out of a lower ranking officer you needed to tell them what to do and hope that they learn from it as they go. Jack realised, as he was thinking of how to share his wisdom with Andy, that the conversation between the two had moved on and he was interested to hear the rest.

'...Digging around and found this on HOLMES.'

HOLMES was the Home Office Large Major Enquiry System, the database used by all UK Police forces to store data about major crimes across the UK.

'There might be a pattern, a spate of robberies up north. Well one in Glasgow, Manchester, Birmingham and then down south in Brighton'

'Hang on, go back a step. What did the informant have?'

'PC Roth said that the informant explained that they were a group of Drag Queen bank Robbers.'

Shilpa looked down at the report she had earlier typed up. 'Roth went on to say that on discussion with his informant, he didn't quite mean bank robbers but in fact thieves who go around robbing gay clubs.

'Good disguise, they'd fit in and not be suspected' Andy looked impressed.

'You're right, and the best criminals are the ones that no one sees.'

'So what of these others you have found on Holmes?'

'Well it is tenuous at best. Four gay clubs, all were hosting a major night such as a talent show or a big act, so it's the busiest night for the club of the week or maybe month. Venues packed out. On three of them, Glasgow, Manchester and Birmingham a manager has come back to the office and found the safe has been broken in to and all the cash has gone. Reading the reports, they all read pretty much the same. Busy night, with lots of people around due to the event. All three of them say they discovered the incident around 3am'ish. It seems to look like standard practice to cash off the tills around 1am and put the money in the safe and then again at the end of the night. Including any takings for the week in Manchester they got away with around £50k. Glasgow was £20k and Birmingham £40k.' Andy was looking interested now.

'So what links them?'

'Nothing' Shilpa sat down next to him 'Apart from it being the same MO, Gay Club, Big Event, and Robbery. That's where I'm at.'

Shilpa realised she might be clutching at straws and seeing something that might not be there.

'Hang on, you said a fourth club, Brighton. What about that? Does that make a stronger case?' Andy asked Shilpa realising he didn't want to dampen her spirit but also thinking this might be just coincidence.

'Well, I kept that separate because we have more information' Shilpa said with a smile, she was beginning to believe that the link was real.

'Sounds promising' Andy encouraged her, not wanting to take it too far and bring her down again when it could turn out not to be anything, but just enough to want to keep her engaged. He had always admired her inquisitive mind and the way that she made connections in seemingly unrelated information. The majority of the time her hunches had been right and they had paid out bringing in arrests when it had seemed there would be nothing. This time, he thought she may be out on a limb. He'd always found to get the best out of Shilpa was to allow her to use that naturally inquisitive mind and then give a bit of direction now and then. She was the type to ask for help when needed, which is exactly what she needed now.

'The biggest difference was there was a witness' Shilpa stopped and looked at Andy. He had sat up in his chair.

'Well that changes things'

'And the witness statement ties in with our informant'

'A significant change then' Andy joked back with her. Jack Daniels still watching rolled his eyes.

'Yes' Shilpa said with a smile. She was feeling more confident reporting back to her superior now.

'Revenge Night Club on the Old Stein near Brighton Pier was holding a...' Shilpa looked back to her notes, 'Wild Fruits Party, during Brighton Pride in 2014' She took a breath.

'The witness statement, albeit brief, states that two unknown drag queens were seen in the office. He had been changing a barrel and on the way back to the bar saw them. He reported this to the manager who went directly to the office to find the safe had been busted and robbed'

'During Brighton Pride?'

'Yes boss.'

'Wow, it must have been a busy night.'

'Busy weekend sir. It was around 2am on Saturday night, Sunday morning. The club was running a weekender for Brighton Pride. It had been open since 10pm on Friday. They got away with over a hundred grand.'

Andy was now sat up and looking through the paperwork.

'So you see a link with the three other clubs and the Brighton club. Could be the same Drag Queens?'

'Yes Sir. And as you say, the best criminals are the ones that no one sees.'

'And no one would notice a few extra drag queens. Especially at Brighton Pride' Shilpa nodded. Happy that Andy was seeing the link she had seen.

'I'm still not sure, it is circumstantial at best. There is no direct link between all four clubs, the only link we now have is that some informant on the street thinks that a group of Drag Queens are actually an organised gang robbing clubs and that something is going down.'

'Well when you say it like that Shilpa' Andy looked at her and she laughed a little. Both looked down at the printed notes and Shilpa's hand written notes on the table and began to read to see if there was anything they had missed. Jack Daniel was becoming more and more irritated by the conversation.

'Right, let's get hold of PC Roth and find out the facts.' Andy sat back in his chair and put the notes down looking at Shilpa. She was pleased with herself. 'There's enough for me to be interested in hearing more.'

'Are you two bleeding daft?' Jack Daniel butted in to the conversation. Both Shilpa and Andy looked round at him shocked as he raised his voice and shouted them down. 'A couple of queers in dresses are seen in an office and suddenly you've got them down as master criminals.'

Still shocked at his outburst neither of them said anything. 'Detective Inspector Grey, a word if you may?' Jack gestured to the private meeting room on the edge of the major incident room they were sat in. Shilpa looked at Andy in shock. Andy widened his eyes and had a grin on his face, he stood up and walked to the meeting room

'I'll be right back' He said as he went.

48

By Thursday afternoon Pip was shattered and it was going to be a long evening. Stopping and looking at herself in the mirror she pulled her hair back behind her ears. Pip was around 5ft 10, in heels she can gain a reasonable height and advantage to most of the clients that came to her business. Today she wore black jeans and a black lose blouse with soft pumps, she needed flats as she was running round like crazy. The chef cooking the three course dinner for twenty guests was new to her and she wanted to make sure everything went to plan as it normally did. The chef being the unknown in the plan at this moment was causing her a great deal of stress due to his constant complaining about the kitchen not being suitable to cook for this many people. Finally getting him set up in the kitchen and happy, she had begun to get the dining room arranged, bringing out the four round tables and setting them up with the crisp white cotton table cloths, before setting them with the fine silver and crystal glasses.

 Tonight was going to be a success, this was the biggest number of guests that had come to one of these events, normally there was around ten people attending, and she wanted to make sure it was extra special. Once the dining room had been set she moved to the outer room on the opposite side where she had created a dressing room. A few years ago when she and Fred had started the club they had driven round all the second furniture places across London and bought as many dressing tables as they could find. The two of them spent a few weeks sanding down and re painting each of the six they had. Now she pulled them out of the storage area and placed them around the room with hairdryers and hair straighteners. Most of the guests brought their own make up in bags with their clothes for the evening but there were a few that left their items with Pip. She brought these out.

Bags of make-up, two boxes, each holding a wig and several dresses that she now hung on a line in the corner of the room. The room itself was quite dark with red walls and a black carpet, not the best to clean makeup stains from the clumsy guests, but it added a certain quality to the room that made the guests feel like they were in a boudoir getting ready for a big night. She then went into her office on the other side of the red room and took a look at her dress. She needed to look the part. It was hard, she knew she was a good looking woman, "understated beauty" was most often the comment; tonight she needed to play it down on nights like this. When they had first started Fred and Pip had decided to wear little make up and matching business-like dresses. Over the last year Pip had realised that the guests, as well as the level of discretion they have when visiting, wanted to think they looked better than the hosts and so Pip had over exaggerated her make-up, in her mind making her look like one of the people working on a make-up counter in a department store and wore a dress that did nothing for her figure. It must have worked. One or two of the guests had even offered her tips in applying make-up recently. She slipped off her jeans and blouse and pulled on the dress and black heels. There was certain big advantage of being the same build as Sam, always a great pair of killer heels to make her feel great when she rooted through his wardrobe.

Applying make-up she began to think back to the weekend, it had been playing on her mind since she heard the guy shouting in the living room at Sam's. She had wanted to open the door and take a look, she knew that she knew his voice from somewhere but couldn't place it. She met so many different people in her line of work it was often hard to remember names and faces but she knew this voice and it was bugging her as to where it was from. Make up on, looking every bit the glamour model, she walked back around the venue taking one last look at everything to make sure all was right. At which point she heard a crash from the kitchen and the chef swearing loudly. As she hurried over she hoped that she had made the right decision hiring this man there was no way she could have the guests over hearing any of this language tonight. She pushed the doors open to the kitchen and he was on his hands and knees picking up peas from the floor.

'Peas are off the fucking menu' He shouted up at her from the floor.

'Oh' Pip was a little taken a back with his aggression.

'Fucking hell, you looked better in your jeans love.' He stood up and looked her up and down.

'Thanks' she said sternly 'What will we do instead of peas?'

'Nothing, we have plenty of other veg so we will have to make do with extra. No time to go out and get anything more now if guests are arriving soon.' Pip raised her eyebrows a little and turned and walked out, then remembered the starter.

'But it's pea and mint soup to start' She said turning back.

'I got the soup covered, just no actual peas left for a side with the Lamb.'

'Ok, well at least we have the soup,' as she walked out of the kitchen looking out over the dining room again, the doorbell rang and almost at the same time her phone told her she had a text message. Reading the message as she walked to the door she was still looking down when it opened. It was from Fred;

'Good luck Superstar, have a great night.' She looked up at the two young men on the doorstep. Christian and John, they were the waiters for the evening. They had worked for Pip many times over the years and knew how to be discreet about the event. She trusted them and they enjoyed working for her.

'Evening boys, ready for another big night?'

'As long as I get to stay a waiter and not be dressed like a lady, all if fine with me' John said as he walked past Pip and into the dining room. Christian leant forward and kissed Pip on both cheeks and walked in.

'I see that you av' in his French accent 'Dressed like the guest one more time.'

'Yes' Pip did a twirl.

'But you still av the eels to killer.' His broken English made his accent sound even more attractive Pip thought, she gave him a cheeky smile.

'We have a new chef tonight boys, he has a bit of a fiery temper so watch out for him.'

'I will go say hello' John said disappearing off to the kitchen.

'I shall set up a bar?' Christian said.

'Abba?' Pip questioned

'A BAAARRR' he pronounced the word better.

'Oh, a bar, I see. Yes off you go. I have got most of the stuff out and ready you just need to get it how you want it. Can you decant the wine for dinner too please?'

'But of course' He smiled and walked away.

Pip kept herself busy for the next twenty minutes preparing lists showing who was on the guest list, who had already paid online and who needed to pay tonight. She was sat by the front door going over the list again when the doorbell rang making her jump up. She opened the door to be greeted by a small man of about the same height as she, without the heels. He had a bald head, a very round face and was wearing a suit that looked like he had got it from the charity shop.

'Mr Weston, great to see you, how are you?' She said as she gestured to take the two bags he was holding so that he could remove his coat.

'Oh you know. So, So.' He smiled and walked in to the dressing room. Pip followed him.

'You are the first to arrive. You have the room to yourself to dress. If you need any help please do give me a shout' she said as she placed the bags next to the dressing table, smiled at Mr Weston and walked back to the dining room. Ten minutes later, the doorbell went again, Pip answered it for another guest and she followed the same process. This happened over again with a steady stream of men arriving over the next thirty minutes. As she brought the next guest, a tall skinny man with fiery red curly hair into the changing room, several others were now ready. She showed the last guest in and brought the now dressed Mr Weston out.

Mary, as he liked to be called whilst dressed as a woman, wore a long dark green dress that almost touched the floor, under this Pip could see that Mary was wearing flat pumps with an emerald brooch on each. A tight black bobbed wig was on the top of the previously bald head and Mary's make-up looked every bit the rich lady of the house that Mr Weston had wanted Mary to be. Mary stood across the room and turned so that the dress cascaded around in the air and looked at Pip.

'What do you think? It's new.'

'What's new, the hair or the dress?' She asked admiring how happy Mary looked.

'Both, I'm a new woman tonight Pippa' Mary twirled again.

'You look fabulous Mary.'

'I can get you the number of the dressmaker if you want Pippa. You really should wear more flattering clothes my dear.'

'Oh you leave her alone Mary' said a voice from behind Pip. Another guest had stepped out of the dressing room. Denise was tall with a long blonde wig and a face holding a lot of makeup to hide the level of stubble that was under it. Bright red lipstick and blue eye shadow finished the look.

'Hi Denise, how are you?' Mary said.

'Hi Denise' Pip turned her too 'you look fabulous too.

'As do you my dear, ignore what she has to say. More money than sense that one.' Denise and Mary giggled with each other as they walked towards the bar. Pip's phone buzzed again, she looked down and saw she had a text message from a number she didn't recognise. It was sent at 19.08. I am here, let me in the office way. It was right then that she knew where she had heard the voice before and it sent a chill across her back and neck.

49

Chief Superintendent Kirsty Brown stood in the major incident room with a smile on her face. Earlier today she had had to break up an argument between two of her senior officers; Detective Inspector Jack Daniels and Andy Grey. Having spent the morning in a round of boring and useless meetings that most senior officers now had to attend, she arrived back at the office to find them in the small meeting room shouting at each other.

'Who the fuck do you think you are giving me management tips you useless waste of space' Andy was shouting at Jack as she neared the room.

'Useless, Useless, You don't know what policing is. In my day....' Jack said but Andy cut in.

'Your fucking day is gone old timer.'

'WHAT' Kirsty shouted over the two of them 'The hell is going on in here?' Both men stood still and looked at Kirsty. Andy looked as if he had just been caught in the act doing something very bad, Jack on the other hand didn't.

'Well' Jack began 'I was just trying to explain to Detective Inspector Grey here the best way to manage his team and he started to shout and get angry' he said looking justified in his actions. Andy sighed throwing his hands in the air.

'I give up.' Andy said 'Sorry Jack, I didn't realise I was wrong and you were right. You should have pointed that out earlier.'

'Now, now Andy. Let's not take that tone.' Kirsty said before turning to Jack 'Jack, please could you give me a minute to catch up with Andy. I will come and find you shortly to hear what you have to say.

'Of course Sir' and he turned and walked out, still feeling smug that he had managed to refer to his female boss as a man.

'What is going on Andy?' Kirsty asked as she closed the door and took a seat. Andy sat down in the seat opposite.

'He is a lunatic.'

'Yes, we know that but what has he done this time?' Kirsty leant forward to show she was interested. Andy recounted the story of Shilpa's findings to her, his feeling about it and that there was enough to interest him further. Then he went on to say about Jack taking him to the room for a chat.

'It was here where it has escalated and Jack had pretty much told me that the lead was nonsense and I should be able to tell that.'

Andy stopped and looked Kirsty in the eye. 'Pretty Little Thing.' He waited winced a little bit 'his actual words. I should tell that pretty little thing to go back to actual policing or go home.' Kirsty looked back at Andy, anger growing inside her. 'It was then that I lost it.'

'Understandable' Kirsty said. 'Right, take a minute to have a breather. It's late you should be getting sorted to go home for the day. Shall we meet tomorrow morning to go through Shilpa's enquiry?'

'Yeah sure' Andy got up 'Sorry boss.'

'You' Kirsty stood too 'have nothing to be sorry about.' She then walked out of the small meeting room and was now striding across to Jack with a smile on her face. As she passed Shilpa she stopped and said, loud enough for everyone to hear, 'I've heard good things about a new enquiry you're working on Shilpa. I'm looking forward to hearing all about it in the morning.'

Shilpa was a bit taken aback by her most senior officer even knowing about the idea never mind actually mentioning it.

'Thank you' was about as much as she could get out. Before she could carry on Kirsty was off again heading in the direction of Jack.

'I hope you've sorted that one out now Kirsty' Jack said as she approached.

'It's Chief Superintendent Brown to you' She looked him directly in the eye. It was obvious from his reaction that he wasn't expecting this. 'In future, the management development, coaching and advice being dished out to other members of this team will be done by me and not you.'

'Well' Jack tried to speak but Kirsty continued without letting him.

'Detective Inspector Jack Daniels, I have said this before and now I am saying this again. This police force was built by great men and woman who have moved with the times and created a culture that fosters a truly great work ethic to protect every man woman and child out there on the streets. Sadly you have not moved with those times and your view of modern policing is at best outdated. You are a sexist, homophobic and possibly a racist individual that has no place in this team or on this force. I want you to know right now that I will be putting a plan of action in place to move you back to community policing if not out of the force all together.' Kirsty was keeping her cool; she had practiced this speech in her head several times but never quite had to right moment to use it. She had been careful not to say any of this in ear shot of the rest of the office so no one else could hear her. Not to keep it a secret as she was quite happy for everyone to know her views but out of professionalism this kind of taking down was best done privately.

'Well your opinion is your opinion.' Jack was set to continue speaking but Kirsty cut in again not giving him any room to speak.

'Yes, and it just so happens that it is the opinion that falls in line the future of this force.'

'Well then Chief Superintendent Brown, we will see about that. I'm sure your dad will have a lot to say about the way you show respect to your fellow co-workers.' Kirsty was stunned by the comment. From everything she was expecting it was not this. Maybe an outburst, shouting, throwing it back in her face even, but to say he was going to tell her Dad had left her actually speechless. She stood there looking at him totally confused not saying a word. With this Jack gathered this things from the table in front of him, stood up and made for the door. 'Good evening everyone, I shall see you all in the morning.'

He turned back to Kirsty 'that is if I haven't been moved by then' he disappeared out of the room.

Kirsty looked over to Shilpa and then to Andy stood in the doorway of the small meeting room.

'I'm actually speechless.'

'I think you might need a drink boss' Andy said, He looked at Shilpa 'you too?'

'I was going home.' Shilpa paused looking at Andy's face 'Yes ok, maybe a quick one.'

'I need more than a quick one, I need several' Kirsty said. The door to the major incident room opened again and Kirsty thought for one moment that he was coming back. She was pleased to see Detective Sergeant Alan Jones walk through the door. Kirsty, Andy and Shilpa all looked at him.

'What?' Alan said 'What did I do?' looking apprehensive.

'Nothing, nothing at all Alan' Kirsty was the first to speak.

'We were just thinking of going for a drink, fancy it?' Andy asked.

'Nothing would make me happier, but I've just got a message from you dad' Alan looked at Kirsty 'Erm, sorry, Tim Brown from the Comms room' he winced at making the mistake of acknowledging it was her Dad.

'Don't worry Alan. I think everyone is aware that my Dad is about.' Kirsty looked at the other two for acknowledgment and to see if they had heard and registered the last conversation in the room.

'Ok, so Tim, your Dad' still flustered he continued, 'has taken a message about a tip off for a robbery taking place tomorrow night.'

'Ok' Kirsty wasn't too interested and began to look around for her things 'Why is he...' She was reaching down under the desk for her bag. 'Sending it our way?'

'Well, it seems to be qualified and reliable. He took a tip off call from someone who was at work today and overheard a group of people he knows taking about a robbery' Alan continued.

Kirsty was stood up again looking at Alan. 'The caller works at a gay bar in Camden and the dance troop. Erm... 'He trailed off while looking at the notes 'The dance troop are Drag Queens and they're planning on robbing G.A.Y at the Astoria tomorrow night.' The news spread across the group of three quicker than Alan had expected and they all dived forward to grab the note in Alan's hand. Shilpa got it first and read through the note.

'It's not just a coincidence anymore' she said passing the note to Kirsty.

50

Pip walked though into the dressing room, passing a few ladies on their way out to the dining room and another one having trouble doing the zip on her dress.

'Here let me' she zipped up the dress smiled and moved on. She took one of the dresses off the rail and grabbed a small leather bag from the nearest table that she had placed there earlier and walked towards her office. She looked back across the dressing room and through the slit in the curtain to the dining room, and thought to herself how surreal it was to have been running a sales training session today for twelve eager new sales people and then just a few hours after to be hosting a dinner party in the same room for twenty transvestites. Her thoughts moved to the task at hand and the voice she now recognised from the weekend. She walked in to her office and placed down the items on her desk and walked to the fire exit door on the other side of the office. Opening the door she looked out at the man stood on the metal platform of the fire exit.

'Hello Michael, how are you today?' Manic Mike stood looking at Pip. His hair was wet and Pip saw that it had begun to snow quite heavily. 'Come on in.' She had trepidation in her voice she was thinking she did not want to have him at the gathering tonight, not now she knew who he was and what he did.

'It's fucking shite out there tonight. How are you?' He asked, almost pleasantly.

'I'm doing well, it's a busy night tonight Michael. We will have twenty guests if everyone turns up, including you. I have brought your things in to the office. I know you prefer not to be seen as..' Pip realised she was talking quite fast and was nervous 'Well, as yourself.'

'Right, are you sure you're ok. You seem a bit' Manic Mike trailed off waiting for Pip to answer.

'Nervous' Pip blurted out and he looked slightly surprised. 'It's a busy night, our busiest yet and I am a little nervous.' Pip smiled back at him hoping he believed her. 'Nothing like a few nerves to keep me on my toes' she said.

'I suppose not. You'll be good, you always are.' He walked to the dress on the table. 'I better get ready then.' Pip smiled and walked out the door back to the changing room. She closed the door behind her and leant back on it breathing deeply. She often wondered about the lives of the men that came to these events, coming along to dress and be like a woman and have dinner with like-minded men. Like Mr Weston, she had decided he was an accountant and worked in a small dull office and led a normal dull life, had a wife at home and some children who had grown up and left home and he liked, once every two months to dress as a woman and come and have dinner.

Then there was Lawrence, who she knew a fair bit about as he was quite happy to chat and tell her about his life. Lawrence was Denise when he was here, a painter and decorator from Epping Forest, he had thought he might be gay for many years and then realised in his twenties he liked woman and also cross dressing. He had never found the right woman to be able to share this with and because of that had had a string of short term relationships. Last time she had spoken with him he had resigned himself to the fact that he was not going to find her and being nearly fifty he was now happy with that.

Sometimes Pip made up stories for the guests and sometime they told her, she was quite often close to the truth. Michael on the other hand she had never thought he would be the person he was. She had thought he was a stunt man or a club bouncer. He had first come to the club a little over a year ago and she knew when he was Michael he might have a few anger issues, but once changed, he made a rather handsome woman and was more mellow and easy to get along with. Now, she knew he was not only a drug dealer but the drug dealer currently threatening the life of her friends, the drug dealer that wanted fifty grand by the end of the week, the drug dealer that until today she had just thought of as a guest at an event and now, now she was scared of him.

'My dear are you ok?' An elderly voice asked from inside the darker room. A lone man sat at a dressing table, the room had now emptied and the rest of the guests were in the main dining room having drinks. She could hear the buzz of the crowd reintroducing themselves.

'Oh, hello, yes, yes I am ok. I'm working a little too hard this evening. How are you?' She said to the elderly man sat at the dressing table.

'I'm afraid I'm a little late this evening dear, I must hurry or I will miss saying hello to everyone.'

'I'm sure you won't. Can I give you a hand?'

'Oh yes please' Pip walked over and sat down next to the guest and got out his make-up.

'Let me do this for you' she said and smiled at him. His open warm generous face looked back at her. Pip spent time applying make up to his face and chatting about him. He was eighty two years old and had lost his wife just two years before, she had always been ok with him cross dressing but since she had died he had had no one to do it with. These dinner evenings were the best thing he had ever been too. As they chatted and Pip helped him in to his dress, the door to the office swung open and Michelle stepped out. She was wearing a hot red dress that came down to mid-thigh level, black fish net stocking and a big black curly wig, tonnes of make-up and bright red glossy lipstick.

'Well hello' Michelle said to the pair in the dressing room. 'Am I going this way?' Without even waiting for an answer, she walked to the curtain and into the dining room.

'I've never liked that one' said the dear old man, who was now a dear old lady. 'There is something quite bad about his character.'

'Yes' Pip said, unease setting back in.

'Mark my words; there will be trouble with that one around.'

'I do hope not.' Pip looked at the curtain now closing behind Manic Mike.

51

As Sam turned the key to the front door of his apartment building he remembered what was important about today. It was Mrs. Pott's 90th Birthday.

'Fuck!' He said out loud as he pushed the door open and thought to himself how could he have forgotten? Checking his mail and seeing that there was a neat stack of what looked like birthday cards for Mrs Potts, and then thinking he needed to get a card. Putting his post back on the side turning and heading back out the door he had just come in and along the street in the direction of Waitrose. On the walk he pulled out this phone and dialled Tom's number. He answered after a few rings.

'Love, how are you?' He said before Tom could speak

'Hello, I'm all good, how about you?' Tom replied and sounded like he was in a good mood.

'Have you remembered that it's Mrs Pott's 90th birthday today? She is having the drinks thing tonight'

'I certainly have.'

'Oh' Sam said shocked.

'I'm guessing you forgot?' Tom asked

'You guessed right.'

'Well isn't it great that you have a friend like me Rockers?' Tom quizzed 'Having finished work early today I headed out and bought our Mrs Pott's a rather lovely silk neck scarf and then a birthday card from us' Tom said quite pleased with himself.

'Well get you, Mr Fantastic, I was just about to go and hunt something down.' Sam stopped in the street realising he could now head home, again.

'Why are you stopping?' Tom asked

'Because I, What?' Sam sounded confused 'Where are you?' Tom hung up the phone.

'Right behind you' He said loudly. Sam turned on his heels to be greeted by Tom holding a Happy 90th Birthday bright pink gift bag, a bottle of something and a card with his work laptop bag over his shoulder.

'I've told you about stalking me' Sam leant in and kissed Tom on both cheeks. 'How's your day been? Fabulous that you got sorted, I've been mega busy all week and totally forgot.'

'No worries' Tom turned and he and Sam walked back towards Sam's flat linking arms.

'Mark is on his way over now too; I tried Ben but haven't heard anything from him.'

'I haven't heard from him all week, probably out shagging somewhere.' Sam rolled his eyes as they turned the corner and down the short path way to the front of the building he lived in. Once again he unlocked and opened the door and headed back in. Collecting his post he realised that Mrs Potts' stack of cards had now gone. She must have been out and got them. He looked over to her flat and could here that music was playing inside her front door was uncharacteristically closed. For as long as he had lived here and known Mrs Potts her door had always been open during the daytime, mostly so that she could keep an eye on the comings and goings of everyone in the building. However she would tell you it was for fire safety.

'Doesn't she normally have the door open?' Tom asked.

'Yeah, yeah she does' Sam looked over at Tom and widened his eyes in a mock shock.

'Maybe she has guests, family over.' Sam turned and walked to the stairs.

'Does she have any family?' Tom asked 'I've never seen anyone.' He said looking back at the closed door on the ground floor.

'Not that I'm aware of.' Sam opened the door to his flat and walked in 'There was a younger, much younger man who used to call round but I think he was an actor friend. I saw him in EastEnders once, back when Pauline Fowler was in it.'

'Right, so she really was an actress?' Tom asked.

'Oh yeah, just wait till you go in her place and see all the pictures.' Sam disappeared off to his bedroom and Tom walked through and sat down on the sofa. Within seconds Caroline came bursting into the flat.

'Hiya love, how are you?' She flopped down on to the sofa next to them.

'Good, how are you?'

'I'm bloody amazing' she said with a huge grin on her face.

'Nice, why's that?' Tom asked

'Well, right, you see.. I met this girl on Tuesday night right and, well she was pretty cool and we got to talking and then went for a few drinks right.

'Right' Tom said, repeating Caroline's favourite word.

'Right' She said looking at Tom, Tom looked back and gestured her to carry on 'Oh yeah.'

She laughed 'Right well the thing is she stayed over here and the next morning when we were having a coffee in the kitchen, we were having it from the Cafetieres because it's nice from there right, so we were talking.' Tom was laughing to himself, he had often thought that when it came to Caroline telling a story why say it in five words when you can say it in five hundred. 'And then she told me where she works right and she only works on the door at G A Y!' She sat up straighter in the chair and looked very happy with herself.

'Oh, right.' Tom wondered if he was supposed to know why this was good.

'Yeah Right' she said, looking at Tom as if he should know why it was great news.

'Erm' He thought some more. 'That's really nice, for her' He said, hoping he could get past this without looking foolish.

'You bloody idiot' Caroline said 'You haven't got a clue what I'm talking about have you?'

'Sorry Caro, I really haven't. Why is it good that she works there?' Tom gave in and looked at Caroline with a questionable face. Sam had arrived back in the room having had totally changed his clothes. He was now wearing skinny fit jeans and a roll neck, green jumper.

'Because Thomas' Sam looked down at the pair of them on the sofa 'Caro here had a very long cup of coffee and then went back to bed and during the pillow talk with the lovely lady she met, she found out all that we needed to know about what happens behind the scenes with all that lovely money we need to get our hands on this Saturday night.' Tom sat up straight from leaning into the sofa, realisation kicking in as to why it was important news.

'See, you all think I'm daft the way I ramble on but I get more information from most people when I do. I think it's like they have a false sense of security when they speak because I speak loads and they speak loads back at me and tell me all kinds. It happens at work too, the other day..'

Sam stopped Caroline from carrying on.

'You're doing it now Caz.'

'Oh, right' She smiled, a very happy smile and pleased with herself for having got the information.

'It's six thirty already, I'm sure Mrs Pott's said six. They all jumped up and walked out of the flat.

52

Pip was tidying away some bits that had been left behind in the dressing room when she noticed that the door was opening. She normally kept the door closed and locked for the privacy of the guests. Someone must have not closed it as they were leaving. The night had been a great success. Most of the guests had already left saying how wonderful it had been. There were just two more guests left and the two boys who had been working. One of the guests was the lovely gentlemen she had had the pleasure of helping dress earlier on, and the other was the one she had been watching all night. She watched him get more and more drunk and more demanding of the boys who were working. She had taken over at one point not wanting them to be caught in anything with him. His bright red dress was as bold as he was. Manic Mike now scared her, she knew what he was like and what he did and she really didn't like him being around her club. She knew, and had decided, at the beginning of the night when she had realised who he was that it was better the devil you know and asking him to leave could have caused her all manner of problems.

She looked around and saw through the window in the door to the kitchen that John and Christian were in there eating the left overs of the food and that the two remaining guests where in the main seating area of the dining room and the door was now being pushed open. She stood up, knowing she had closed it behind herself. As she walked towards the door she began to feel even more confused. She watched as a man walked in through the door and stood still, chest out with a menacing look on his face starring right passed her and at the two guests sat talking; a large grin now crossed his face. Pip couldn't work out what was going on, why was Mark here?

Mark stood in the doorway but looked slightly different, had he changed his hair?

'What are you doing here?' she said confused. As she did so, she saw the scar across his face 'Oh my God, what happened to your face?' She blurted out. Tony Cash focused on her and looked confused.

'Go back in that room and keep out of my business' He said and pointed at the room. Pip was even more confused now, his accent was all wrong too. The two guests sat talking in the main seating area turned to look up. The set of events that happened next happened so fast that both Pip and the old man from earlier had no idea what in fact did happen. Manic Mike saw Tony Cash stood in the doorway and jumped to his feet, running across the room as fast as he could go in the stiletto heels he was wearing knocking the older man from his chair as he went. Pip dived forward to try and catch him and missed but was there to help him up. The man in the doorway gave chase after Manic Mike and they both flew towards the office with the Mark lookalike catching Manic Mike just inside the door.

'Are you ok?' Pip realised she had totally forgotten the gentleman's name. 'I'm sorry I seem to have forgotten your name' She apologised.

'I'm ok dear, yes yes, I'm all ok' He said as she helped him back in to his seat 'I'm Trevor my dear, Trevor Booth. It'll be the shock, my dear that made you forget. Are you alright?' He said in his lovely smooth voice.

'I best see what's happening.' She was still holding on to Trevor's arm as she was looking towards the office where she could hear a commotion. Trevor gripped Pip's arm and wouldn't let her go. There was crashing furniture and shouting coming from the office now.

'My dear, your furniture is expendable but you are not. Please stay away, I told you he was bad news' Trevor said, wanting Pip to stay away from what now sounded like a pub brawl. Pip continued to look in the direction of the office, still confused wondering why this man looked so much like Mark. Where was her mobile phone she wondered to herself? She had left it in the office at the beginning of the night not wanting to be distracted by it whilst working with the guests.

'Mr Booth' she looked down at him 'Trevor, I'm so sorry that you are here for this. I know it must be quite scary, but I do need to go find out what is happening. I'm responsible for.' She was cut down from continuing when Manic Mike flew through the office door and landed on the carpet in the dressing room right beside the curtain. He lay there for what seemed to Pip like minutes but was in fact just a few seconds while he caught his breath. He stood up and launched himself back towards the office and the man he was fighting with. There were millions of different thoughts flying through Pip's mind right now. Was

Mark attacking Manic Mike for the threats he had made to Sam, Dean and James on Sunday? Why would he do that, why would he come here to her club and do that?

Anger was building up inside her now. How dare Mark come here and ruin everything she had spent years building up. She broke free from Trevor's hold and walked over to the office. She was going to put a stop to this and was going to tell Mark what she thought of his little power play with a drug dealer. As she did so, as she got close to the office she could hear what was being said.

'You little fucking puff! Here you are dressing as a woman and drinking fucking tea. You make me fucking sick you do' Tony Cash had Manic Mike pinned against the wall, his arm across his chest and a knife in his hand pinned close in to his neck almost cutting in to it. Pip could see that there was blood across Manic Mike's forehead and all around his lips. Then she realised that it wasn't blood it was the glossy red lipstick he had been wearing.

'Listen Boss, this has got nothing to do with work' Manic Mike said, his voice trembled.

'Shut the fuck up' He moved his head in closer.

'But..'

'I don't want no fucking but's. I want my fucking money. You stole from me you little shit and you think you can get away with it? You took my drugs and kept them for yourself and put dodgy fucking scumbag knock offs on the street' Tony's voice was calming a little now.

'The only reason I haven't put you in the river already is that I want my fucking money back. You owe half a million and if I don't have it by Sunday when I leave' He took a deep breath. 'You're coming with me sunshine and I'll show you what it is really like to steal from me.'

'I'll have it, I will. I promise' Manic Mike's voice sounded like a scared child. Pip looked in amazement as who she believed to be Mark crush this man she had been so scared of all evening.

He stood back releasing Manic Mike who dropped to the ground, turned and walked towards Pip. He pushed his hands in his pockets and pulled out a wad of money.

'Sorry love, made a bit of a mess of your office back there. This should sort it' He pushed a wad of twenty pounds notes into her hand and turned to look at Trevor 'Are you ok there love, he didn't hurt you did he?' His voice had gone from hard aggressive killer to soft and gentle.

'I'm ok, thank you' Trevor replied. He turned back to Pip.

'You saw nothing.' And walked to the door and disappeared. Pip looked down at the cash in her hand realising there must be nearly two thousand pounds. Then she heard movement in her office, she walked through and saw the back of Manic Mike, now back in his regular day wear, walking out through the fire exit. She looked around at the devastation in the office seeing that chairs were broken and her computer lay on the floor. No wonder he had given her a wad of money but who, who was that. How could someone look so much like Mark and be so totally different and, and what had just happened?

'I think you may need to call the police my dear, I'm happy to be a witness if needed.' Trevor had got up and walked over, on his way closing the front door and bolting it. As he did so John and Christian came running through, both out of breath and both looking shocked. Christian was picking up a chair that had toppled over in the dressing room.

'What the fuck just happened? We were taking the bins out and got back to your mate looking a bit dodgy and that guest being thrown about?' John asked. Pip looked round at all three of them. She was still confused, her voice sounded it. The three men looked back at her, waiting for an answer. It wasn't coming any time soon.

'I'm not quite sure myself. But whatever it was I don't want any further trouble. Is the door locked?'

53

Sam, Tom and Caroline walked down the stairs to the ground floor to Mrs Pott's flat. The door was still closed and Caroline turned to Sam, giving him a look to acknowledge that it was odd. Sam nodded back and walked up to the door. Nervously, he gently pushed the door, it opened and he looked at his companions and smiled. Turning back and walking through the door he shouted out.

'Is the birthday girl there?' Sam looked down the hallway passed the door to the bedroom on the right and the bathroom on the left to the door facing him at the end of the hall way. The cream coloured walls were covered from top to bottom with framed pictures, mostly black and white pictures that could be fifty to sixty years old and then some more recent pictures in colour. Sam walked down the hall towards the room where he could hear music, Caroline followed him.

Tom, who was visiting the flat for the first time was looking at the pictures. The walls looked like a who's who of early cinema. He looked at a very young Mrs Potts in black and white leaning forward on a white leather sofa. She looked stunning and every bit the movie star she reported to be. Her white dress hugged her figure and was quite modest compared to today's styles, wearing her neck scarf in what looked like matching colour. Tom took a moment to quickly look at all the pictures she was in and noticed she wore a tied neck scarf in them all. A good spot he thought and felt good about the present he had bought. He continued to look and noticed some of the photos of her with others. It was a group shot that looked like it was taken of the set of a film or show. Mrs Pott's stood to the side of a group of men and women, there were six of them. A woman in the middle sat on a director's chair and Tom through he recognised the actress, he thought for a minute trying to place her looking at the men and another woman in the picture trying to work it out.

'I love Lucy.' Caroline's voice came over Tom's shoulder, making Tom jump a little.

'Really?' He looked closer 'Oh yeah, it is. She looks amazing.'

'Yeah she really does. Have you seen his one?' Caroline pointed to a smaller black and white picture that looked like it was a paparazzi picture. 'It's a cutting from a bigger picture that's over there. She was in the background' Caroline paused for Tom to take a look.

'Elvis!' Tom looked up at Caroline 'Bloody Elvis. She got about a bit' Tom laughed. Caroline smiled at him. As he did he looked passed Caroline and down the hall he saw that Sam was now stood in the door to the living area still and staring. As Tom looked down the hall to Sam stood about two meters away from him, he saw Sam raise his hand over his mouth in shock. Tom looked to Caroline who was now noticing what was happening, both of them walked towards Sam. Sam looked round to Tom and Caroline walking towards him and then back at what he could see in the living room. Tom walked through the door first, closely followed by Caroline, both stopped in their tracks and stared at the scene in front of them.

The room was filled with flowers, every flower you could think of across the whole of the room, some on tables some stood on the floor. All of which looked like they had been delivered with cards sticking out. A lovely smell was coming from the kitchen that may have been from bread baking.

Across the other side of the room was a large dining table laid out with a buffet that could feed the entire street, to the left of this hung a ball gown. The dress was bright blue and covered in sequins and what looked like feathers around the bottom. Mrs Potts was stood on the tips of her toes with one leg in the air behind her on a small stool at the window with a feather duster in her hand cleaning the top of the curtain rail wearing just her underwear.

'Mrs Potts, what on earth are you doing?' Sam said out loud, it was more blurted out as he still had his hand over his mouth. Tom looked at Sam shocked and back at Mrs Potts, he couldn't see what Sam was talking about. Sam was now pointing towards Mrs Potts.

'She's going to break her neck' he looked at Tom and Caroline.

'Hello my dear, you're just in time to give me a hand getting in to this.' She made her way down from the stall in one quick and dancer like motion and was stood at the dress before any of the group could get over to help her.

'Do you love it?' She asked looking round to the three people stood in her living room.

'It looks fantastic love. Just what you need for your special day' Caroline said walking over to her.

'Let's have a look' Caroline had lifted the dress from where it was stored on the dado rail and had started to take off the plastic sheet covering it. 'Right, here we go. Are you ok to lift your arms up?'

Mrs Potts lifted her arms in the air as Caroline put her hands through the dress and lifted it towards her head.

'Tom' she said looking over to the two of them. Sam was still stood in shock.

Tom walked over and gave a hand getting her in to the dress. Caroline was now kneeling down pulling the dress down and gathering it in the right place 'Have you got shoes?' She looked up at Mrs Potts.

'Yes dear, those ones there' She pointed at a box sat on a chair near the dining table. Tom grabbed the box, opened it and held it out for to Caroline.

'You look lovely,' Caroline stood up, 'doesn't she Sam?' Caroline turned to Sam trying to get him to comment.

'Yes' He stumbled over his words 'Yes' shaking his head in action and back in to the moment.

'Happy Birthday, you look absolutely fabulous.' At that moment, the door was pushed in to him knocking him slightly. 'You really shouldn't be up on stools like that Mrs Potts. You should call me or Caro to come down and do that for you.'

'Wow, Sam's right, you look fabulous Mrs Potts.' James said walking in to the room followed by Dean. 'If you were thirty years younger Mrs Potts I would be all over you.' 'Happy Birthday' Dean said from behind everyone.

'More like fifty years younger James, I know your type' She chuckled to herself. Tom looked at her and realised she was not wearing a neck scarf. Having been caught out getting ready she mustn't have put one on just yet.

'Mrs Potts, we have got you a gift and I think it would be perfect for you right now' Tom said as he handed her the bag. She opened the bag and pulled out the scarf that was an almost perfect match for her dress. As she did so her hand moved to her neck and she realised she wasn't wearing one.

'My dears this is just lovely' and in a swift move the neck scarf was around her neck and tied in a perfect bow.

54

Mark walked out of Angel tube station and turned right along Upper Street taking another right down Duncan Street and a quick left in to Islington High Street. He walked along slowly looking for the building. He didn't recognise any of it. He looked back where he had come from and none of the buildings looked like they were the one he had spent a large part of his weekend in. It was now going dark and it was cold, he had heard on the news earlier that it was going to snow tonight and it may be quite thick. He loved London in the snow, it didn't happen very often but when it did London became magical. As did most places he thought. It was especially nice to be in London when it snowed as people became much more relaxed and made eye contact with each other, like the snow everywhere, it gave them something in common. As he continued to walk along the street hoping he had not missed the entrance he thought back to the time he had spent with Stuart inside the mysterious Institute of Gentleman. Having spent most of the week's free time searching for anywhere that had made reference to the club he had drawn blanks everywhere. Even when he had spoken to his friend Troy, who was the world's best stalker of anyone and anything online, even he couldn't find anything, so he had decided to go back to the building and find out more. His mission wasn't going to well at the moment. He realised that when leaving the club on Monday morning he was in a bit of a daze and his body was on auto pilot. It had gotten him to work and now he couldn't quite work out if he was in the right place or not.

Earlier, knowing that he was going to be quite close to Ben's flat, he had called Ben and asked him about the club. Given Ben's extensive sexual activity and living quite close to the club he thought he may have been. Sadly he hadn't and all the phone call had done was ignite an excitement In Ben at the prospect of being able to go to the club. Ben was going to come and find him, which Mark had tried his best to get him to stay home, but Ben wanted in on the action and wasn't going to let it lie.

Mark had told him the general area he was going to be looking but not specifically the street. Vague was good and may even mean that Ben might not actually find him. He continued to walk looking in shop doorways seeing clothes, passed a Butcher's and an Estate agents and then reached the end of the street. He looked down the enclosed alley way that was the continuation of the street, it had pebbled floor and was a little darker than the open part of the street. Had he walked along this part of the high street? He didn't think so. As he did so he looked at the shop in front of him and recognised the crockery in the window. He had looked at this before, on Monday morning when he had admired himself in the shop window in the suit. He looked to his left and realised he must have walked along the pedestrian part of the high street to get there. He turned and walked faster now, just as he had on Sunday morning. He took a few more steps and walked passed the door set back from the main high street hidden away. It was now dark and he would have missed it had he not been diligently looking around for it. He almost stumbled making himself stop and stood looking at the doorway. The same black and white tiles on the floor and the old solid door painted the exact same colour as the walls. The golden lock was the only identification the doorway had, carved in to the gold 'I o G'. He had found it. He looked around for a doorbell whilst doing so remembering his Monday morning attempt and not finding one.

There was the small black electronic key fob on the wall and nothing else. He pressed it just in case. Nothing. He looked around at the people walking passed on the street to see if anyone might be heading this way. Nothing. So he stepped up to the door and knocked on it very hard. Nothing. He waited what seemed like minutes until he felt it was an ok amount time to knock again, this time harder. Nothing. There were no lights in the alcove so Mark couldn't see if there were cameras or the speakers that had been used on Monday morning. Nothing. This place was becoming more and more mysterious by the minute. Had he been to some secret society in the centre of London? A secret society for gay men to go and watch other gay men have sex and then nip off to a room to have sex themselves. Yes, that was exactly what had happened. And now, now he wanted to go back and experience it again he had no way of doing so.

How was he going to contact Stuart again? The guy that he'd had an amazing time with and really wanted to do it again but had no number to call him on. He knocked on the door again hoping that finally it may get answered. Nothing. Stepping out of the doorway he moved across the small street and leant against the wall opposite looking at the door. Maybe it was the mystery that was so attractive. Maybe it was the mystery of Stuart that was so attractive. As he stood there, wondering if he would make it inside again and if he would even see Stuart again he began to think of the other men who were there, did he recognise any of them?

'Alright our kid' Mark was dragged from his daydream by the harsh accent of his brother. Tony walked a little further and stood in front of Mark and giving him a slight punch on the shoulder.

'No fancy suit today?' He asked

'No' Mark said 'What are you doing here?' Mark looked up and down the street to see if there was anyone else about. There were several people about but mostly going about their own business, until he looked along the High Street and saw Ben walking in their direction. He sighed and looked at his brother.

'What do you want?'

'Don't flatter yourself Marky I was doing some business down there.' He pointed his thumb over his shoulder down the lane in the direction he had come from. The opposite direction to where Mark had walked earlier. Mark looked to his right again to see Ben getting closer and as he did so the front end of what looked like a very expensive black car pulled up.

'Looks like my ride is here. You need a lift anywhere little bro?' Tony said as he started to walk along the street.

'I'm good thanks.' Mark watched as his brother rounded the car and disappeared out of sight.

The car pulled away to reveal Ben stood looking at Mark with his mouth wide open. He gestured, keeping his mouth open at Mark and then the car, a knowing look of 'What was that?' Mark walked to Ben, rolled his eyes and spoke.

'You've seen my brother then?'

'Oh my God, I kinda knew you had a brother but one that is the spitting image of you.'

'Well there you go, you've seen him now.'

'Actually, he is more attractive than you.' Ben said and smiled back at Mark.

'How can he be more attractive, we are identical twins?' Mark said with a little shock in and humour in his voice.

'I think it's that fuck off big scar down his face. It just says danger. Danger, quick come shag me.'

'What?'

'Your face does not say danger to me.'

'I should hope not, and it better not say come shag me. I've done that once, never again.'

Mark looked at Ben and smiled.

'You wish.' Ben said back and hit Mark in the arm in the exact same spot his brother had done moments before. 'No luck with the dodgy sex society building?' Mark looked over Ben's shoulder down the street to where the door was.

'No nothing. I bet I wasn't even round here.

'Knobhead, I'm not going looking for some dodgy vice ring if you can't even be bothered to remember where you were' Ben said to Mark as he took out his phone and read a text message he had just received.

'It's from Pip, that's strange. It says: What the fuck is going on?'

'Oh fucking hell you don't think something else has happened with that lot do you?'

'Erm, not got a clue. I spoke to Tom about an hour ago and all was good. They were at Mrs Potts' birthday thing. I said we would head over that way next.'

'Then what is Pip on about?'

'Only one way to find out,' Mark pointed down the lane. 'Her office meeting place is down there.' Mark started to walk in that direction the direction Tony had walked from.

'Oh my God, Pip might know about your dodgy sex club. I can't believe we didn't think of her first.' Ben grabbed Mark's arm and started to walk.

'Bloody hell, who knew that Angel was the dodgy sex club capital of London?'

'Pip's place isn't dodgy sex.'

'So she says.' Ben rolled his eyes 'she has never invited me' He spoke as they continued the walk down the street. As they did so, they passed the door to the Institute of Gentlemen. Mark looked at the door and smiled sadly, thinking to himself that he may not get to see the inside again.

'I didn't think dressing up as a woman was your thing?' Mark asked.

'It isn't' Ben replied sounding shocked.

'Oh yeah, I forgot what the dinners were for. Maybe that's why she hasn't invited us.' Ben said sarcastically.

'Yeah maybe.' They continued to walk down the street holding themselves tight into their winter coats. It seemed have gotten colder today than it had been all week. Mark thought back to the club at weekend and hanging out outside with Tom, they weren't cold at all, and now it seemed to be the depths of winter. As they walked and he thought about the cold the snow started to fall.

It took them nearly five minutes to make it to Pip's building, by the time they had reached the entrance the snow was coming down thick and had covered the streets in a crunchy white blanket. As they neared the building Mark could see the two guys that work for Pip on nights like this. They were helping an elderly man from the building and in to a waiting taxi. The two friends continued to walk towards the entrance. John and Christian had finished and were now walking past them. John gave Mark a funny look that he thought was quite odd, the times that he had met him in the past he had always seemed pretty nice. Christian had the collars of his coat turned up and they both walked off in a hurry.

Mark and Ben both stepped inside the entrance and Mark pressed the button for the lift. It was an old building and the lift was a caged lift, the type you see in old hotels. The stairs rose around the outside of the lift shaft and up in to the building. They heard the clatter of the lift on the floor above and a voice shouted down that it was stuck and they would have to take the stairs. Ben, once again, rolled his eyes then walked passed Mark and started up the stairs.

'What did this place used to be?' Ben asked Mark as they walked up the first flight of stairs.

'What do you mean?' Mark wasn't focused on what Ben was saying.

'Used to be, it must have been one building rather than separated like it is now.'

'Oh right yeah.' Mark was still thinking about how John had been outside. 'I think it used to be a department store, hence the old lift.'

'Yeah right' the conversation continued up the stairs. They passed two people on the third floor, a couple who looked like they were leaving work for the day and ready to go out into the cold. The man was trying to get the gated door of the lift from its open stuck position and the woman was on her mobile phone having a heated conversation with what seemed like someone who was supposed to be fixing the lift. They continued passed smiling at the pair and up to the fifth floor and to Pip's place. The door was closed and the landing was dark. It was the top floor and there was no natural light on this landing, just the door to Pip's place, the lift and the stairs.

Ben knocked on the door.

'Who is it?' the timid voice of Pip came from the other side. The boys looked at each other, instantly knowing something was wrong from the sound of her voice.

'It's me.' Ben said 'Ben and Mark are with me.'

The door swung open and Pip stood looking at them. She was looking directly at Mark and what was previously a timid scared voice was now turning in to anger.

'What the fuck are you doing back here?' She shouted at Mark. Mark was shocked. He didn't know what was going on and could see that Pip was getting angry.

'What?' Mark looked at her and looked at Ben.

'What's wrong?' he asked Pip.

'WHAT THE FUCK'S WRONG?' Pip shouted 'YOU!' She stopped. The anger in her face had changed to confusion. 'Why did you get changed?' She was slightly calmer and now her questions were sounding confused. 'And..' She hesitated then stepped forward in to the doorway.

'And where has your scar gone?' Pip looked at Mark, even more confused than before. Suddenly, Mark began to realise what was happening. He was the one now beginning to feel angry.

'Pip' He said sternly and looking her directly in the eye 'Have you just seen someone looking like me but with a scar?' Pip nodded her head 'Are you ok?' Pip shook her head, tears now welling up in her eyes.

'Is she talking about your brother?' Ben asked. Mark had now stepped forward to hug Pip but she wouldn't let him. She walked backwards in to the room behind her.

'Pip.' Mark was now upset. Pip had been one of his closest friends since he had moved to London and now she was scared of him. His fucking brother! 'Pip, it wasn't me. I have a twin brother. It was him. What happened?' He tried to calm the situation and let Pip know that it wasn't him and she was safe.

'Your twin brother from Manchester?' She asked, her voice trembling.

'Yes' Mark said, not adding any further information. Pip knew about why Mark had left Manchester and moved away. There was a look between them, Mark's eyes pleading for Pip to understand and Pip looking at Mark, a knowing look of what had happened here this evening. Pip jumped forward and threw her arms around Mark and both of them were crying. Pip's uncontrollable sobs of fear were contrasting against Mark's quiet happy tears that his friend was still his friend.

'I'm so sorry. I don't understand why he would be here.' The pair stood there holding each other for a few more minutes.

Ben just stood watching. He had looked round and could see a mess in the room beyond the door and was even more confused than both Pip and Mark.

'Come in' Pip had calmed down, her voice still trembling she let go of Mark and moved back in to the dressing area of her offices. Mark and Ben walked in behind her and saw Pip's office with all the broken chairs and tables inside. There were papers lay around the floor. Pip walked in to the dining area and shouted through to the boys.

'Close that door and lock it. I need a drink!' Pip poured three very large glasses of vodka with a splash of tonic and some ice. She took a large gulp and began to tell the story of what had happened. She explained about Manic Mike being a guest and how uneasy she had been once she made the connection of him being in Sam's flat, she told them about the arrival of the guy that looked like Mark with the scar on his face, and the fight and what she had overheard and she ended with him giving her the wad of cash.

'How much?' Ben asked when Pip had finished.

'Eighteen hundred' She replied 'I had just counted it when you arrived.'

'Bloody hell' Ben said

'It will probably just about cover the damage. I think my computer is dead.'

'Pip.' Mark said. He felt guilty that it was his brother who had done this. 'I'm... I'm so sorry' he said and he looked down at his drink.

'No. You don't need to be sorry Mark. Now I think about it I don't think this has anything to do with you. In fact I think it has everything to do with James and Dean.'

'Oh right, those two little shits fucking things up again.' Ben said. It was his turn to be angry. 'I will fucking kill James when I get my hands on him.'

'Ok, calm down' Mark said giving him a look that told him to shut up 'Why do you say that Pip?'

'Think about it. The drugs have gone missing and your brother must be Manic Mike's supplier. He wants his money back and Manic Mike is trying to get it back from the boys.'

'Oh yeah, you're right. It makes sense. Sorry it had to happen here.'

'Hang on a minute' Ben jumped in, having had a realisation 'This big hard drug dealer who everyone is so scared of is a tranny?'

'Transvestite' Pip corrected him. Ben pulled a face at her. 'You'd be surprised the people that come through the doors Ben. It doesn't make him any less scary outside of the doors.'

'So we think that Manic Mike works for my brother?' Mark asked

'I would say so' Pip replied

'Can't you just have a word with your brother and make all this just go away?' Ben asked Mark.

'Not on your life. All is fair in love and war but if my brother gets wind of any of us being involved in this he will have the lot of us.' Mark looked worried as he replied.

'Kill us probably.' Mark replied.

'Something doesn't quite work out.' Pip said, she was looking up, visualising the fight from earlier.

'He said he had stolen from him.'

'Who?' Mark asked.

'Your brother, Tony,' She continued. 'He said that he had stolen his drugs and put scumbag knock offs on the street.' Pip was lost in the memory recounting what had been said. Finally she looked at the boys and said 'Manic Mike stole half a million pounds worth of drugs from Tony and put dodgy drugs out on the streets in place of them.' Pip looked pleased with herself.

'What?' Ben asked

'Yeah, Pip. What?' Mark joined in.

'Don't you see? The pills that Dean and James had the accident with are just a very small part of this. They have to be, fifty grand is nothing compared to half a million.' Pip's voice was back in control. Her well-spoken accent was shining through.

'Boys I think Dean and James are mixed up in the middle of something much bigger.' She looked at the two boys who now looked as confused as they had when Pip first answered the door. 'And I think I know of a way of getting them out of trouble.'

55

'Running club?' James said again to Dean.

'Is that a bit like fight club?... Well no it couldn't be as you're talking about it.' Dean replied

'What?'

'First rule of running club.'

'Fight club' James cut into Dean's reply.

'Yeah fight club.'

'Running club is different. It's like all hipsters that run together and you are named after animals depending on your speed.' James explained about the new club he had joined.

 'Like Cheetah and Wolf' he looked at Dean. 'Well, you start at Beaver and work up.'

'Beaver?' Dean laughed as he asked.

'Yeah.'

'Where are you?'

'I'm a cat.'

'You're a cat, impressive.'

'Depends on the type of cat I guess.' James thought about the cat and that he didn't know what type of cat his group was.

'I'd be a Gazelle!'

'Babe, I don't even think that's a cat.'

'I run like I dance, so I could be a Gazelle.' Dean declared.

'What are you two talking about?' Sam had walked over to them.

'You're right a gazelle isn't a cat, James they're going to sit you down at running club and say we have reassessed your membership and you are classified as a sloth.' Sam laughed out loud and Dean joined in.

'That's not fair.' James said looking at them both.

'Anyway, how the fuck have you managed to ignore the fact that you are about to be killed by a drug dealer and go off and join a running club?' James tried to reply to Sam but he continued. 'You are gonna bloody need running club pretty soon. To run the fuck away from here and not get caught.'

'Drug dealers dear?' Mrs Potts was stood next to Sam now having left the other guests in the sitting area of the open plan living and dining room that led in to her kitchen in her ground floor flat. 'Who is in trouble with a drug dealer dear?' She looked at Dean and gave him a dirty look.

'Is it you?'

'No.' Dean said, as he did he wondered why this old woman didn't like him. He had come to her birthday party what more did she want? Then he realised he had lied and it was in fact him that was in trouble with a drug dealer.

'Oh, well not just me, him too.' He felt like she was one of his parents asking questions and he had just been caught out. Maybe it was her age, being so old he knew he had to be respectful of her.

'I was a dancer once dear. Back when dancers were glorious and wonderful.' Mrs Potts said to Dean.

'They still are' He got up from his seat and pushed passed her and walked over to Tom and Caroline sat at the table.

'Youth is wasted on the young isn't it Sam?' She said 'Now my dear James, what is this bother Dean has gotten you in to?'

'It's nothing for you to worry about Mrs Potts, let's get that Champagne out of the fridge for you and your guests.'

Sam walked in to the kitchen and to the fridge pulling out a bottle of Verve Cliquot. 'Where's your glass my love?'

Mrs Potts had a little excited giggle when she saw the fresh bottle. Sam looked back at the fridge and saw that there were three more waiting. He was going to have to stop drinking now as he was performing later tonight. He walked back to the group in the sitting area. James had now joined Tom, Caroline and Dean and they were deep in a conversation. There were two other elderly ladies sat on the sofa with another man, the one Sam had seen coming and going from the flat over the years, who he thought he recognised from the TV. Cracking open the champagne he offered it round, Mrs Potts now sat up in a chair opposite her friends offering out her glass and the others awaiting their refill too. He walked over to his group of friends to refill their glasses.

'So, at midnight all the money is taken from the front desk and to the office. The office is across the other side of the building so they have to walk across the dance floor to the bar to get it. Behind the bar is a long corridor that goes right across the back of the bar, to the cellar and at the other end up to the stage. The office is at the bottom end before the cellar.' Caroline said to the group. Sam realised what they were discussing. For the majority of the night Caroline and been hatching a plan with Dean, James and Sam about how they were going to get the money.

G.A.Y idol was on Friday night and they had decided Sam, Dean and James were going to go for it. At first Sam had joined in, he was now scared that they had turned in to petty criminals and that the now very real conversation was taking place. Caroline was going over the plan with the others one last time and it was now that Sam began to feel the dread of the situation. Tomorrow night he was to finish his act, change and head to town to meet the others and they were all going to go in to G.A.Y together. Caroline had said that she could get them on the guest list but they had decided this wasn't a good idea as they didn't want their names registered at the club.

Sam's show was earlier on the Friday so he could be at G.A.Y for around midnight. Once in the club they would find their spot and watch G.A.Y Idol. Keeping an eye on the door and for when they moved the money to the office. Once this had happened, they, separately, were going to get themselves into the corridor at the back. It was going to be busy with all the acts getting ready for their part of the show so they would be able to blend in. Once they had made their way to the office, Dean was going to keep watch while Sam and James went inside. Caroline had found out that the till drawer would have a padlock on it and the money is generally left inside. All they needed to do was to break the padlock and get the money. Once done get out as quickly as possible, before anyone even knew they had been there.

'It all sounds way too easy. Why isn't everyone trying to rob the money?' Sam said as he filled the glasses on the table.

'Well you see the thing is Sam.' Caroline attempted to answer.

'It was rhetorical.' He smiled at Caroline who smiled back, rolled her eyes and chuckled.

'And what are you two going to be doing while we are back there?' James asked of Tom and Caroline.

'Well, I'm am going to be enjoying the show and watching my idol as she presents on stage. I can't wait. I'm really looking forward to it actually' Caroline said 'Mel C, right there in front of me.' James watched her talking and was confused.

'Are you sure Mel C is actually there. There's been no advertising around it? He questioned. Caroline gave him and upset look.

'Of course she is, everyone is talking about it' She replied

'And anyway, why aren't you coming back with us?' James asked

'This is not my party James. It's yours.' Caroline said, in the most unusually succinct way.

'Too right!' said Tom. 'I'll be there for moral support right up until you go back stage and then I will stay outside with Caro's idol.'

'Oh my God, do you think we could get to meet her?' Caroline asked Tom.

'Yeah' He laughed 'Why not. We could walk up and say something like. Hi, were your number one fans. Do you know the quickest way out, only my mates are robbing the place?'

'Ha ha that would be dead funny.' Caroline replied.

'Neither of you two are funny. This is serious' James said back.

'What's not serious about that?' Sam asked.

'It's about as ridiculous as this situation is.' Sam had finished filling the glasses and looked at his watch. 'I'm going to have to make a move soon. Thursday night is a big night. New routine. Me and the Tranny Ninjas.'

'The what?' Tom and Caroline asked the same question at the same time.

'The dancers, tonight they will be the Tranny Ninjas my dears.' Sam replied with a theatrical voice.

'That sounds like fun.' Tom said 'Fancy going with him?' He asked Caroline.

56

'Don't you see? This is the answer we have been looking for.' Pip said to Ben and Mark both looking across at her from their seats on the opposite side of the tube. It was busy tonight and a lady stood in front of them so Pip had to keep moving a little to be seen by both of them. The woman seemed to be having a problem with her underwear as she kept adjusting it making her move the position she was stood in and thus making Pip move. This was much to Pip's disapproval having to watch a woman play with her knickers.

'Sorry Pip. I'm not with you' Mark was now for the second time tonight completely confused by what Pip was talking about.

'Me neither.' Ben added.

'You.' she looked at Mark 'You are the answer.' she said with a beaming smile.

'You sound like Rockers' parents now.' Mark laughed and looked at Ben, who was looking back confused. 'The reborn son of God thing?' Ben still looked confused 'You don't know that story about Sam's Mum and Dad thinking he was Jesus?'

'No' Ben sounded excited 'Tell me that at once.' He said looking at Mark. 'I thought he hadn't had contact with them for like,' Ben thought 'twenty years?'

'He hasn't and that's why, I thought you knew.' Mark replied

'Can you two stop for a minute please?' Pip butted in 'I was in the middle of explaining if you have quite finished.' Mark and Ben looked back at Pip and both saying sorry at the same time.

'As I was saying;' the tube came to a stop and Pip looked up to check if it was their stop. The man sat next to Ben did the same and realising it was his stop jumped up. Pip stood and the woman adjusting her knickers was about to take the seat when Pip shot in to it. She released a sigh loud enough for everyone to turn and look and then took the seat that Pip had just vacated. Pip smiled at her and was about to explain that she wanted to sit next to her friend when the woman gave her a disgusted look and looked the other way.

'As I was saying, this is the answer.'

'What's the question Pip?' Mark asked.

'Dum ass.' Pip rolled her eyes. Ben gave Mark a look and mouthed that he didn't know either with a shrug of the shoulders.

'Three of our friends are caught up in a..' Pip looked around not wanting anyone to hear what she was saying.

'An indiscretion at the moment.'

'That's an understatement.' Ben said 'That fucking James.'

'Ok, calm down.' Mark said 'Why am I suddenly the answer?'

'You're not' Pip said back and giggles to herself.

'Have you taken something Pip? Are you still in shock?' Mark said.

'Tony is the answer.' She replied.

'Bloody hell Pip, make your mind up. Is it Mark or Tony?' Ben said 'Who is Tony?' he looked at Mark this time then realised. 'Oh right, yeah. Tony. I'm still lost.'

'I'm not!' Mark's tone had changed and he was no longer joking. 'Whatever you are thinking right now it is not going to happen.' The tube came to a stop again and this time it was their stop. Mark got up and walked out looking physically upset. Ben looked at Pip and mouthed the word 'What'. All three of them climbed the stairs and walked out on to the street. Mark was ahead of the other two and Pip was almost jogging to keep up with Ben's large strides. Suddenly Mark turned around.

'I can't believe you would even think of it Pip. What the fuck?' He was now stood still in front of them and Pip stumbled forward a little as she came to a stop.

'Think of what? What has she done?' Ben said to Mark looking at him and then back to Pip.

'She wants me to pretend I am my brother and go to Manic Mike and tell him to forget about the money and stop chasing the boys.' Mark said looking at Ben 'That about sum it up?' he looked over to Pip.

'Yeah' Pip said casually 'Yeah that's about it' Mark turned and continued to walk along the street in the direction of the building that Sam lived in. 'Mark, slow down, I can't keep up' Pip shouted along to him.

'Run then Pip.' Mark said over his shoulder 'because that is what we will all need to do if.. .'

He stopped and turned again 'One, we get involved in this and two, if I have anything to do with pretending I am my brother he will literally kill me, and you.' He looked at Pip and then to Ben.

'And you!'

'Whoa, slow down, this is her idea nothing to with me.' Ben said stepping back slightly.

'But you admit it is a good idea don't you Ben?' Pip tugged his arm.

'As ideas go it is better than robbing G.A.Y.' Ben said.

'Sorry Ben.' Mark replied 'Did you not hear the bit about my brother being a fucking psycho that will kill us all?'

'When you say it like that it sounds bad. But would he actually find out?' Pip chipped back in.

'Would he find out? I haven't heard from him in 10 bloody years and I came home the other night to find him sat in my living room. As far as I knew he didn't know my address never mind how to get in' Mark was beginning to calm down as he spoke his words were less hurried and his volume had dropped.

'How did he get in?' Ben asked

'Not relevant.' Mark looked to Ben raising an eyebrow.

'Sorry' Ben said.

'But if we could set it up so that you meet with Manic Mike as Tony in his place he wouldn't know who it was. We could give him a message that the boys are protected then we could actually pull it off.' Pip was beginning to sound reasonable.

'We could get Mike to come round to Sam's place; he has been there before and would not think it is a strange request. Tony couldn't possibly know that you have anything to do with Sam. You can be there as Tony. When Mike gets there you can be in character and have a go at him for harassing the boys and tell him he has to leave them alone.'

'Why would Tony be at Sam's flat?' Mark stopped Pip from talking.

'What?' She replied.

'Why would Tony be at Sam's flat? Don't you think that Mike would ask that question?' Pip thought for a while. They continued to walk along the street, this time all at the same slower speed alongside each other.

'He wouldn't!' Pip finally said back. 'I have seen him around Tony. The moment he saw him he bolted and tried to run for it. He is really scared of him. He didn't ask why he turned up at my place and he won't ask why Tony is at Sam's place. He would be too scared.'

Mark looked at Pip thinking the scenario was becoming much more plausible. He wasn't about to give in though. The thought of being his brother was scaring him, the thought of being caught was even worse.

'Listen. I know you are thinking of the boys and this does seem like a good idea if it was ever to work.' Mark took a deep breath, Pip was about to say something but he continued taking a step forward so that the others would follow his lead.

'When we were younger we used to do it all the time. We would pretend to be each other to catch people out. I used to think it was a great game and would laugh my socks off when people found out we had switched. There was this one time at school that I got caught doing something I wasn't supposed to be, and instead of owning up I said that I was him. He hated it. He went in to a rage and beat me up. Like really beat me up, I was off school for a week while I got over it. My face was black and blue.'

'Oh bloody hell Mark' Pip said

'Sorry.' They continued to walk. 'Sorry I have brought that back up for you. But you were teenagers then a..'

'We were seven,' Mark butted in to what Pip was saying, stopping Pip's speech and shock covering her face.

'Seven?' She questioned, Mark nodded his head.

'It was worse when he got me back in the opposite direction. Only this time we were teenagers and he had been arrested. At thirteen I had to stand up in juvenile court and tell everyone the drugs I had on me, were for my own use and not to sell.'

Both Ben and Pip had now stopped walking and were looking at each other. Pip walked to Mark and put her arms around him and said sorry in to his chest as she hugged him.

'Anyway,' he said in the hug, 'that is all in the past. But at least you know why your stupid fucking, mad as a hatter idea scares the shit out of me. Even though…. it could possibly work.'

'What?' Pip said jumping back. 'You mean?'

'It needs further discussion,' they continued to walk down the street.

'Why didn't you tell them in court that it was your brother?' Ben asked a few minutes later.

'That really is the stupidest question yet Ben,' said Pip.

'Didn't want another beating love,' Mark said as they approached the block that Sam lived in. They could see through the windows to Mrs Potts' flat on the ground floor that there were people still there. Mark looked through and couldn't make anyone out for definite and hoped that Tom and Sam were still there.

57

Sam waked back stage at the Black Cap and down the thin corridor towards the dressing room. A walk he had done countless time before, but tonight it felt like a long tunnel. The enormity of the world around him at this moment in time was fast beginning to take over him and overwhelm him completely. Just need to get through tonight, he thought to himself as he entered the changing room to find the four guys he had been working with for the past six months bent down over the table looking at what seemed to be like a floor plan.

'What have you got there girls?' Sam asked as he dropped his hold all bag on to the chair at his changing area that took pride of place at the top end of the room. One of the boys looked up, looking bit flustered.

'Erm,' he looked at the others 'Have you seen this?' He turned back to the others and pulled a newspaper from underneath the document they were looking at, as one of the others folded it away. His stage name was Tinker-Belle, being the smallest of the four, his real name was Araf. His warm brown skin and high cheek bones meant he didn't need much in the way of make-up. But being a Drag Queen he piled it on anyway. He hadn't even started to apply this evening's war paint and stood before Sam in a black vest and a pair of jogging pants. At twenty three years old he was also the youngest of the troop. He handed Sam the newspaper.

'What is it?' Sam asked.

'Check out page 3,' Araf said as he let go. Sam looked up at him with a disappointed look.

'I don't go in for that sort of thing sweetheart.'

'No, no. It's the Daily Mail.'

'Then I really don't go in for that sort of thing,' Sam aimed the newspaper back at him. He took it and opened it to page three and turned it back on Sam.

'Isn't that the guy that tried to start a fight with you on Saturday night?' Araf handed the newspaper back to Sam. He looked down and saw a picture of a man wearing a baseball cap. He was in his mid to late thirties and looked familiar.

'It is isn't it?'

'What's it all about?' Sam looked up at Araf in a little shock.

'I thought it was,' Araf took the paper back and took a moment to find the bit he wanted to read.

'After a drunken night out, Shaun Simpson 39 from Lewisham, made his way across London to Little Venice where he took his own life. Police are asking for any witnesses to get in touch. As of this article going to print they are yet to piece together how he made it from his last sighting in Camden to being found on Hampstead Heath by a dog walker the following morning.'

Araf looked down at Sam.

'Give me that.' Sam took the paper and read it again for himself.

'Looks like he left here and couldn't face what he had done so ended it all,' Billy, another one of the dance troop said as he walked over.

'We were just reading it when you came in.'

'Poor bugger, the fight he started with you must have been a cry for help.' Araf said

'A cry for help? He dragged me off the stage.' Sam said back to them both.

'Well. I thought homophobe at the time but isn't that always the way? The ones who shout the loudest and all that,' Billy said.

'I know, the fucker could have really hurt Rockers,' Araf said back.

'Hey, the man's dead. Less of the character assassination,' Sam stopped them both.

'You're right. Poor guy,' Billy said.

'Didn't your Dave deal with it?' Araf asked.

'What?' Said Sam puzzled.

'Your Dave. He was there. Didn't he take the guy outside and get rid of him?' Araf had now turned away and started to walk towards the one large dressing table in the middle of the room that the four had been using as a bench to look at the paper when Sam had walked in.

'Firstly, he isn't my Dave anymore and hasn't been for a long time,' Sam continued.

'Secondly! What? He was here on Saturday too?'

'Yeah,' Billy replied 'Thought you knew. When you went back stage to sort out your wig and adjust ya tits, Dave stepped in and took him outside with the security guy.'

'Oh. I didn't know,' Sam turned to look at himself in the mirror.

'Why does he keep showing his face?'

'That's why he is still your Dave,' Araf said as he walked over and dropped his arms around Sam kissing him on the cheek. Sam kissed him back from the corner of his mouth.

'Now then boys it is high time we got our shit together and turned this wreck into Rocky Star.'

'In other news,' Araf said, all four of the dance troop now lined up behind Sam looking at him through the mirror he was facing. With Billy and Araf, now stood Jo and Louis. In a row stood Miss T, Tinker Belle, JoJo Galore and the oldest of the group at 34 was Lou the Bitch. Sam still hadn't gotten to the bottom of why Louis had decided his stage name was Lou the Bitch considering he was the least bitchy person Sam knew.

'What?' Sam asked looking through the mirror at them. Jo spun Sam around in the chair he was sat in.

'We have big news' He said to Sam. Almost simultaneously the four men bent their knees and dropped down to eye level with Sam. Sam chuckled to himself knowing they must have rehearsed the move.

'What, you want to change the routine last minute? Sorry girls I don't have time to learn any new moves.'

'No Rockers,' Louis now spoke.

'Bigger news than us being out there tonight.'

'Right before you came in Rocky Star, we took a phone call for you, for us,' Billy said.

'Right, hold on a minute,' Sam was beginning to get confused at who was speaking and telling the story.

'Only one of you talk, you're confusing the fuck out of my pretty little head.'

'Ok,' Jo took the lead.

'About an hour or so ago we took phone call saying that the warm up act for tonight's show had to pull out due to health issues and they want us. US!'

'Who does?' Sam Asked

'Bloody fool' Louis pushed Jo out of the way. 'If you're going to tell a story, at least tell the whole story. Sam, have you heard that Gay Idol is on tomorrow night at G.A.Y?' Sam began to feel a little uneasy. Why were they now talking to him about the event he had spent the whole evening talking about?

'Yes,' he said slowly.

'Well, they had a drag show opening the night at 11pm and they have all gone down with,' He looked at Billy. 'Food poisoning!'

'Food poisoning?' Louis continued 'And they have called to ask if we could do the act. One song, do the routine and off.' He stopped talking with a smile on his face. Sam sat for a moment trying to work out how he felt about it. He was excited to know that the group were thought well of and they had the chance to do a big show and get some exposure. On the other hand he was filled with dread. Would he be able to do the show and pull off a robbery at the same time? He thought through the facts. It would make it easier for him to be back stage without getting caught, or if anyone was asking questions about why he was back there. Also, if there were any complications he could slip out unnoticed.

'Sam,' Louis raised his voice. 'Are you ok?'

'Why?' Sam replied.

'You drifted off there for a minute love. What do you think? Are you in?'

'Well' Sam thought a little more. 'By the look of it you are all up for it and I might not have much choice.' All four of them were nodding their heads. 'But we are nothing without Rocky Star. We are just a group of men in dresses dancing round without the star performer!'

'Right then,' He looked at them. 'I guess I'm in then.' Sam jumped up from his chair as the four boys starting cheering and hugging each other. 'I'll be right back.' Sam left the dressing room and ran up the short corridor to the toilet at the end, he burst through the door closing it tightly behind him, he was sick. He wretched a couple more times and then slid down the toilet wall to the floor. 'What the fuck am I doing now?' He said out loud as he held his head in his hands. Sam sat on the floor for the best part of fifteen minutes, until there knock at the door.

'Rockers, are you ok in there?' Louis asked.

'Yes love,' Sam wiped his face with some toilet roll and threw it in to the toilet, he stood up and looked at his face to check all was ok and flushed the toilet.

'Have you seen the time? We are on in thirty minutes.'

'What the fuck, how long have I been in here?' He opened the door to the toilet.

'About thirty minutes.' Miss T now stood outside the door looking at him. Her face was fully made up, contoured, sparkling, a jet back bob wig cut harshly just below her ears. She was wearing a back jump suit that had a hoodie in the back that wrapped around the back of her head. As she looked at Sam she did a twirl.

'What do you think?' Raising her arm in the air.

Sam looked down the corridor and saw the other three dressed exactly the same. 'We give you the Tranny Ninjas!'

58

'The time is seven thirty pm on this lovely Friday evening in December. Thank you everyone for coming out in the cold. I know below freezing is not the best weather for an operation like this.'

DCI Kirsty Brown stood at the front end of the briefing room. They were making use of a mobile briefing unit that had been pulled in to place earlier that afternoon on the opposite side of Soho Square, facing the street that led down to the entrance of The Astoria night club, the current home of G.A.Y.

'I will be handing you over to Detective Inspector Andy Grey who is the officer in charge of this operation. I just wanted to say,' she stopped and looked at everyone ensuring she made eye contact with each person in the group. There was a team of twenty officers gathered together, her usual team plus a few police officers from the local beat. The majority of the group were in plain clothes apart from four local officers who were to be used as back up and to give visibility to gathering crowds should anything go wrong. 'This is a major tip off for us.' She continued making eye contact with everyone in turn. 'And we are going to get these thieves tonight. Thank you again.'

She turned 'Andy, over to you' She stepped away and let Andy take over.

'Thank you ma'am' Andy stepped forward. 'I don't need to mention again the sensitive nature of this operation. The management of tonight are cooperating but don't share our belief that something is going to happen tonight.' Andy swallowed and continued to brief the group on the operation. Kirsty sat and watched, admiring how Andy was taking control and running this. She knew he needed this after the week he'd had. She needed this to; she had spent the best part of the last 24 hours convincing her senior officers that this was a real and pertinent operation. She had split the floor of her office last night, not for the first time in her career and certainly it wouldn't be the last. She looked at her officers and knew that she had a great team working for her. She was constantly amazed at the brilliance they brought to her each and every day.

Then she looked at the thorn in her side, DI Jack Daniel. She sighed inwardly to herself. He had ended up part of this team by accident due to being in the right place at the wrong time. She thought her senior officer had planned it this way in order to get him off their back and under someone who can manage him. She knew she could, she wasn't scared of being harsh with him and mostly wondered how on earth she was going to find the moment that would move him on from her. Then she kicked herself, the pride she had for the rest of the team stemmed from the amount of work she put in coaching and developing them to make their own decisions and come to her with information rather than questions. She spent time with each and every one of them, rank did not matter to her, getting policing done did and she knew how to get the best out of people. Right now she was kicking herself at not being able to get the best out of Jack. Some people just aren't able to change. As long as someone has a belief that they are correct in their actions then they will never change. Kirsty resigned herself to the fact that she would not be able to find his best points and in fact he would be better elsewhere. In her opinion out of the police force but she knew he wouldn't ever move on.

'Rocky Star and the Tranny Ninjas will be performing the opening act at 11pm. We believe they will return to the dressing rooms directly from the performance and then they will make their way to the office and the theft will take place.' Kirsty caught the end of Andy's speech.

'Gov?' one of the uniformed officers asked, Andy looked at him and indicated he could continue. 'The previous crime reports associated to the group, reference four Drag Queens committing the crimes.'

'Yes' Andy said. He looked at Shilpa who had compiled the reports.

'Well, there's five of them in't there?' He said looking over to Shilpa too 'The Tranny Ninjas,' He chuckled to himself 'And this Rocky Star.'

'That's correct. We are unsure at the moment as to whether Rocky Star, or Sam Rockwell as is his given name, has anything more to do with the group other than being the star of the show so to speak.'

'Oh, or the mastermind?' The officer questioned.

'Bloody mastermind?' DI Jack Daniel butted in 'Mastermind, were talking about a que...' he stopped himself before he said the words. 'A bloke who prefers to dress as a woman and dance on stage.'

'Enough.' Kirsty shot down Jack's outburst and he slouched back in to his seat feeling reprimanded. The uniformed officer looked angered at the interaction and turned to Kirsty nodding his appreciation, and then back to Andy.

'The research we have shown us that Sam Rockwell, Rocky Star, has been working at the Black Cap for the best part of twenty years on and off. The dance troop working with him tonight, have only been there for the last six months.' Once again looking at Shilpa and nodding his thanks for the intelligence. 'Unless they recruited him fast then our suspicion is that the Black Cap and Rocky Star is their cover.'

'Time will tell, by the end of the night we will know,' the officer said 'let's hope he doesn't end up a casualty of the situation.

'D.I Daniels,' Kirsty said as she walked across the room. 'A word outside please.'

59

'I'm telling you now for God's sake.' Sam shouted at James 'I found out last night and haven't been able to get hold of you all day.' He was gripping the phone tightly in his hand. The stress of the week had been too much for him and he had finally snapped. James had been uncontactable all day and Dean was no use whatsoever.

'So, the plan to get the money from robbing a bloody club is out the window. It was stupid plan anyway.'

'What the fuck are we going to do Sam? He wants the money tomorrow and right now we don't even have enough to pay for his parking.' James was now shouting at Sam too. Sam took several deep breaths trying to calm down.

'James I really don't know what to say.' He was calm and talking at a normal level now.

'I can't get out of doing the act, which means my name is all over that place tonight, there is no way I can be part of a robbery where my name is plastered all over the bloody walls,' Sam had tears in his eyes. He was glad this was over the phone, not wanting James or anyone to see how scared he was. How was he supposed to perform in this state? In about an hour he was supposed to do his regular act at the Black Cap and then shoot across town in a taxi to do the opening number at G.A.Y Idol. He could hear James talking to someone else in the room with him at the end of the phone.

'Who is with you James?'

'Dean just came out of the tube station.'

'Where are you?'

'On our way to your place.'

'Why are you coming here? What are you... .' He trailed off not knowing what he was saying or what he wanted to say.

'I'm heading out myself in a minute. I have to get to work. Anyway, this really isn't a safe place to be. It's the only place your wonderful lover knows where to find you and he might come looking.'

60

'That's it!' James looked at Dean. They were both sat on a wall opposite the entrance to the tube station from which Dean had just appeared. 'Sam is out and we are fucked.'

'He is as fucked as we are,' Dean said.

'No he isn't. Mike knows it was us and is using Sam to make sure we pay up. He won't do anything to him, just us.' The boys sat on the wall for a few minutes more.

'We could always do it ourselves,' Dean said looking at James.

'We know the plan and if it is as easy as Caro says then we could do it. The less people that know, the less there is to go wrong.'

'What? You want to rob a night club on your own?'

'No, not on my own, with you, we can do it.' Dean was sounding much more confident than he had ever sounded before.

'All we need is the door opening so we can get behind the scenes. And Rocky will be there to do it as he passes, by accident like,' Dean stood up and looked at James.

'We can do this. We have to do this.' James was beginning to be convinced.

'So say we did do it, what if we get caught?'

'Exactly the same excuse as before. We were lost and we camp it right up and play dumb.'

'I still think that is a weak part of the plan.'

'James it is all we have. Let's go round and see Sam face to face and see what he says.'

The two boys grabbed each other's hands and ran down the street in the direction of Sam's flat. As they ran down the street they saw Sam run from his building and in to a waiting taxi.

'Sam.' Dean Shouted 'SAM.' But he didn't hear them and the taxi drove passed.

'What are you boys up to?' The voice of Mrs Potts travelled across the cold air in the street.

'Oh, Hi Mrs Potts how are you?' James said. 'We were looking for Sam but have just missed him.

'Yes you have boys. He just left for work, a busy night it is. He seemed quite stressed about it all.' Mrs Potts turned to head back in to the building and shouted over her shoulder 'You better come in out of the cold.'

The two boys sat on the sofa in Mrs Potts' living room. Dean was sat at the end next to the window looking out on to the street and James in the middle. Mrs Potts crossed the room carrying a tray with tea and biscuits.

'We can't be hanging around here we need to get off,' James hissed at Dean.

'I know, but I am freezing and have nowhere to go,' Dean kept looking out of the window.

Two people had just walked in to the entrance and he couldn't see who they were. He wondered if Sam had come back but realised they were the wrong shape to be him.

'Then let's have a cup of tea and then head off.'

'Here you go boys.' Mrs Potts placed the tray on the table 'Now,' she looked at them and waited for them to both be focussed on her. 'Which of you is going to tell me what is going on and what has got Samuel so stressed out this week?' They both looked at each other, as Dean was about to lie to Mrs Potts and tell her nothing that they were aware of, James spoke first.

'Oh Mrs Potts it's all a right bloody mess. Last week we accidentally had an accident and this,' he hesitated before he said it was a drug dealer, 'Nasty man,' He breathed out, 'now says that we owe him loads of money and he is a scary bloke who could really hurt us.'

'Accidentally had an accident?' Dean questioned James.

'Well' He stared at Dean hoping he could read his mind as he thought he was about to mention drugs.

'And is this all drugs related young Dean?' Mrs Potts turned to Dean who hadn't really said much to her since he arrived.

'Well,' he felt nervous, as if his mother had just found him smoking or taking something that wasn't his.

'Well, yes actually it is.' He held his hand to his mouth and then blurted out 'But not me. I wasn't taking them,' he defended his actions. 'I was trying to stop him from taking them.' Mrs Potts looked at James with disgust and then back to Dean.

'So you didn't take any?' She asked.

'No Mrs Potts, I never have and now we stuck in a situation where the drug dealer might actually kill me and I have never even taken them.'

'There is irony in that young Dean,' Mrs Potts poured the tea and passed a cup and saucer to Dean. 'Now tell me, how does this nasty man and the drugs have anything to do with Samuel?'

'He followed us back here last week when it all happened.'

'I think I need to know the whole story from start to finish.' Dean sat back as James started to speak. He was less frenzied now and speaking calmly and filling in the detail that he hadn't before given. They spoke for about twenty minutes and Dean added in bits of information as needed. Dean felt like a load had been lifted off his shoulders just by telling the story. It didn't help the situation but it did help him get things clear in his head. James sat back in to the sofa feeling much the same.

'And so, what is your plan now boys?' Mrs Potts asked.

'Well we were going to go ahead and do it ourselves.' Dean continued and explained the new plan to do the robbery themselves and get away without being caught. If they were, the camp option would spring into action. Mrs Potts chuckled to herself listening intently to what they boys had to say.

'Well it seems to me that you need the help of someone a few more years wiser than you.'

As Mrs Potts was talking and about to offer the boys a solution Dean shouted out loudly and jumped from his seat on the end of the sofa.

'Bloody Hell.' He looked back at Mrs Potts and James; both shocked at him jumping up and turned back to the window to watch the shadow of the man walk through the door. 'He's here.'

'Who dear?'

'Mike,' Dean looked at James. 'The drug dealer.'

61

'I don't think it is going to work.'

Mark was sat in a chair in Sam's bedroom. Pip, Ben and Caroline stood over him. For the past twenty minutes, since he and Ben had arrived, Pip had been applying make up to create a scar across the centre of his face and Caroline had been coaching him on getting back to his Manchester accent and working out what he was going to say. Ben had mostly been pacing around the room. Earlier this afternoon, Pip and Caroline had stolen Sam's phone and sent a text message to Mike to tell him to be at his flat at 8pm in order to get his money.

Having decided the invite was better coming from Sam rather than either of the boys. They knew that Sam would be out of the way and off to work by the time Mike arrived and they would have time to get ready for the show. All four had agreed that they would tell no one of what the plan was apart from them four and after the night they would not talk about it again. Mark was feeling uneasy about it. He knew that he could pull off being his brother, being as angry and aggressive wouldn't be too hard. Deep down inside the anger and resentment he had for his brother began to stir and he knew he could use this to become the mad man he had always seen Tony as. His unease was not at being his brother and convincing a crazy drug dealer that he was his boss, it was at what happens after. The four of them were aware there may be consequences for what they were about to embark on, they knew that should Tony find out he wouldn't be happy. Having not even been in contact with Tony for the best part of ten years and having nothing to do with him for nearly 15 years he didn't know, none of them did, what the consequences might be.

The act, as they were now calling it, had been well thought out. Ben and Pip were master wordsmiths and Pip had, to the best of her ability used NLP to script out what should be said. Managing what was to be said so that Mike didn't try to have this conversation with Tony next time he sees him would be key to limiting the damage that Tony could create.

'Of course it's going to work Mark. Or should we call you Tony?' She held the mirror up to his face and he looked at the image. Looking at him was his brother, knowing it was his own face he was seeing he could tell that the scar was make up. Ben had shaved Mark's head first to just the right length to be like Tony's, this was where the illusion stopped.

'It's not going to fucking work; you can tell that it is make up.' Mark flopped back on to the bed, the world beginning to swirl around him. Before he could let it in and feel any more stressed Pip had grabbed both his arms and pulled him back up.

'I don't give a fuck what you think Mark Cash. I know this is going to work and you need to buck your ideas up. If you think it is not going to work then it bloody well won't work.' She took a breath, Mark, Caroline and Ben staring at her in shock at her sudden assertive behaviour.

'But if you believe it will work, then it will,' she looked around at all three of them and then back at Mark and smiled. 'Low level lighting my love.'

'What?' Mark spoke; he liked Pip being like this. Normally whenever they spoke and he was unsure about something she would spend time to coach him in to making a decision that was right for him. There was none of that this time. Sometimes people just need to be told, he smiled.

'If the lighting is quite low in the room then he would need to be right up in your face to see that it is make-up.'

'She's right,' Caroline said.

'I'm about three feet away from you and I can't tell' Ben added 'in fact, you look just like a bloke I saw in the street the other night.'

'You're too kind.' Mark looked up at them all. He stood up and walked over to the suit that was hanging in the back of the bedroom door. Thinking about the first time he wore the suit just over a week ago. Right now the excitement of wearing it was totally different. But he was beginning to feel that he could actually pull this off. Stood in just his Calvin Klein boxer shorts he took the shirt and pulled it over his back and buttoned it up.

'So Caro, go through it again for me.'

You and Pip are going to be here in the bedroom and Ben and I are going to be out there in the living room?'

'Right, so we will stay in here because Pip cannot be seen or he might wonder why she is here as he already knows her. I've got nothing to do with it so I'm saying out the way.'

'You very much *have* got something to do with this right now,' Mark butted in.

'Well I'm still staying out the way.'

'Fair play,' said Mark with a shrug.

'So, Ben opens the door and lets him in acting all uneasy. He'll make out that there is an issue and try to tell him not to come in. Mike will walk in and find Mark.' She laughed a little. 'Sorry, Tony stood in the living room,' she looked at Pip. 'With low level lighting, and then.. .' Caroline stopped talking, interrupted by a knock at the door. All four of them froze. Caroline was the first to speak in a low whisper. 'It's eight o'clock' everyone looked at Mark who had now pulled on the suit trousers and jacket and was slipping his feet in to a pair of black shoes. He patted himself down turned and looked at everyone else. No one spoke, Ben and Mark walked out of the room and Mark took up his place as Ben walked across the room to open the door. As he did, Pip bolted back into the room and in front of Ben, signed for him to stop. They stood still as she raised her hand to the dimmer switch and lowered the lighting level. Mark and Ben mouthed the word 'FUCK' to each other as Pip ran back to the bedroom and closed the door. She and Caroline instantly kneeled behind it.

Pip listened to what was being said and Caroline was looking through the keyhole watching what was happening. Her view of the front door wasn't very good but she could see Mark stood in the living room with his back to the bedroom. As she watched she could hear Ben speaking and then a louder voice but she couldn't quite hear what he was saying.

In the living room, Ben was being pushed out of the way by Mike.

'Get out my way, where's Rockers?' Mike demanded.

'Erm, there's something you should know,' Ben said sounding very uneasy.

'What's that dickhead?' Mike said as he stepped further in to the living room.

'Me,' Mark said loudly, assertively and in the thick Manchester accent of his brother. He was shitting himself inside, his stomach was in knots and he thought he may have been shaking. But he wasn't and as he heard his own voice, a voice he hadn't had for a long time, his confidence grew. The room was silent. Mike was stopped in his tracks stunned to silence, looking as Tony Cash unexpectedly stood in the room.

'Why are you here?' Mike's voice was quiet, he sounded scared and confused.

'More to the point, what the fuck are you doing here?' Mark questioned him.

'I'm here to...' he didn't know what to say.

'Listen little Mikey, if you lie to me right now you're gonna end up face down in that canal outside. So before you answer, have a little think about it.'

'I'm collecting on a debt,' Mike said. At the same moment a large thud came from the bedroom. Pip had moved to look through the key whole and fallen. Mark, Ben and Mike all looked at the door. Mark's heart jumped.

'Collecting a debt from the scared Drag Queen hiding in the bedroom?' He was speaking before he had even realised what he was saying. It was a good call, up until now, none of them had an explanation as to where Sam would be given that he had invited Mike over.

'Erm, well his mates,' Mike still sounded nervous.

'The two kids?'

'Yeah, where are they?'

'Don't matter where any of them are. You're dealing with me now Mikey.' Mark could tell that calling him Mikey was annoying him; in just the same way it annoyed him when Tony called him Marky. He decided to keep on using it as much as possible.

Mike, looking at Tony was feeling very uneasy. 'I've sorted with them, the Queen and the boys. You don't need to worry about them anymore.'

'Why?'

'Are you fucking questioning me Mikey, you little shit?' Mark was becoming more aggressive as he spoke and Mike was becoming more scared. He didn't want to take another beating from Tony and he was also very unsure what was happening. He didn't have the money to pay Tony and he didn't have the drugs to give back to him. He was screwed, and now the money that he thought he could run away with was gone. But why, why was Tony here and how did he know about the money? It wasn't making sense.

'How did you know about the money they owe me?' Mike asked nervously.

'Still questioning me Mikey?' Mark was now sounding patronising, in exactly the way his brother always had, 'I know fucking everything Mikey, everything.'

'So where's the money?'

'You should stop worrying about that money Mikey and start thinking about where my half mil is. Because if I remember rightly you have until tomorrow to get it to me or,' he pointed at Mike's feet flicked his finger round and then pointed up. Mark was thinking to himself that he wasn't quite sure what the gesture was that he just made. Mike watched wondering what the hand movement meant and guessed that it was something to do with being dead and buried.

'But what about them robbing the club?' Mike said. Mark was shocked, how did he know that they planned to rob the club?

'What club?' Mark replied, shit, he may have just blown his 'I know everything' cover.

'Rockers and his mates where going to rob a club to get me my money,' Mike replied.

'Ain't happening Mikey. As I said, I've sorted all this and they don't owe you a penny. But you still owe me' Mark didn't gesture with his fingers this time, still trying to work out why he had done it the first time anyway.

'But what am I?' Mike trailed off.

'Guess you've got a club to go rob then haven't you Mikey?' Mark could hear the words coming out of his mouth and realised he had now gone way off script.

'Who the fuck are you?' Mike said, with a small hint of confidence but still sounding scared.

Mark looked at him. Shit, does he know I'm not Tony? The only option now was to shout enough to scare him in to leaving.

'Who the FUCK AM I?' His voice boomed across the room and as he did so he stepped forward, just one step. It was enough. The step forward sent Mike jumping back and covering his head.

'I'LL FUCKIN' AV YOU!' Mark shouted, Mike turned and ran for the door which was locked and bolted by Ben a few minutes earlier. Mark adjusted himself.

'Remember Mikey, you leave these boys alone now.' he walked towards the door and Mike started to fiddle with the lock, trying to get as far away from Tony as possible.

'Right right, yeah,' he said as he managed to unlock the door and open it.

'Oh, and Mikey,' he said.

'What?' Mike turned and looked at Mark.

'My money. Tomorrow. See ya!' With the final comment Mike disappeared down the stairs and out the front door.

62

Ben watched from the window, with the blind slightly pulled up so that no one would see him, as Mike crossed the road and got in in to the huge black Range Rover with blacked out windows.

'He's gone,' he said to the others behind him. Not looking back as he watched the Range Rover drive along the road and then speed off round the corner. He turned and looked at Mark stood in exactly the same spot he was stood in when Mike left the flat. Caroline and Pip and stepped out of the room and stood in the door way as if they were ready to dive back in should there be another knock at the door. All four of them looked at each other, none of them knowing what to say and all still feeling very nervous.

'See ya,' Ben was the first to break the silence. He camped it up a bit when he spoke a second time 'Seee ya,' he was looking at Mark who looked terrified.

'What on earth was that?'

'What?' Mark trembled when he spoke. 'I was fucking shitting myself the whole way through.' Pip let out a loud laugh and slowly Caroline and Ben joined in. 'Why are you laughing? What the fuck did we just do?'

'Well Mark,' Pip spoke, 'I see we have a man of many talents in our group. I for one totally believed every single minute of the performance. And having seen Tony in action,' she looked at Ben and Caroline before returning to Mark. 'I'm the only one who can justifiably judge it.'

'Fuck off,' Caroline's strong northern accent chipped in. 'You may have seen Tony in action but so have bloody I.' She walked over to Mark and threw her arms around him. 'I was scared of you Mark you were like a different person.'

'Do you think?' Mark asked the tremble in his speech becoming more relaxed as he himself began to calm down.

'The big question is,' Ben said as he looked back out the window up and down the street, Did Mike believe it and is this the end of it?' He turned back to the others. 'He hasn't come back, and I'm not surprised,' Ben was now the calmest out of everyone, thinking and speaking rationally.

'It really was a great performance Mark. I have to say I was shitting myself before and thought it was a ridiculous plan. Truthfully I didn't think you would be able to pull off the thug drug dealer. I was wrong. Good work!'

All three of the others looked at him and burst out laughing. Mark had finally calmed down and with Ben's sudden serious nature, he had seen the funny side. Caroline, Mark and Pip flopped on the sofa.

'Seriously though Mark' Caroline said 'I did think it was all gonna fall over in the last minute when you said See Ya!'

'What was wrong with that?' Mark asked.

'Well, it was a bit camp. You were well tough all the way through and then added a little See Ya at the end. I fell over and Pip had to catch me.'

'I did,' said Pip giggling.

'Well, he seemed pretty scared as he shot out of the room,' Mark said.

'That step forward was genius. It was like you were about to start hitting him,' Pip added.

'I stumbled and almost fell,'

'What?' Pip sat up.

'I didn't even mean to move but I was so grounded in that spot and shitting myself that I stumbled forward as he moved and it looked like I was going for him.'

'Fabulous' Pip jumped up 'Mark just scared a drug dealer off by falling over.'

63

Mike sped off from the parking spot quickly, wanting to be away from here as fast as possible. He slammed his brakes on at the junction and then turned quickly and put his foot down again, almost knocking a cyclist over and shouting out his window at them.

'Fucking move moron.'

'Boss, are you ok?' said a squeaky voice from the passenger seat. Sonny had been waiting in the car for Mike while he was seeing the Drag Queen. Whilst he waited he had been playing a game on his brand new iPhone and also sending various people text messages. He had worked for Mike for about two years and was now working closely with him and saw himself as his right hand man.

'Did everything go ok? Have you got the money?'

'No it did not go ok. Fucking Rocky Star has got protection.' Mike swerved passed a parked car in the street and almost mounted a crossing then swerved back in to the road, putting his foot down again.

'What do you mean protection boss? Is someone moving in on our turf?'

'Tony fucking Cash was in there.'

'Woooowww Tony Cash is protecting Rocky Star? That is big news innit?'

Mike was getting angrier by the minute and Sonny wasn't helping. The boy had his uses but he wasn't the sharpest tool in the box and until now had only really been used for running around picking up packages and delivering stuff.

'Yeah big news and it means we are fucked.' Mike slammed his brakes on at set traffic lights.

'Why are we fucked boss?'

'Because we are in debt to Tony Cash and the money Rocky owes us isn't coming to us anymore.'

'So, Tony Cash, the big gangster from the north was in that flat?' Sonny questioned.

'Yes he fucking was.'

'Are you sure boss?'

'Course I'm fucking sure. What the fuck kind of stupid question was that?'

'I is just asking innit boss.' Mike was beginning to get angry at Sonny now. He was sat in the passenger seat asking stupid questions and having text conversations with someone. It was worse than having a child. Still looking down at his phone and not really paying attention to what was being said.

'So what ya gonna do now then boss?' He asked. Mike was thinking now, his driving had become less erratic and he was calming down.

'We need to find the money and get it to Tony Cash.'

'But you got the money ain't ya boss?'

'Not all of it. Tonight's takings aren't going to be enough either.'

'So where is the rest boss?' Mike sat in the driver's seat in the slow moving traffic going in to the centre of London. As bus drove passed and he looked up at the advert on the side, a young blonde muscled boy in hot pants was holding a microphone. He looked at the boy and began to think of the dirty things he would get up to with him. He read the sign next to the model, G.A.Y Idol. Still thinking of the boy and then reading the sign again, it hit him.

'We are going to rob G.A.Y.'

'What the fuck boss?' Sonny looked up from his phone.

'The club that Rocky and his dickhead mates were going to rob. They ain't doing it no more so we can move in with their plan.'

'Aww boss, I ain't sure about that innit'

'Not fucking sure about it? It's a fucking perfect plan. Believe me, Rocky Star ain't fucking stupid and I know the plan they made. It's good to have eyes and ears everywhere you know.'

Sonny chuckled to himself at this and went back to send the message he was working on.

64

The London Astoria is a music venue located at 157 Charing Cross Road. During its lifetime it had been a cinema and ballroom, before being converted for use as a theatre in the 70's. In the 80's it was again converted and became the well-known popular music venue and night club. When it was first constructed it was four storeys tall with a decorative frieze cornice surrounding its exterior. The original interior was styled as a square proscenium theatre with a panelled barrel vault ceiling supported by large columns, a viewing balcony and false viewing boxes. The basement had a large ballroom. In 1985 after a period of being closed and renovated, the London Astoria re-opened to be a music venue and night club with capacity for around 2000. In January 2009 the venue was compulsory purchased by Crossrail Development, despite public outcry, and is now set to be demolished to make way for the new Elizabeth Line, Tottenham Court Road station for the London transport system.

The nightclub G-A-Y had been homed in the London Astoria from 2000 and in July 2008 moved its residency to Heaven. Tonight, it was back for one night only and to say a fond farewell to such an iconic venue. G-A-Y Idol was taking place and the queue outside 157 Charing Cross Road was the longest the security had ever seen it. Most people had been stood out in the cold for the last hour and were beginning to argue with the security on the door about opening the venue doors. The promoters of the event had decided to keep everyone outside a little longer due to the imminent arrival of the star of the show; it would create a great showpiece for the photographers on the door. G-A-Y Idol is a one night only music competition to find a new singing talent. Entries had been auditioning over the past three weeks and the shortlist of eight acts was now on posters around the whole of the building. The show has one host and the judging panel is everyone in the audience. The venue has a text based voting system and by the end of the night G-A-Y's first Idol will receive the boost to their career in the form of a cheque for £10,000. The cheque was already written, it was oversized like the ones you see on Children In Need when someone has sat in a bathtub full of beans and collected money. It was currently in the dressing room of the star of the show, the presenter that had the crowds flocking to the doors.

The guest presenter was currently having her hair blow dried. It was the finishing touch before she put on her dress and went out through the exit to get into a car waiting for her, so she could be driven around the corner to the front door and open the venue. As she stood up, wearing just her knickers and bra the door swung open and in walked Sam.

'Oh my good gosh, I am so bloody sorry.' Sam said as he looked over at her, who was a little shocked that someone had just walked in and she was grabbing a towel to cover herself 'They told me this was my dressing room.'

'No worries' She laughed, 'I think the next door along is a bigger dressing room. We'd be a bit cramped in here together.' She laughed off the intrusion.

'I'm so sorry.' As Sam stepped back to leave the room his hold all bag finally gave way and the contents came crashing out and all over the floor. Wigs and make up landed, filling the space. Sam starred at the floor and then looked up, his hand over his mouth and then back at the floor before looking back up again. 'I'm...' he was lost for words.

'You know how to make an entrance don't you love?' She was now wrapped in the towel bent down to start picking up wigs and lipstick.

'Oh no you don't!' Sam shouted 'I'm not having one of my all time favourite artists on the floor picking up my war paint. Sam knelt down and started to gather his stuff trying to stop her from doing it.

'War Paint,' laughing back to Sam 'I haven't heard it called that in years.'

65

Tony Cash sat in the passenger seat of the black Range Rover, the blacked out windows shielding him from the outside world while he observed what was happening. From his viewing point he could see down the street that led to the place where the police had set up the Porta cabin, which gave him a good view of what and when things might start happening.

He could see to the entrance doors of the Astoria giving him a good view of who was going in and out. He looked down the queue and could pick out everyone he needed to in it. There were four undercover police officers in two groups about ten people apart in the queue. Behind, stood one of the low life dealers who worked for Manic Mike, completely unaware that he was stood in front of the undercover police officers, who were also unaware of the amount of drugs the low life had on his person. There were two other dealers in the queue that worked for Manic Mike and also another lone dealer that Tony wasn't sure about. He wondered if Manic Mike was aware of other people working his patch. Or if in fact, this was a new scumbag working for Manic Mike peddling his dodgy drugs.

Tony's main mission tonight was to find out where Mike had moved his quality merchandise to and where he had got his dodgy, shouldn't be on the street, drugs. It was still early and he knew that the kids in the queue at the moment were just there to get the gear in to the club and later the actual dealers would arrive, taking the stash and sell it across the club. Tony had been sat watching for about 5 minutes and had been receiving text messages the whole time he was sat there. He had three phones on him tonight. A new iPhone he was still trying to work out how to use. This was his Manchester business phone and it had been mostly quiet. The second phone was a Nokia 3310, a phone he had had for about ten years and still preferred it over the new fancy gadget phones, he had tried. This was his personal phone and he kept it on him at all times. There were only a handful of numbers on the phone and only a handful of people had the number. His mother and his wife were the main people who called him on it. The third phone was a Motorola phone where he had been receiving text messages for the last hour. This phone was a new disposable phone and only had one person's number in it and there was only that person who had the number too. The text messages that were coming through were a minute by minute update of what was happening with the person sending them. That person was informing Tony of what one particular person was doing tonight.

There was a loud cheer from the crowd that was stood outside the Astoria, Tony looked up to see that a car had pulled up outside the main entrance and a young woman with long dark hair was stepping out wearing a red evening dress. She looked familiar to him but he wasn't sure where he knew her from. The crowd were cheering for her and getting quite excited. He suspected she may be famous. Celebrities were a far more lucrative part of his business dealings than the run of the mill dealing, he made a mental note to work out who she was.

Looking up above the entrance he saw the sign for the night, G.A.Y Idol and the young woman was pictured on it. An member of a big girl band, probably a Spice Girl or an Aloud Girl he thought. He took a closer look realising he not had any dealings with her. She walked from the car and to the crowd where she chatted with a few people at the front of the queue and photographers took several pictures before she then walked in to the entrance and through the doors. Minutes later the doors where opened once again and the queue of people started to pour in to the venue. Tony looked down the street towards the place where the police were and didn't see anything of significance. Looking back at the venue the queue was now almost gone. Either there hadn't been as many people as he thought or the club were working quickly to get people in and out of the cold. That would be good for the dealers getting the stash in to the club. Security would be paying more attention, at this early time, to getting people in rather than doing full searches. Something they would be doing for the rest of the night. The driver's side door to the car opened and a man in a suit climbed in to the seat. He was a fifty three year old man with a shaved head, broad shoulders and a skin head. Tony often referred to him as Grant after Grant Mitchell from EastEnders. This annoyed Paul as he didn't like to be associated with a, in his words, 'Southern Wimp'.

'She is getting ready to walk up this way now,' he said looking around the street without actually looking at Tony. 'They did a briefing and then she stepped outside to talk to an old guy who wasn't too happy.'

'About what?' Tony asked with interest.

'She was ripping him a new one,' Paul continued. 'He seems a bit old school, a bit too old school if you know what I mean. He had wanted something from inside and she had stopped him. She brought him outside to pretty much tell him she wanted rid of him and how crap he was.'

'Good work. Maybe we get to do Detective Superintendent Kirsty Brown a favour at the same time as she does us one.' Tony smiled back at Paul who was now distracted by something he had seen and hurried to change the subject.

'That could complicate things.' Paul looked over to the entrance of the Astoria. 'I doubt you want your little brother getting stuck in the middle of this?'

Mark was walking along the street where just moments before there had been a long queue. The queue was not a quarter of the length it had been. He was with Pip, Caroline and Ben and they were aiming to join the queue.

'Turns out our Marky can look after himself,' Tony said as he opened the car door and stepped out in to the road. He walked across the street and directly towards Mark and his friends. As he approached, Mark and Tony locked eyes on each other. Mark stopped the conversation mid - sentence and the other people with him turned to look at what had distracted him. All four now stared at Tony as he walked up.

'We need to have a word Marky.' He continued passed the queue in the direction Mark and his friends had just come from. Mark followed him and his friends followed Mark.

'No,' Mark said to them. 'Wait here. I will be ok.'

66

As superstar entrances went, that was and ok one. She had walked red carpets many times. A crowd was a crowd and this one seemed really excited and up for it. She walked back across the dance floor, through the small exit door at the side of the stage and along the walkway back to the dressing room she had left about fifteen minutes before. As she did, she passed the doorway to the larger dressing room where Sam was now applying his 'war paint'.

Sam and she had chatted about his performance and the fact that he was going to do a Spice Girls mix up to get started. He had told her all about the Tranny Ninjas and the number they would do together and then he was going to move in to a Spice Girls medley to get the crowd going before she was introduced to the stage. Together they had then discussed the options of doing something different. Sam realised quite quickly how persuasive an she could be, and before he knew it they were rehearsing a duet of 'Viva Forever'. He was going to finish the Spice Girls medley and then she would join him on the stage.

'But I will be in full drag' He had said to her when she suggested it.

'I know its genius. The girls would love that you know,' It hadn't taken much time to persuade Sam.

'And this way you get to actually sing on stage rather than mime.' At this point Sam was in. He was one of a small selection of Drag Queens that actually liked to sing and had a decent voice.

'Ok then,' he had said. 'Let's do it.' At this point Sam had begun to have a surge of excitement he wasn't expecting. He wasn't really one to have big public shows of emotion but he had jumped up and hugged her and let out a giddy high pitched, 'YAY'.

'It's not every day I get to duet with a Drag Queen called Rocky Star.' Both of them had hugged each other. 'No you better help me get this frock on or the crowd outside will leave before we even make it to the stage. Sam had then grabbed the rest of his things and made his way through to the main dressing room to apply his make-up. When he arrived he found the boys of the dance troop were already there and already dressed as the Tranny Ninjas, although one of them was missing.

'Where is Louis?' Sam asked as he walked through and dropped his luggage next to a spare seat in the room. The boys all looked at each other.

'He just went to the loo,' Billy replied. 'Will be back any minute.'

'Ok, so are we all ready for tonight. You boys got here early how can you already be ready?'

'You know us,' Billy continued to speak with Sam as the other two went back to the mirrors they had been looking in to when he arrived.

'Always ready. We wouldn't be very good Ninjas if we weren't always ready would we?' he winked at Sam and returned to the other two boys. Sam continued unloading his luggage and getting out his wig and make up. He was humming to himself and thinking of how exciting it was going to be. Considering the week he'd had, no one was going to take this away from him. He was also thinking that he needed to let Caroline know about what had happened and that fact he was now best friends with her idol.

'It's all sorted boys.' Louis walked in to the room and said loudly to everyone that could hear. At this point Billy dived up from his seat and shouted at Louis even more loudly.

'Look Sam is here. It's Rocky, Rocky Star.' Billy looked at Louis and then at Sam. 'Rocky Star!' He explained in a theatrical voice. Sam was confused.

'Oh, hi Rocky, how are you?' Louis addressed Sam.

'I'm good' Sam now sounded confused. 'What's all sorted?' he asked and stood up to get closer to Louis. Something was wrong with the boys tonight. They weren't themselves and now Louis was acting strange. Sam wasn't sure but over the last 24 hours he had begun to doubt the group of boys and there was an element of mistrust. He had gone along with their planning of this night. It was working in his favour, and was getting better with the new friend he had made. But it was their secretive way of getting to this stage that had made him mistrust them and only now he was realising what that was.

'Erm' Louis said. Looking like he had been put on the spot and found out for doing something wrong. Sam was watching the change in him and thinking a guilty look often means someone is guilty. 'I have just' Louis hesitated and then looked at Billy. Araf and Jo now standing next to Billy also looking just as guilty as Louis did. Alarm bells were ringing in Sam's head

'It's a surprise' snapped Billy, a little too forced. Or was Sam just seeing what he wanted to see now he was suspicious of them?

'We have arranged a surprise for you. We were going to tell you after the show.' The boys all nodded their heads and muttered something along the lines of 'Yeah Surprise.'

'What sort of Surprise?' Sam asked wearily.

'Well it wouldn't be a surprise if we told you what it was now would it?' Billy asked Sam.

'Stop trying to spoil it.'

'Hmmmm, well.' Sam thought for a minute 'We will see.'

Louis stepped passed Sam and over to the other three and as he did so, revealed a man stood in the doorway. The man was wearing a black t-shirt and black jeans. He was in his mid-thirties with a shaved head and a headset over it with wires going down to a Walkie-Talkie on his hip.

'Evening ladies' he said as he looked at everyone in room. The boys gathered together and saw this as a welcome distraction. They shuffled over to talk and mumble to each other away from Sam. Sam watched them again with an air of suspicion and turned to the man in the door.

'Hello love, it's Dave isn't it?' Sam had recognised the man who had showed him in to the changing rooms earlier.

'Yes love.' Dave had a strong Welsh accent.

'What can I do for you Dave?'

'Well you see, the thing is, I have just had the lady in the room next door asking me about changing the music set list for the opening of the show and I wanted to run it passed you to make sure all is correct.' The Tranny Ninjas all turned round and looked at Sam.

'Yes, that right. We are going to sing a duet after the Spice Girls Medley.'

'Oh, right you are then' Dave replied and placed down the black box he had carried in.

'You'll be needing to be miked up then if that's ok. Singing live are you?'

'Well for the duet I will. We will still be miming to the Spice Girls medley.'

'Right you are then love' He had opened the box and took out some electrical equipment.' Bend over then.'

'Dave!' Sam said fanning her face. 'Boys have normally bought me at least one drink before they ask me to do that.'

'You need a drink do you love?' Dave asked, completely missing the point. It was at this point that the stage manager had walked passed the changing room and put her head around the door.

'Are we all set Sam?' She asked.

'It looks that way. Dave is just bending me over now,' Sam said winking at her.

'Bloody hell Dave, you're a quick mover aren't you?' She said.

'I'll get it done as fast as I can,' once again, missing the reference. He fumbled behind Sam dropping the mic box a few times.

'Do you know what you are doing Dave?' The stage manager asked form the door, stepped in and took over.

67

The venue was deadly silent. The volume of the crowd had been turned down to just a few whispers here and there. Rocky Star stood in the middle of the stage in darkness. A few people in the crowd could just about make out a figure standing there, waiting for something to happen. Rocky fidgeted with the battery pack that Dave had attached to her belt. He had had to come back several times once Rocky was in full outfit. She stood on the stage and looked out at the packed dance floor. She began to feel the rush of energy she felt at the start of every performance, and this one was no different. The venue had pulled out all the stops and any second now the show was about to start. Rocky took a deep breath, looked up and saw the feet of a Tranny Ninja. The iconic opening bars of the song Kong Fu Fighting by Carl Douglas blasted across the Astoria. As Carl began to sing the first line all the lights turned on the stage and Rocky Star was bathed in a red glow and she exaggerated her mime to the words. As she did so the four Tranny Ninjas ascended from the ceiling. Arms out stretched and legs positioned out as if they were jumping in a Ninja pose. By the time they made it to the floor the song was a third of the way through. Quickly releasing themselves from the harnesses they were wearing and all fell in line whilst the fast movements of the ultra- coordinated dance took place. All five of the men in full costume looked like the perfect dance troop. Their coordination was impeccable and Rocky Star led the way lip syncing every word. By the time the song had ended the crowd were going wild. Rocky and the team could feel the energy surging up within them.

'Good evening everyone, are you having a great time?' Rocky said down the microphone attached around her head. The crowd cheered and quite a few people at the front jumped up and down. 'Easy there you at the front you don't want to do yourself and injury before we get our G...' She paused between each of the letters 'A... Y... Idols on the stage.' The crowd cheered even louder. Rocky was loving every minute of it. The Tranny Ninjas had reformed behind her and stood wearing their black jumpsuit and heels the size of their arms. 'What do you think of my Tranny Ninjas?' The crowd screamed and cheered for them. 'I never leave the house without them. You can't be too careful in this part of London. Always good to have protection.' There was a loud cheer and laugh from the crowd and someone from the front shouted back at Rocky, something along the lines of being able to look after yourself.

'Of course I can look after myself dear, the Ninjas are there to protect anyone that I start on.' The crowd went wild once again. 'Anyway my lovelies, we need to crack on with the show as we have a treat for you. You know who the presenter and judge for tonight's show is don't ya?' The crowd screamed and cheered once again.

'Bruce Forsyth,' Rocky shouted 'Oh no, crap that's the other show.' Rocky laughed and then started to speak again. As he did the wires in the microphone fell lose and no one in the audience heard a word he said. He just stood on the stage speaking and wondering what was happening. As she did so the first line of Spice up Your Life boomed out across the venue. The Tranny Ninja's pulled away the black jumpsuits to reveal what they were wearing underneath. Each one of them was wearing an iconic outfit of the Spice Girls. Sam saw the lose wire and pushed it back in.

'Allow me to introduce the ladies' Rocky said, his voice boomed out louder than before across the venue with the lead now connected. 'We have Jo Jo Galore, our little Baby Spice' Jo walked forward pulled off the hood she was still wearing to reveal a blonde wig with pig tails, the crowd cheered. 'And here we have Tinker Belle as the Scary Spice herself with another of my friends Miss T as Ginger as they come.' Araf and Billy stepped forward and took a bow. 'And here we have Lou the Bitch who makes a wonderful Posh don't you think?'

Louis stayed stood in the same spot and pouted her lips to the cheering crowd. 'And as for me, well you'll see….' Rocky repeated the famous line from the song. 'Slam your body down and wind it all around.' The crowd went wild as the medley, starting with Wannabe, blasted out and the performers on the stage danced right the way through. At the end of the medley Rocky stayed in the middle of the stage and the rest of the group disappeared off. Rocky took a moment to catch her breath and looked out at the crowd. Seeing the whole dance floor filled with every manner of person you could imagine. She looked over towards the bar knowing that a group of her biggest fans would be stood watching. Ben, Caroline and Pip were cheering and waving.

'Ladies, Gentlemen, Gays and Girls.' She took another deep breath. 'What did you think of that?'

The wild crowd cheered even louder. 'Well if you liked that, have we got a treat for you tonight.' There was more cheering from the crowd. Rocky was beginning to really love the feeling of a huge crowd. Having spent an entire career working in small pubs and clubs being on a stage in front of what looked like thousands of people really suited her. She was now building up to bringing on to the stage the star of the show. Knowing that this is what the crowd were there for and knowing the moment of fame would soon pass once the big star arrived, she took this moment to relish it. As she did so she saw Dean and James weaving their way through the dance floor. She gave them a smile and then felt concern as she looked at their faces and the determination of their walk as they crossed the dancefloor towards the door that led backstage. Oh Fuck. Were they still continuing with the plan? They couldn't be. Had they not got the message? 'Well the wait is almost over and G.A.Y idol is about to begin. The crowd went wild and she lost sight of the boys on the dance floor. They were gone. Then she heard music playing, the cue to start the song and louder than she expected another voice boomed across the dance floor.

Rocky stood and stared at her. She gave Rocky an encouraging look, a smile that beamed across the stage and almost on auto pilot Rocky started to sing the duet.

68

Mark walked through the crowd around the edge of the bar listening to his friend speaking to the crowd on the stage. He admired the way Sam became Rocky. Going from the mild mannered Sam to the fierce Rocky Star, applying his war paint was part of his ritual to be able to stand on stage and perform night after night. He loved the fact that tonight was Rocky's night and she seemed even more on form than usual, he watched as music kicked in and then he stopped in his tracks as he saw Rocky stay stock still on the stage. Was Sam star stuck? He couldn't be. He seemed to be looking in to the crowd. He was now frozen as mega star celebrity walked on the stage and started singing. The crowd went wild and he got knocked over. He stumbled forward as a crowd of young lads ran forward towards the stage. By the time he had steadied himself Rocky had started to sing and the show was going on. He looked up and gave a cheer himself joining in with the crowd and continued to walk over to his friends who were waiting for him.

'Oh my God Mark, what happened?' Pip saw him first and jumped forward hugging him.

'Hey,' Mark said 'calm down its all good.' He looked at his friends who all stood looking at him, waiting to hear what had happened. Mark had walked down the road leaving his friends and turned the corner on the orders of his brother.

'Alright Marky, what have you been up to?' Tony turned and stood close to Mark, closer than he liked. Too close. Tony seemed different to him tonight. Was it to do with the way Mark was feeling? Having become his brother and walked in his shoes for a while, did he now have a new understanding of him? Or, was Tony actually acting differently towards him?

'What are you doing here?' Mark asked 'Why are you still in town?'

'Thought I needed to keep an eye my little bro.'

'Why would you need to keep an eye on me?' Mark was beginning to wonder if the whole act had not worked and Manic Mike and been and told Tony everything.

'Well it looks like I don't, don't it?' Tony stared at Mark and stopped speaking. Mark began to feel uneasy. He knew. And Mark was about to find out what he was going to do about it.

'You'd better be careful Marky Boy, cutting your hair all short like mine, people might start thinking you are me.' Mark knew then that Tony knew what he had done. He kept quiet, looking passed Tony and realising that he had positioned himself badly to make a run for it.

'You see the thing is our kid.' Tony put his arm around Mark's neck and over his shoulder. 'Getting low life drug dealers off your back by pretending to be me is one thing,' Tony gave a slight push and the two of them stepped forward a few paces in the street. 'But you don't want other people thinking you are me, let alone have others think you are even in contact with me. We don't want them following you again do we?'

'What people?' Mark was confused 'Have you had people following me?'

'Always Marky Boy.' The two were looking in to each other eyes. 'Always. See I thought I needed to keep an eye on my little bro in case he got in to any trouble.' He took a breath and stepped back from holding his arm around Mark's shoulders. 'You seem to like to partake in the product that I put out there and I didn't want anything nasty happening to you. So, I have one of my guys keep an eye on you from time to time. But that's not who I am worried about. You see Marky Boy, those coppers that came around asking questions the other day.' Tony looked at Mark and waited for his recognition. Mark acknowledged this, and Tony continued. 'Those coppers want to know what I am up to and if they think you have anything to do with me then they will follow you, as they have done before.'

'What the fuck, that's harassment,' Mark was getting angry.

'Not if you don't know about it our kid. Anyway, it seems you can look after yourself when it comes to scaring the fuck out of a low life drug dealer.'

'You know about it then?' Mark asked, almost stand offish.

'I know everything Marky Boy. What I didn't know is how you got in to that trouble anyway?' The statement was posed as a question and Mark felt the need to answer. After explaining to Tony what had happened with Dean and James and the money, Tony leant back against the wall and took a deep breath.

'Next time anything like that happens you call me right.' Tony demanded of Mark.

'I don't plan on anything like this happening again,' Mark sighed. He looked at his brother and he saw a different person. For the first time in his life he was having an equal conversation.

'So, is this why you're here?'

'No, I just heard about all this and it got in the way. I was going to deal with it and you got there before me. I gotta say our kid. You look damn fucking good as me' Tony laughed, Mark joined in.

'I can't cope with the hair,' he said.

'Not gay enough?' Tony laughed some more.

'Maybe I'll add some glitter.' Mark couldn't believe he was having a laugh with his brother now. Tony was thinking the same. All the years they had not been in contact, all the years he had spent having people watch him and now they were friends.

'Do it. But I tell you what. Impersonate me again and you'll need more than glitter to look good.' The warning had been said in jest but Mark fully understood the meaning behind it.

'Now then, the trouble ain't over. Your dickhead mates were planning on robbing this club, right?'

'Right. But I think they don't need to now.'

'Well it seems our mutual friend is planning on taking over and is on his way to do it.'

'What the fuck?'

'Get your mates out of there. Shit is going to happen, and I want you and your mates far enough away, so they don't get caught up in it.'

'Right' Mark looked at Tony again. Not sure what to do or how to take what he was saying.

His brother was really looking out for him and in a moment where Mark had expected to be killed he was now working with him.

'Now give your big bro a hug and fuck off' Tony stepped forward, hugged Mark and started to walk away. Mark stood in the street in shock. 'And give Mum a ring. She worries about you more than I do.' Tony turned the corner not looking back and was gone, leaving Mark alone in the street. It took him a minute to gather his thoughts and then act. Shit, he needed to get inside and take his brother's warning seriously. Having explained the whole thing to his friends at the bar in the Astoria they all stood and looked at him.

'What are we going to do?' Ben asked first.

'Leave,' Pip said.

'Yeah, in a minute,' Mark said looking over to the stage whilst still talking to his friends. 'First we need to get hold of Sam.' they all looked up at the stage to watch Rocky Star finish singing. Mark looked up to see Rocky taking a boy and on the other side of the stage, all he could see was a set of out stretched arms so everyone could take a moment to cheer for Rocky, but he could not make out what was being said over the roar of the crowd.

'We'd better go back stage and get him.' Mark shouted at his friends, but they couldn't hear him. He mimed to them and pointed in the direct of the door that went back stage to the dressing rooms. He mouthed to them LET'S GO GET SAM.

69

Dean stood by the door that led back stage, he felt sick and the roar of the crowd was making him feel worse. James looked around to see if anyone was watching them and pushed his hand on the big sign saying 'PRIVATE'. The door was open and without much effort it pushed to reveal a long corridor leading to the back of the bar in one direction and to the back of the stage in the other. He stepped inside and reached back to grab Dean. To the right, along the way to the stage were a series of doors, mostly open and people walking in and out of them. To the left there were just two doors further down, one leading to the back of the bar and the other to the office. The office, James thought, was the one on the right hand side and a good distance away from the other rooms for them to get in and out noticed.

'What about Sam?' Dean asked.

'What about him?' James looked at Dean for the first time since they arrived at the Astoria.

'Well we need him don't we?' Dean was sounding nervous now.

'Yeah, he saw us. He will come off stage any minute and we can go for it.'

'I don't remember him being on stage as part of the plan.'

'It wasn't, but it will give us a good story if anything is wrong. We were just here to see him.'

'Here to see who?' A strong Welsh voice bellowed from behind the two boys stood in the corridor. Dean and James turned on their heels to face Dave, still wearing his black t-shirt and headset.

'We are supposed to be meeting Sam Rockwell here. He is Rocky Star and he is on stage and we were supposed to meet him here, only he is not here because he is on stage,' Dean rattled out his excuse for being here.

'Ok son, calm down and take a breath,' Dave said back to the boys. 'I'll take you to his dressing room. He should be done at any minute.' Dave led the boys to the dressing room. James was looking at Dean and trying to tell him to stop speaking without saying anything. The subtleness of the widening of his eyes seemed to have been lost on Dean as his nerves took over.

'Thank you very much for showing us here to Sam's.' Dean stopped to correct himself 'I mean Rocky's dressing room.'

'You're welcome so you are. Now it is going to get quite busy back here real soon with all the acts coming through here. I think Sam will have packed his things and be ready to leave so it shouldn't affect you too much,' he took another step and stopped. 'Here you go, don't get in to any bother while you are in there.' As he opened the door James heard the cheer of the crowd get suddenly louder as a door opened into the corridor. Through the door stepped a young man carrying a tray that looked like it had a lock on it and with him two security guards. The money from the door takings James thought as he looked at Dean. Dean looked back at James having seen the same thing and got a little excited. James pushed Dean forward before he could say anything and they stumbled in to the room together. The door slammed behind them.

'Jesus Christ!' Louis shouted as all the Tranny Ninjas jumped from the shock. 'What are you two doing here?'

'Erm.' Dean was now stuck for words.

'We are here to meet Sam.' James answered. 'We said we would meet him here after the show.'

'Oh, right. He never said.' Louis looked at the other three people in his team and down to the map he had out on the dressing table. With a nod Billy folded the map and tucked it in to the front of his ninja outfit.

'How come you have put your Ninja outfits back on?' Dean asked sounding a little puzzled. 'Are you doing another act tonight?' The four men all looked at each other. Around the room, were various parts of the previous costumes. A ginger wig and a union jack dress the most obvious parts of the act they had just finished.

'We erm,' Louis started and then stopped.

'We are going on to a party and prefer the Ninja look to the Spice Girls' All six of the men stood looking at each other for what seems like hours but was in fact less than a minute.

'Ok, so we will wait over here. Is this Sam's stuff?' James looked over at the olive green holdall bag he had seen Sam carrying on many occasions.

'NO' Louis shouted, he quickly calmed from the shout and dived over to the bag. 'That's ours.' He lifted the bag and it seemed very full and quite heavy.

'This is Sam's.' Billy guided the boys towards another dressing table with the exact same bag sat in front of it. It was empty and all Sam's things were on the dressing table. Dean sat down at the seat and James stood next to him. The four Tranny Ninja's took their place on the other side of the room and started to chat to each other.

'Do you need a hand tidying up?' Dean asked the group. 'Only that man who showed us in said that the contestants were coming in here any minute.'

'What's that?' Louis asked.

'Tidying up?' Dean asked again.

'Oh right, erm,' Louis looked at the others in his group and then turned back to the boys.

'No, no. Someone else is using this room you said?'

'Yes, that man who showed us in said the contestants were coming in once Sam has packed his stuff up.'

'Ok, well we are going any minute now.'

'Ok.' Dean turned on the swivel chair and started to look at the pictures on the wall. As he did so the door burst open again in the same way it had done when they had burst through about ten minutes earlier. It made him jump in the same way the dance group had jumped and Dean found himself shouting out the same curse Louis had done previously. 'Jesus Christ!'

Rocky Star came through the door, first stumbling forward followed by Mark, Pip, Caroline and Ben. Moments before, Rocky had finished the performance on stage and exited, coming down the small set of stairs at the back of the stage and entering the corridor leading to the dressing rooms. Mark, Pip, Caroline and Ben had made their way across the dance floor and slipped through the exit door that Dean and James had used previously. Meeting Rocky in the corridor, Mark explained quickly that they needed to leave and the reason why.

'Thank God you two are in here,' Sam shouted at Dean and James. In the corridor Sam had explained that he had seen Dean and James go back stage but didn't know where they would be. Now feeling relieved that they had not got far enough to take action on the now cancelled plan.

'We have got to get going Sam.' Mark said.

'Where's Tom?' Dean asked looking at the group. With none of the sense of urgency everyone else seemed to have.

'What?' Sam asked.

'Where's Tom?' Dean asked again.

'Not here,' Mark replied. 'Now listen boys we have got to move fast.' He turned to Sam. 'Your stuff?' he questioned. Sam bent down and picked up the empty holdall and began in push all his things from the dressing table in to the bag. The room was now cramped with ten people in it moving around. The door had closed behind Caroline who was now on the floor next to Sam collecting his things and pushing them in the fast filling bag. The Tranny Ninjas were also moving around quite quickly and everyone was beginning to fall over each other.

'Hold on, Hold ON!' Jo shouted from the far corner of the room as he had fallen down having been pushed in the rush to pack things away. Everyone looked up. 'Let's just calm down for a minute, we are not getting anywhere fast like this. There are too many people in the room for us to be comfortable like this.' Just as he said this, the door slammed open and shocked the whole group again in the same way it had done before and everyone at the same time shouted 'Jesus Christ!'

'No,' said the thick east end accent of Manic Mike. 'And I ain't your fucking saviour either.'

Mike walked in to the room with Sonny behind him. Now with twelve people in the room it was pretty hard to move and Mike stood close to Mark. Looking puzzled, Sam had fallen back slightly on to the dressing table and held on to it. Caroline still on the floor zipped up the holdall and pushed it over the floor so she could stand. Everyone looked at Manic Mike.

'What the fucking hell is going on here? Who the fuck are you?' Mike said to Mark. Mark began to panic. Mark knew that he looked like Tony still. He no longer had the scar and had changed out of the suit back in to jeans and trainers but he looked like him, his hair was the same and they were all about to get found out.

'I.... I'm,' he couldn't speak. Neither could Ben, Pip or Caroline. The act had been so good before but they didn't expect to see Manic Mike again.

'You're taking the piss out of me. I'm going to fucking kill you,' Mike was getting angry.

'I don't know what's going on here guys but it doesn't seem to be anything to do with us.'

Billy stopped forward and grabbed their green holdall bag. 'So, if you don't mind we will make our way out and give you some more room.' He tried to step in the direction of the door urging the rest of the dance troop to follow.

'You ain't going anywhere Billy.' Manic Mike said. 'I know who you are and I know what's in that bag.' The whole group now looked at Billy and the bag.

'I don't know what you're talking about,' Billy said as he tried to step further towards the door. As he did there was a loud scream as Jo Jo Galore flew through the air to attack Manic Mike pushing him over and nearly taking out Mark and Ben at the same time. Jo landed on Mike and pulled a ginger wig over his face.

'Fucking run!' Jo shouted as he wrestled with Mike on the ground. Everyone began to flee from the room. Sonny stood in the corner watching and even opened the door so everyone could get out. Billy fell over the wrestling Ninjas and drug dealer on the floor dropping the bag. Caroline grabbed Sam's bag and shouted to the others to get going. The Tranny Ninja's grabbed their bag, grabbed Jo by the arm and dragged him out in to the corridor. Sonny walked over to Mike on the floor, pulled the ginger wig from his face and helped him up. The room was now empty apart from two of them.

'Hurry up fuck wit. We need that bag.'

James was at the back of the crowd as they moved quickly down the corridor heading towards the door that led back in to the main club. Ben was in front of him with Dean, Mark, Caroline, Sam (still dressed as Rocky) and Pip up front. The Tranny Ninjas had all run in the opposite direction towards the area that led to the stage and then to a door which was a fire exit to the back alley of the Astoria. The first thing James knew about Manic Mike following them was his hand grabbing the back of his neck. Before he knew it, the grip tightened around his neck, almost strangling him from behind and pulled him off his feet backwards. He let out a scream that all the others heard and stopped and turned around. Mike was holding on to James from behind.

'Where's the bag with the money?' He said looking through the group and seeing Caroline holding the olive-green holdall. 'Give it me.'

'This isn't it,' she pleaded. 'Let him go please.'

'The fucking money you robbed. Give it me.'

'We didn't do it,' Sam replied stepping forward. 'We didn't go through with it. I had to be on stage, so we didn't do it. We don't have your money.'

'You fucking bunch of twats, do you think I'm stupid. The money. NOW!'

'Boss. Boss.' Sonny said from behind 'It's them four in black who were doing it. They went that way.' Mike tightened his grip on James and tears rolled down his face. As he did so, Ben stepped forward.

'Leave him alone you fucking knob' Ben squared up to Mike.

'What're you gonna do about it?' Mike questioned. Before he could finish what he was saying, Ben had punched him square in the nose sending him flying back and releasing his grip on James who fell forward into Ben who grabbed him and held him tight. 'Now fuck off after your money or I'll carry on.' Ben stepped backwards and the rest of the group turned back together to the door to leave through the club.

70

Before the commotion of Dean and James entering the dressing room, the Tranny Ninja's had all removed their heels and pulled on trainers. They had a map of the side streets next to the club and knew the best way for them to get to the bikes they had parked on the other side of Soho Square. The quickest getaway in central London was going to be motorbikes; the traffic was always too bad to rely on getting away fast. Billy was the first to bounce out of the exit door followed by Jo who was carrying the olive green holdall and then Araf and Louis. Louis slammed the door shut behind them.

'He didn't follow us,' Louis said to the group.

'Who the fuck was that?' Araf asked.

'I don't know but he seemed to have a bigger issue with Sam and friends than he did with us. And he didn't look like someone I wanted to hang around and find out about,' Louis said gasping for breath.

'I told you a job in London wouldn't go well. We have never had to run from a job before.' Araf continued speaking. 'What are we going to do now?'

'Same as we planned,' Jo said walking to the three others. 'The bikes are that way. We get on them and drive away. The fight is their fight and not ours.' Jo walked on down the alley way at the side of the Astoria. There was a car parked and the driver lay asleep in the front seat. 'Come on.' They all continued down the alley way turning into Sutton Row and heading towards Soho Square.

'Nip through the park,' Louis said. 'The gates are still open.' They walked towards the open gate of Soho Square Park. The light covering of snow from earlier was now thickening and coming down heavier. Billy shivered at the cold.

'We didn't think the weather through much did we. These outfits are going to be freezing on the back of a bike,' Billy said to the others who were all now catching their breath and walking towards the opposite side of the park. They passed the small rotunda in the middle and towards the entrance facing Carlisle Street.

'We have coats in the bikes. They will keep us warm for the bike ride.' Araf said. 'And it's only ten minutes anyway.' He leant over and grabbed Billy's shoulders 'I'm sure your pretty little face can take that. Out of nowhere Billy's legs were taken from under him and he fell to the floor dragging Araf down, who fell on top of him. Billy felt a foot meet with his face as he fell to the ground. Araf, who saw what was happening but was unable to do anything as he fell, saw that Manic Mike had kicked Billy in the face. Jo and Louis turned to see what was happening and Louis was met with a punch.

'What the fuck do you think you're doing?' Jo stepped in to stop the attack. Mike stood in front of him, his face was covered in drying blood and it looked like he had broken his nose.

'Give me the fucking bag.' Mike said to the group.

'No, fuck off!' Jo stood his ground.

'Give me the fucking bag or I will kill the lot of you fucking puffs.'

'I might be a puff sweetheart but that doesn't mean you are able to kill me.' Jo dropped the bag towards Louis, took a small step forward to ground himself and make his stance more solid with his fists in the air. Mike did the same and tried to land the first punch. Jo tilted back and the first flew passed his face missing him. Ready to make a move Jo sprung in to action and landed a punch in the exact same spot that Ben had done so several minutes before. The pain shot through Mike's face. The broken nose from the previous punch still hurt and now Jo had punched him even harder in the same spot. Everything around Mike seems to go slow and then black as he passed out.

He hit the ground with a thud. Sonny stood further back in the park watching as the four men from the dance troop helped each other up, grabbed the bag and ran out the exit to the bikes. Mike came round as he heard the bikes speeding off.

'FUCK' he shouted after them, blood spilling out of his nose once more. He grabbed the bloody cloth from his pocket that he had used after the first punch and wiped some of the blood away.

'Don't worry Boss' Sonny said as he walked over. 'I got the bag.' He put the olive green holdall bag down in front of Mike and helped him up from his knees. 'I swopped it over when they weren't looking boss.'

'Good lad Sonny' Mike said and managed to crack a smile through the blood. Sonny grabbed the bag and walked Mike back towards the exit they had entered the park from.

Mike's Range Rover was sat at the exit where he had slammed the brakes on when he had seen the group in the square moments before. Mike grabbed the bag from Sonny and walked round to the driver's seat.

From the corner of the road looking up at Soho Square, near Greek Street, Tony Cash hung up the phone he was on and stood and watched the whole situation unravel. Sonny looked over and caught his eye, Tony winked and Sonny slipped away from the other side of the car, back through Soho Square Park and away down the street the Tranny Ninjas had escaped down. Tony continued to watch as Manic Mike climbed in to the car. Confused as to where Sonny had gone he stood up on the sill of the car to look. There was no sign of him. He climbed in to the driver's seat with the olive green holdall on the passenger seat and leant over to open it up.

Looking down at the bag he was now confused, it was not full of the cash that the thieving dance troop has stolen from The Astoria. Mike looked down at the bag full of ecstasy pills, small, light blue pills in plastic bags. He rummaged through the bag, there must be about ten thousands pills in here he thought. Still confused as to why the group would have so many drugs, he then wondered what to do with them. This was worth more than a bag full of money to him. He sat back in the driver's seat doing the calculation in his head taking another look at the bag and smiling through the pain he felt across the middle of his face. As he did so he heard the screech of several cars skidding to a stop near him and then the blue flashing lights of a police van that had just pulled up in front of him. Before he could work out what was happening Detective Sergeant Alan Jones had opened the door and pulled Mike out, tripping him over and landing him on the ground.

For the third time tonight Mike's face blasted open as it hit the ground sending blood everywhere. With his knee in Mike's back, Alan Jones, pulled Mike's hands round and placed hand cuffs on his wrists and began to read him his rights.

'Guv, look at this, the tip off was right.' Detective Inspector Andy Grey was stood at the passenger side of the car with the olive green duffel bag open exposing the drugs to Chief Superintendent Kirsty Brown. She smiled at Andy and looked down to Manic Mike lay on the floor.

'Finally got you Mike,' she said sounding confident and happy. 'You're going away for a long time now scumbag.' She looked at Alan still sat holding Mike to the ground. 'Good work Sergeant Jones, bloody good work.' She turned to walk back to the unmarked police car she had jumped out of and she saw him. Tony Cash still stood in the same spot watching everything that was happening. Her heart skipped a beat and she so wanted to arrest him then and there, but for what? She knew she had nothing on him. She knew Tony Cash well enough to know that she may never have anything on him. She also knew deep down in her gut that he had everything to do with this. She stood and stared at him and he stared right back and then he took a step forward and walked over. It may have taken him about twenty steps to reach the scene where Mike had now been lifted from the ground and was being walked to the police van. As he walked over he saw Tony and began to struggle.

'You fucking wanker, you set me the fuck up,' Mike shouted at Tony. Tony didn't even flinch.

He watched as the low life he had been trying to get rid of for a long time was pushed in to the back of the van, face covered in blood. He hoped to himself that it was his little brother that had punched him but suspected it wasn't. He looked at Chief Superintendent Kirsty Brown and smiled.

'Good evening Chief Superintendent how are you today?' His polite nature took her by surprise. 'Seems you've had a busy evening, who was that man you arrested?' He asked sounding as if the question really was rhetorical.

'Anthony.' Kirsty replied nodding her head. 'I think we both know that you know full well who that was and why he has been arrested.' Kirsty was beginning to pull together the events of the night in her head. All of her team had been in place including the undercover officer Dave who was posing as part of the crew for the night. Dave had radioed through that the dance troop, not including Sam Rockwell, had completed the robbery of the office and safe and where getting ready to make their exit. The whole team were ready to jump in to action to arrest the troop when Kirsty had received a call on her mobile from an unrecognised number explaining that the dance troop had already exited the club, were in Soho square fighting with a drug dealer who had a considerably large stash of drugs on his person. In minutes they were mobile and made it to find Manic Mike sat in his car with the drugs as explained. She noticed something on the street next to Tony's feet.

'I think you have dropped your mobile Anthony?' she said pointing down.

'Not mine Chief,' he looked down at the mobile phone 'You may want to take that, it could be evidence from the scene' He said and smiled at her. His smile unnerved her, as it did everyone she suspected. His teeth were pure white his eyes looked slyer than before and the scar across his face seemed to widen.

'I suppose, if I was to call the last number to call me, it might ring?' She said looking at Tony.

'I'm not sure why I would know that Chief Superintendent.'

'I don't know what you have to do with this Anthony Cash. But I know you do.' She kept looking at Tony and dialled the last number to call her phone. The Nokia 3310 phone that lay on the floor began to ring, the screen lit up and her number flashed on the screen. Without taking her eyes off Tony she spoke, 'Detective Inspector Grey, there is a phone on the floor and I believe it to be the phone that made the anonymous call to let us know of this situation. Please could you collect it and bag it as evidence?' Andy Grey looked at his boss talking to Tony Cash and slowly walked over to retrieve the phone.

'Looks like it has had a good clean Ma'am, but is still in full working condition.' He looked up at her, holding a cloth in his hand with the phone in it he opened up the screen. 'Last number dialled is,' He paused for a moment, 'You're right Ma'am, yours was the last number dialled and there is a missed call from you too. They are the only numbers dialled on the phone.' He took another minute to look through the phone. 'Ma'am there are a series of received text message from another number.' He took moment to read through them 'It seems we have the minute by minute actions of Mike for tonight in text messages.' He looked up at Kirsty who was still staring in to the eyes of Tony Cash. As they continued to look at each other a car pulled up behind Tony.

'Know anything about the phone Anthony?' She said as he took a step backwards towards the car.

'When you want someone off the street Chief Superintendent Brown, I feel you are always the best to handle it. Hopefully now those poor kids that died will get justice' He smiled at her and walked back opening the door of the car, climbing in and driving away.

71

The snow was falling heavily and had turning into a blizzard, the wind blowing it almost horizontal in to the group. Mark couldn't separate where the road and the pavement were as he ran along Charing Cross road away from the Astoria. He could barely see if there were cars in the road as he ran over Oxford Street to continue north. Ben had been the last to come through the door into the club and the group had fought their way across the crowd. It had proved hard work and the wrong decision to make as everyone instantly recognised Rocky Star and wanted to touch, talk to or hug and dance as they crossed the dance floor to the main entrance. Once they had made it to their exit, Caroline had then been grabbed by the security guard she knew who wanted to say hello. After explaining they were in a rush, the security guard asked Caroline to call her, and they were finally able to get out of the club. James tumbled down the steps in to the street with dark red patches on his neck that looked like they were already starting to bruise.

'I think he is following us,' James coughed to the group. 'I saw him get up and he looked mad.'

'Following us?' Mark questioned. Deciding there was no time for an answer, 'Fucking run.' He had turned into the blizzard and was now running away leading the group as fast as he could.

They crossed roads and turned corners until they found themselves running in to the entrance of Hyde Park. They continued to run up the central pathway, so covered in snow that they were now slipping as they ran. Mark's phone began to ring and he saw that it was Tom.

'Can we stop running?' Sam shouted from the back of the group. They all came to a stop at the same time and made a small circle. 'Are we sure we are being chased? I can't see anyone and I have massive heels on that are making it impossible to run through snow.'

'And I'm carrying this bloody bag.' Caroline's northern voice echoed across the group. 'What have you got in it Sam, it's so bloody heavy?'

'Well,' Mark said. 'I don't think we are being chased.' He was looking around in the direction they had come from. Dean, James, Mark, Pip, Ben, Caroline and Sam all stopped, taking in big deep breaths trying to calm themselves down and breathe normally. Mark's phone started ringing and it was Tom again, he answered and stepped to one side to speak to him. Another phone started to ring, it was Ben's he answered it and started to have a conversation with the caller.

James watched him. He admired the way he took the call and spoke to the person. He looked at him and thought about how he had just saved his life when the drug dealer had tried to kill him. He knew right there that he loved Ben and would never love anyone else. Ever.

'What's that?' Dean said seeing something behind the group in the distance through the snow. It looked like the headlights of a car coming forwards them.

'I think it's a car,' said Pip.

'It can't be a car we are in Hyde Park,' Mark joined the group having finished his call with Tom.

'It is a car,' Dean said as the lights slowly got closer.

'It's going bloody slow if it is,' Pip said.

'What if it's?' Mark said as the whole group realised that it could be Manic Mike. As they looked back, they could hear music playing. The Dam Busters' song was playing at full blast, as a classic Rolls Royce pulled up in from of them. The car came to a very steady stop due to it driving so slowly.

'What the fuck?' Sam said she he leant over the car, 'Mrs Potts what are you doing?'

'You look like you need a ride my dears,' Mrs Potts shouted from behind the steering wheel. Her eyes could almost see over it. 'Jump in and we will be home in no time.' The group of friends all looked at each other.

'Well I'm not staying out in this snow all night.' Caroline was the first get in the back with the olive green hold-all followed by Sam and then the others all climbed in. Pip and Mark shared a place in the front passenger seat.

'Who knew there was so much space in one of these old things?' Pip said to Mark as she climbed on to his lap.

'How rude dear, I'm not that fat.' Mrs Potts laughed back. 'Here we go dears,' she shouted as she put her foot down on the accelerator and the car began, very slowly, to move forwards.

'We would have been better walking,' Dean said to James under his breath on the back seat. Dean and James were crammed in together on the floor while Caroline, Ben and Sam had more space across the back seat. Caroline was fidgeting with the bag.

'It's too bloody heavy,' she said. 'Something is digging in to my legs.'

'It's only wigs and make-up it can't be that heavy,' Sam said. 'Let me have a look,' Sam reached over and unzipped the olive green holdall. 'OH MY FUCK' he shouted when he saw the contents of the bag. He looked up at Caroline who now looked down and saw what he saw and was gobsmacked.

'What is it?' Ben said casually as he looked down. 'What the' he trailed off.

'What's happening back there?' Pip said looking over Mark's shoulder. 'Bloody hell where did that come from?' Pip said.

'What is it?' Mark asked unable to move and look himself. Mrs Potts continued to drive at around twenty miles an hour out of Hyde Park and in the direction of home.

'The bag is full of money!' Pip said to Mark.

72

The bag full of cash sat in the middle of the table in Sam's flat and the group of friends sat around it staring. Every now and then one of them would look at another in disbelief. It had taken them over an hour to make it home. Mark had stopped Mrs Potts from driving and took over himself, driving slightly faster but still slow due to the snow blizzard. Once they had arrived back and the classic car had been returned to the garage, Sam had taken Mrs Potts home where she had explained how she had managed to be out in the blizzard. She had been worried about James and Dean and had decided to go to the club and bring them home so that they didn't continue with their silly plan. When she had arrived at the club, she saw everyone run off down the street and thought it best to follow.

'What an adventure my dear,' she had said as Sam tucked her up warm in bed with a hot drink.

'What an adventure indeed. Who knew you would be still on adventures at your age.'

'There's still life in the old dog yet.'

'Where did you get that fabulous car from Mrs Potts?'

'Oh that, it used to be Bruce Forsyth's.' She lay back in the bed and began to sound sleepy. 'He wanted to marry me you know,' and she rolled on to her side and went to sleep. It was now nearly 4am. Sam returned to his flat where he showered and joined the group.

'Have you counted it?' No one spoke. Sam stood looking at the group sat around the table, thinking about how they had sat in almost the same place just a week before, looking at a pile of drugs and thinking about the terror that was about to fall upon them. What a difference a week makes. A drug dealer had threatened to kill them, a plan to rob a nightclub, which could have gone so terribly wrong. Sam thought of his one night at the Astoria and singing a duet live on stage. Actually singing live. He looked at James and saw the terrible bruises around his neck and thought about the moment Manic Mike had got hold of him and how Ben had stepped up and surprised everyone by flooring him. Pip had explained about Mark's brother arriving at her loft and the insane plan that they had hatched to get the boys out of trouble. Now they were here with a bag full of cash and a brief idea of how it might have happened.

Dean explained how the boys in the dance troop had the same olive green bag as Sam and the rest of the story had fallen in to place. Sam took his place at the table.

'I'm going to count it,' Pip said and pulled the bag towards her.

'I'll help you,' Caroline said and the two sat at the head of the table with the open bag.

'I'll get some drinks,' Ben got up and walked towards the kitchen, energy began to sweep across the room and everyone busied themselves doing something. Ben and Mark started to make drinks. Dean and James walked to the sofa and turned on the television. Within a few minutes they landed on the news.

'Oh my gosh, look at this,' Dean shouted to everyone in the flat. 'They are in Soho Square.' He was turning the volume up on the news as a female police officer was being interviewed.

'At approximately 1am this morning during a routine investigation, where local nightclub security and the police have run a joint services operation, we arrested a known drug dealer holding a quantity of tablets that we suspect are ecstasy with a street value of around five hundred thousand pounds.' Flashes of cameras went off around the lady being interviewed on screen. The name across the screen read Chief Superintendent Kirsty Brown. 'We have taken a male, 35 years old; into custody that is helping us with our investigation and we are hoping to charge the said person within the next few hours.' The female officer looked around the group. 'If you have any questions please direct them to our press department.'

'Do you think they got Manic Mike?' Dean asked Mark and Ben who stood by the edge of the sofa watching.

'This night just got bat shit crazy,' Sam said as he walked over to the sofa too. 'So, how did he end up in Soho Square with a bag full of drugs after Ben floored him?'

'It only just got bat shit crazy?' Pip asked rhetorically

'I'm guessing my brother has something to do with it,' Mark said.

'How'd you know that?' Sam said.

'Because I just got a text message saying we don't need to worry about Mike anymore, he has taken care of it.' Mark handed his phone to Sam so he could read the message.

'But this is from someone called Auntie Anne,' Sam handed the phone back to Mark.

'Yeah, that's my Aunt. I'm guessing he saved that number in my phone in the same way he got in to my flat.'

'How was that?'

'Bloody magic I'd say.' Mark sat on the sofa.

'Twenty-two thousand,' Pip said as she walked over to the group.

'What's that?' Mark asked.

'Twenty-two thousand in the bag' Pip said.

'If all those bundles are the same' Caroline said. The whole group stood looking at the pile of money once again.

'So we wouldn't have got enough anyway' Dean said, everyone looked at him in surprised agreement.

73

Mark walked down the street towards the building he lived in. Dean was behind him sending a text message. 'Come on hurry up,' he said to Dean, 'it's bloody cold.' The snow had stopped and the whole of London had come to a standstill. The snow was up over their feet as they walked. There were no taxi's on the streets and busses were parked up in bus stops with no drivers, so Mark and Dean had to walk back from Sam's apartment. It had been a long trip. As a group, they had all decided that, in light of the threat that was now gone, they needed to return the money back to its rightful owner, the Astoria. As Mark and Dean were the ones needing to go back across town, they decided to make the drop. They had returned to the Astoria and gone down the alley at the back. They could see through to Soho Square and the crime scene.

'It might be best if I don't get seen around here with this haircut,' Mark said to Dean.

'Do you think he really believed you were your brother?'

'Of course he did. Look at me.' Mark laughed, 'I'm a total crime lord.' He nipped to the door at the back of The Astoria that the Tranny Ninjas had used earlier and dropped the bag. The door was open and he could hear people talking just inside.

'And do you think he will still come after me?'

'Who? My brother?'

'No, Mike.'

'Why would he?'

'It's all my fault.'

'Yes it is.' Mark looked at Dean. 'But I think it is over now and you are bloody lucky. I think James came out the worst.' The two of them walked along the streets as the sun started to come up over a white London. The blanket of snow made the city look magical and very bright.

'Wait a minute,' Dean said as he tried to pick up the pace as they got closer to the apartment block. A taxi pulled up in the street next to them, it had been driving slowly, taking caution in the snowy conditions.

'Hello boys!' Tom jumped out of the taxi and stepped into the snow 'Are you only just getting home?'

'Says you,' Mark said.

'I've been in bed all night. Gavin just went to work so I headed home.'

'At least he has a serious name now then. Had fun?' Mark asked.

'Yeah. Lots.'

'Right then, so you have done the deed?' Mark smiled and walked on. The three walked the rest of the way down the road and up to the apartment building. Mark explained what had happened during the whole night including the news report about the drug dealer, the text message and then the bag drop at the Astoria.

'Hang on,' Tom said at the top of the stairs. 'Mrs Potts at ninety years old driving a Rolls Royce through the worst snow storm London has ever seen?'

'We could have pushed the car faster.' They laughed as a person stood up from sitting on the floor outside Tom's flat. They had been sat in a bundle with a big winter coat on and a very big ruck sack next to them.

'Hello,' Tom said. 'Can I help you?'

'Are you Mark Cash?' The person flipped the hood from the winter coat and black hair fell around her shoulders. She looked young and very cold. She was not wearing any make-up and Tom thought she was about sixteen years old.

'That's me.' Mark looked at the young lady stood in front of him and then looked over at Tom and Dean, before returning to her. 'Are you ok? Should you be out this late?'

'Yeah, I'm ok,' she said. 'I think you're my Dad.'

Printed in Great Britain
by Amazon

25021198R00165